Henri's Last Gift

GILLES JAITOUR

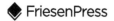 FriesenPress

Suite 300 - 990 Fort St
Victoria, BC, V8V 3K2
Canada

www.friesenpress.com

Copyright © 2021 by Gilles Jaitour
First Edition — 2021

All rights reserved.

I have used Wikipedia as a source for many of the historical, factual and scientific references as well as some of the images used. I have a References/ Sources document where I have copied most of my source URL's and relevant text.

I also must credit Dr. Dan Siegel, author of *Mindsight*, for his definition of brain function – the brain transforms energy into information.

ISBN
978-1-5255-7359-0 (Hardcover)
978-1-5255-7360-6 (Paperback)
978-1-5255-7361-3 (eBook)

1. *Fiction, Visionary & Metaphysical*

Distributed to the trade by The Ingram Book Company

Henri's Last Gift

PREFACE

When I was growing up in small town Ontario, copies of *Reader's Digest* were everywhere in local shops and offices. My favorite article was 'The Most Unforgettable Character I Have Ever Met'. I quickly became addicted and looked forward to a visit to the barbershop or doctor's office to discover more admirable characters. This passion carried over to books and biographies became a preferred genre.

Once "Henri Deault" moved to our village and befriended me, I was sure I had met a person worth memorializing. He quickly became part of our family, employed me through my summer school breaks and took care of many of my siblings through their formative years. I was convinced an understanding of his past would explain his character and anchor my story. I intended to write his biography but he didn't want to talk about his past. That I get since I didn't want to talk about mine either.

Using the few clues he left, and many inspirational messages from the Muses, I followed a dimly lit trail laid out for me in dreams over many, many years. The trail revealed a few of Henri's experiences and loved ones but not enough for me to feel comfortable putting pen to paper. Then, with some supernatural help, Henri opened a flood gate exploring his past and mine. A past we had both buried but one that in his final hours he knew would be his greatest gift.

CHAPTER I

Henri's Last Days

It isn't enough. It never is. None of my morning routines inspire me to seize the day. Thank God I have a mindless morning drill and enough time alone. I make my way to the kitchen; our cat leads the way. I turn on the radio, make coffee, then open the back door. Our cat sniffs the air and refuses to go out. Unusual. I follow him to the front hall. He takes a left into the living room and settles onto his favourite couch. I continue to the main entrance for the morning paper. A cold, blustery wind hits me when I open the door. Some of the marigolds in the flowerpot on the front porch are brown, dying. The newspaper is halfway out of its wrap, soggy. Damn that paperboy, and the weather. I shake my head, shiver, slam the door, and go back inside.

It's never enough, but the solitude comforts me. When the family gets up, they will disrupt the silence and my regular rituals. I escape their noise and clatter by leaving before they stir. The coffee tastes bitter this morning. I pour it down the sink. I'll get a decent cup at work. On the radio, the irritating voice of the woman reading the weather report prattles on about clouds moving in fast from the northwest, bringing chilly air and thunderstorms. Even though I'll be inside, the lack of sunshine will bother me. My head begins to pound.

The phone rings. "Yeah?"

"Josh."

I instantly recognize the voice. It's Paul, my youngest brother. Maybe the day won't be so bad after all.

"Oh, hi, Paul. I thought maybe it was some asshole from the plant ... Paul?"

"Josh, Henri's gone. Last night in his sleep."

Another death I don't want to deal with. Emptiness overwhelms me. I swallow and take a deep breath before answering. "The old bugger was over seventy, Paul. He'd been in hospice for two months. We knew it was only a matter of time."

"Still, when they called, I was shocked, Josh. I was there until ten. When I was leaving, Henri said, 'Come back tomorrow, *mon ami*, and tell that frisky nurse I'm alone now if she wants to fool around.' He was so nonchalant, joking and being his cheery self. I didn't think it would be so sudden. I should have stayed with him."

I don't answer. I know Paul well enough to know what he's thinking. He wishes he'd been there to say goodbye, to see death firsthand as he envisaged it: peaceful, while asleep, loved ones close by. Perhaps it would have helped erase the memory he had of our father's death, five years earlier. Paul and his wife had taken Dad and our stepmother out for dinner, agreeing in advance they would play a few hands of cards when they came back. While Paul was setting up the card table, Dad went to the washroom. He never came out. Paul found him sprawled on the floor, covered in vomit, his pants around his ankles. When he called to tell me, my burden was released. After I delivered the eulogy and witnessed his internment next to Mom, I was relieved. And I wouldn't ever need to see my stepmother again.

Paul's voice brings me back to the present. "No one should die alone."

It's an awkward moment. Paul is no doubt thinking about Dad and Henri. Meanwhile, I'm thinking of a far greater personal loss that happened almost 40 years earlier ... Ronnie, a brother who died before Paul was born. As Paul is haunted by Dad's death, Ronnie's death disturbs me. On July 10, 1961, Ronnie drowned at age nine. I was just a year older. The funeral was open coffin, but Ronnie wasn't in it. It was the body of a stranger—bloated, puffy-cheeked, and pale. I remember crying out, "That's not him! That's not Ronnie!"

Chest pains bring me back to the present, compounded by my headache. I have to get off the phone. "The last few months have been hard for all of us, Paul. Listen, I'd better phone the office and tell them I won't be in. I'll call you later."

It's going to be one hell of a lousy day.

Pushing away thoughts of other times and other deaths, I recall my last encounter with Henri, two days earlier. When I arrived at the hospice, he was sitting in a vinyl-covered chair in his half of the room, with his back to the window. A green blanket is draped over his legs, and he is peering at a framed picture in his lap. I watch as he cradles the picture, holding it as if it were a kitten. I recognize it: a young blond man, average height, with a happy and handsome face. When I'd first seen the photo—sometime in the mid-seventies I'd asked Henri about it. His answer was curt: "That's Dieter, someone I once knew well." Something in his tone told me to drop the subject.

Behind Henri the sun was setting, giving the room a warm saffron glow. When I said hello he turned the picture face down and told me to sit on the edge of the bed. Pulling his bathrobe close around his bony chest, he smiled at me, and then gazed over my shoulder with a faraway look in his eyes. It was so unlike Henri to seem lost in reverie.

I study his face. His large hazel eyes, normally alert to all that went on around him, are misted, focused inwardly on a private thought. He tugs at one of his elephantine ears, puts his hand under his chin, and then sighs. "I hate this place, Josh. It's a hospice. Only one way out. The guy beside me's on life support and never says a word. I never see any doctors. They don't bother with me. Why should they? And the nurses? They act more like funeral directors. They're pleasant enough, but there's no passion in any of them. I'm just another body, soon to be removed. In the meantime, they feed and clean and inspect me every four hours to see if I'm still alive."

I don't like to hear Henri talk this way. Can't he see the look on my face? I stand up and go to the window, wishing he would change the subject.

He continues, "I'm cut off from everything I enjoy. There's no one to talk to. Once I've read the paper, there's nothing to do—no one to visit, no place to go. I need to be where there's some action, some excitement."

He stops, pushes back his shoulders, and shakes his head. "I can hardly believe I said that Josh. It's not like me, but I'm lonely, I'm dying, and for the first time in my life, there isn't a damn thing I can do about it. If it weren't for you and Paul and others coming by, I'd have probably said, 'Kiss my ass!' to this world months ago!"

"Henri, you've always told the world to kiss your ass! I've known you for nearly thirty years, and you've been a crusty old bugger all that time. If you ask me, the problem now is that you have no freedom. You can't do what you used to, and I can see it's getting to you. You're turning into a bitter old man!"

Henri laughs. "That will never happen, Josh. The nurses around here call me a dirty old man, but they've never called me bitter. It's just that, since I've been here, I'm by myself too much. Too many hours with nothing to do but think of the past, wait for death, and wonder if I've done all I could to make a difference."

"How could you ever doubt that Henri? After all you've done for our family and for others? All those children you helped when no one else would? How do you think Paul and the others would have turned out if you hadn't stepped in and given them a father's love? You were also there after my mother was diagnosed with cancer and was in and out of hospital. You looked after Eddie, Willie, and Ben off and on for four years."

I didn't say a word about my brother, Luke. I didn't need to. Henri and I had that conversation before. Luke, and everyone around him knew he was "different" and moved into a home where gay boys were tolerated.

Henri looks at me, and squints his eyes. He takes a deep breath, rests both hands on his knees, and leans forward in his chair. "Yes, Josh, shortly after your mother died—what, twenty-four years ago now? I did take in Paul and Matt. Eddie, Willie, and Ben were older. They didn't need much attention. They all turned out to be good men, but they didn't have a mother and your stepmother did everything she could to get rid of them. I don't know why, but this has been bugging me for days. What do you think?"

Henri expects an answer, but when he sits back and folds his hands in his lap, I know that he wants me to think about his question before answering. My reply is important to him—it will somehow make a difference in his last few days. I go back over everything I know about him and his relationship with our family. Why is Henri raising doubts about what he'd done? Why is he asking for my opinion at this point? If Matt and Paul had had a mother figure while they lived with Henri, would they have been better off? Mom was an alcoholic, then an invalid. She hadn't been much of a mother as far as I was concerned.

I duck the question, buy some time to answer it. "We could all be different people, Henri, if things didn't happen as they did. Why is this bothering you now? You personally never had any use for women except in a ballroom or bedroom."

Henri takes the picture from his lap and hugs it to his chest. Rocking from side to side in his chair, his eyes to the floor, he says nothing.

In the hallway, the sounds of people walking by and talking in muted voices bothers me. I wish they would laugh or say something more spirited. Does this hospice have to be so funereal? I get up from the bed and sit in the chair next to Henri.

He looks over at me, the picture still in his lap. "I'm trapped in this room and dying. I have too much idle time, Josh, way too much time. I hear strange ghostly voices, and I have strange thoughts. I hear Beethoven music and the number twelve keeps popping up. It's weird but ..." Henri stops, just for a moment or two, and then he continues. "Look, forget I asked. I'm tired of sitting in this chair. Help me into bed, won't you?"

Henri puts out a gaunt, trembling arm. Once he's in his bed resting against the pillows, I sit in the armchair. The nurse comes in with some pills.

Henri suddenly smiles. "I thought we had a deal, nurse. No pills, just vodka or gin."

He takes the pills from the nurse and then tosses them in the waste-basket when she leaves. Typical Henri.

I laugh and shake my head.

"Josh, I need you to deal with one or two loose ends. Piclow, that high-priced lawyer on Main Street, will call you once I'm gone. I've had a good life. I've lived pretty much as I pleased and have few regrets. My house is pretty much in order, except for one thing, which I've left for you to resolve."

"You've left something for me to resolve? That's not like you, Henri. What do you want me to do?"

The corners of his mouth turn up just a little, and he opens his eyes a bit wider. "You'll see, Josh, soon. Yes, quite soon, you'll see very clearly." He continues to stare deeply into my eyes.

I don't like it and look away. The sun has almost set. Henri taps his fingers lightly on the picture frame to get my attention, then says, in a business-like manner, "You're executor of my will, Josh. You're one of the few people I trust in this world—so responsible, so serious. I don't have much, but I want you to take care of my mementoes and say good things about me at my funeral. Here, take this." He pushes the picture towards me, his hand trembling.

I can't believe how weak he's become, but Henri doesn't want my pity or sympathy. I quickly relieve him of his burden and then look at the photo. Standing in front of a meadow, a forest of pine trees off in the distance behind him, is an attractive young man smiling self-assuredly—tall, powerfully built, probably in his late teens. Turning it over, I read in Henri's distinct, almost unintelligible handwriting, "Dieter–1958. Timmins. Soon to be college boy."

I don't want any more responsibility. I don't want to think about Henri's death, or anybody else's for that matter. I'd attended too many funerals starting at too early an age. I just want to be left alone.

"Listen, Henri. You're too ornery and stubborn to die anytime soon. Besides, I don't know much about this Dieter guy, so I don't understand what it is you want me to do with his picture. Any time I've asked you about him, you've brushed me off. Same thing when I asked you about your family and roots in Belgium. Why don't you just hang on to it?"

I try to put it back in his lap, but he waves me away from the bed. He says nothing for a moment, just grins at me in a knowing way. Finally, he speaks. "We've known each other a long time, Josh. You know as much about me as you need to know for now. Promise me you'll look after my things."

"Dammit, Henri, you know I will. I just can't see the point, and you're not making it any easier. What makes this picture so special? Why won't you tell me?" Henri is silent. Is he reading my body language? Quickly I stuff my emotions back into the dark abyss where they normally hide.

Henri resumes. "All in good time, Josh. Soon. Relax and don't worry about it. Just make sure you go through my things after I'm gone. Then it will be clear. In the meantime, take this picture home with you. I won't be needing it anymore." Henri turns his head away from me, looking out the window. It's his way of telling me the discussion is over.

I don't know if I can handle this. Henri got to a tipping point and shut down. Just like me.

7

The sun is gone by then. The crows have settled down outside, no longer raucously vying for bedtime perches. All is quiet. Henri is not going to say any more that night. I know it's useless to probe. It never works. Anytime I ask him to tell me about his youth, he ducks the question. Few of his stories go back beyond the time he immigrated to Canada, in 1946. Anything he says about his childhood and adolescence are factual and terse, without elaboration or colour.

Our silence is broken when the nurse comes in. She is young and shapely. Her gait reminds me of a model walking down a runway. I start towards the door.

Henri sits bolt upright, grows, and casts a mischievous grin at the nurse. "Yes, Josh, time for you to go. *Cette jolie jeune femme* wants to be alone with me."

As I'm leaving, he says once more, "Don't forget what I said about my things!"

I just shake my head and leave, promising I'll come back and see him the following week. In the parking lot, I look up to the window to Henri's room. A smile on her face, the nurse is closing the blinds, her head turns sideways, no doubt intently listening to whatever Henri is saying. He has a way with the ladies, as always.

As she closes the blinds, my gut closes too. I bend over and do what the psychologists and psychic healers told me to do: take three deep breaths and focus on a pleasant memory. Like always, it only works for a few seconds, then the pain returns. My master. When it does subside, I'm a zombie, empty inside for hours, hollow, devoid of emotion. My shrink calls it apathy. In my ACOA/ACA meetings, the more experienced Adult Children of Alcoholics called it an avoidance state.

∞

The clock in the front hall strikes seven times, waking me from my reverie and bringing me back to the present. Henri is dead, leaving me with the burden of burying him and disposing of his worldly goods.

Once again, I'm Mr. Responsible. The calm, dispassionate guy who keeps cool while everyone else wails, sobs, wrings their hands, or completely freezes. But I'm no Walter Mitty, wasting my days in grandiose daydreams; I'm busy solving everyone else's problems. I don't have time for wallowing in any emotional snake pit. Besides, none of the counselling sessions, whether one-on-one or in groups, do any good. They just resurrect more ghosts and add to my burden.

"Don't forget what I said about my things!" His parting words now make me queasy, unsettled. The familiar burn in my gut returns, Henri didn't care much for "things." Why did he try, at the last, to tell me otherwise? What was he getting at? And why had he alluded to Beethoven, numbers, and strange, ghostly voices?

What will I be thinking about on my deathbed? It's not a question I want to answer now; better to deal with the immediate problems, like calling my office and getting the number for the funeral home.

I do my chores, staring blankly out the window over the stainless-steel sink, and then sit at the kitchen table. Poor Henri. At least he went in his sleep, which is what the nurse told Paul. Had she told Paul that it was a peaceful death? I can't remember. I just assume that anyone who dies in his sleep goes peacefully. Is it possible to die asleep, in torment? Can a nightmare kill you? Henri said he'd been troubled in his last days, but we'd never finished that conversation. I don't like to talk about emotions any more than I care to show them.

I look at the clock on the stove. It's seven-thirty. Soon my wife, Jackie, and the kids will be up. I will have no peace or solitude once they stir.

They have to know about Henri. He'd been such a close family friend. I quietly make my way up the carpeted stairs to the bedroom to tell Jackie. She can tell the kids. She's good at that sort of thing, better than me. When I open the door, the radio alarm clicks off. Jackie is lying in bed with the quilted eiderdown cover pulled high to her neck. She's even less of a morning person than me, but she likes having breakfast with the kids. After she sends them off to school with big hugs and kisses, she goes back to bed until ten or so. I have never been able to sleep during the day. Once I'm up, I'm up.

Jackie peers at me with half-closed eyes. "What are you doing here? It's after seven-thirty."

"Paul called while I was having breakfast."

"What did he want so early?" Jackie kicks off the covers and sits up on the far side of the bed, leaning on her arms. Yawning and stretching, she makes her way to the closet and pulls her bathrobe from the hanger. She then turns and shuffles towards the bathroom.

"He wouldn't have called so early if he didn't have something important to say."

Jackie stops, folds her arms, and gives me a stabbing look. "Don't play games with me, Josh, please! I'm not a mind reader!"

My chest pains and headache intensify. I wrap my arms around my gut and stifle the sobs and sadness trying to surface. I shove them back into the abyss.

"Henri died last night, about two hours after Paul left. Paul was pretty shaken up about it."

Jackie turns around, coming close to me but stopping when she sees me backing away. For an instant, her eyes cloud; then she picks up on my last words, while heading towards the bathroom again. "I imagine he was. Henri was like a father to him, your sister Annie, and most of your brothers. Poor Paul. Are you going to see him?"

"Later. I asked him to let the rest of the family know. I have to look after the funeral arrangements and see Henri's lawyer. Henri insisted, probably because he knew Paul would fall apart. And you know Matt, he doesn't have the wherewithal to do any of it."

Jackie has her green-handled toothbrush in her hand as we talk. She puts it down, turns off the tap, and comes to where I'm standing, just inside the bedroom door. She hugs me, her left hand rubbing my back, her right cradling my head. "I'm sorry, Josh. Henri was a good man who did a lot for your family—for a lot of other families too. It's too bad he got so sick and had to spend his last days in a hospice. He was such an energetic old devil before, despite his age. I can't believe he wouldn't take their painkillers; afraid they would cloud his judgment. Such a stubborn man. He would rather suffer pain than risk a loss of consciousness. That was Henri, feisty and spirited to the end."

"That's what Paul said ... on ... the ... phone ... too." I'm gasping for air as I finish the sentence. Jackie's embrace is like a straitjacket, stifling me. I need to escape.

Jackie doesn't let go completely. She slides her right hand down to my left hand, gently squeezing it, resting her other hand on my shoulder. "I know you don't want to talk about it, Josh, but I'm here if you change your mind. Henri was right to ask you to look after his affairs. You'll see that his will is honoured, and when you deliver the eulogy there probably won't be a dry eye in the chapel."

She knows I prefer presentation to conversation, because when I have time to prepare—to choose words and phrases to arouse others— I can do it. Very well, others tell me. Too bad I can't do it spontaneously or naturally.

I can't let go. I never could, even as a child. Not in front of others. I can't express emotion. It causes too much pain. It makes me feel like I'm in a giant cement mixer filled with shit and scents that I inhale and swallow. I can't go there. From an early age I'd found a way to escape— put all that crap behind a steel trap door from which nothing escapes, leaving emptiness and numbness. Now, with the door slammed shut I can carry on. I back away.

Jackie winces, takes a deep breath, and then looks at me like a child would look at a puppy she can't take home from a pet shop. "Josh, I'll look after getting the kids to school and telling them about Henri. Why don't you go down to the study? I'll bring you a coffee once the boys are gone."

"Tell the kids I'll see them later. I'd like you to come to the funeral home during visitation hours, but I don't want them there, okay? They can come the last day, after the coffin is closed. I want them to hear what I have to say about Henri, but I don't want them to see his corpse. We'll put his picture on top of the coffin."

"The kids know how much Henri meant to you and your family, Josh. I think they're old enough to decide for themselves whether they want to be there earlier. They know we're all mortal. I think we should leave it up to them."

"Jackie, please! After what I went through when Ronnie died, I just don't want our kids being scarred like I am …. like I was."

"We've had this conversation before, Josh. You can't keep all these things bottled up. It isn't healthy. Look at you. I can see what you're feeling even though you think you're hiding it. You'll have to learn to say goodbye at some point!" Jackie slams the bathroom door behind her.

Good, now I can be alone. I go to the basement, closing the door at the stairwell as I descend. We have both retired to neutral corners, away from the world and each other.

The basement is soundproof, something I insisted on when we finished my office. The contractor had to stomp around on the floor above before I would let him close off the basement ceiling. I sit at the cherry-wood desk, then pick up a framed picture I have of Henri with my two youngest brothers, Matt, and Paul. They were just boys then. The photo is at least twenty years old. Henri's arms are around them, protective and proud. I have no pictures of Mom and Dad hugging me. I push that thought away. Better to focus on the job at hand.

"You were a good man, Henri Deault, and I'm gonna make sure no one forgets!"

I put the picture down and take a pencil and notepad from the desk drawer. Within an hour, I've filled more than six pages. Not hard to do when you have more than thirty years of personal experience and family anecdotes to choose from. I read it over. Tears and sobs try to surface. I force them away. No time and too many bad memories to handle. Satisfied that I can do no more, I look at the picture Henri had given me of Dieter. What was their relationship, and why was Henri so sure I'd find the answer?

Before I can take the thought any further, Jackie opens the stairwell door. "I've got a cup of coffee for you, Josh," she says. "Do you want me to bring it down?"

The tone in her voice tells me she's forgiven me. It's safe to ascend. "No, I'm coming up."

The cat is lying on the carpet at the top of the stairs, looking at me with half-closed eyes, his tail limp. He knows better than to expect anything. I step over him and onto the white ceramic tile in the kitchen. Jackie sets my coffee cup on the table, next to the kids' dirty dishes. I glare at her. She knows I like a tidy kitchen.

She ignores the look and studies my face. "What were you doing down there?"

"I wrote some things about Henri ... for the funeral. It's on the desk. Why don't you look at it? Tell me what you think."

I sit at the round oak table, drinking my coffee. My stomach is empty, acidic. I haven't eaten anything yet. I can't stop thinking about Henri's death and our last conversation. Outside, the clouds are moving in, blocking the sun, and robbing the room of warmth. I shiver. Is it in response to the weather or the thought of Henri's death ... or the memory of Ronnie's death?

Jackie puts the dishes in the sink. I hear her making baby talk with the cat before she goes back upstairs.

I get up to distract myself, to ward off the memories flooding my thoughts. I stand by one of the long, thin windows, seeing nothing, swirling my coffee. It's hot. Steamy. I can feel its vapour rising inside my nose. The phone rings again. Damned phones. Now who's calling?

I pick up the receiver. "Hello, Bencet, here." I suddenly realize what I've said and how I've said it. I used my usual gruff office voice, the one that implies I'm busy and this better be important.

It's Henri's lawyer. He asks me to come over to pick up a copy of the will and the key Henri had left with him. Recalling Henri's wishes, I grab my green down-filled jacket from the closet, and from the hall rack, car keys for my five-year-old, dark-red Ford. I turn on the radio to distract further thoughts, and go straight to the lawyer's office.

Besides the ache in my stomach and the burning in my chest, my forehead tenses up, amplifying the pain already there. I tell myself it's the change in weather. The sun is gone, covered by clouds in varying shades of grey. On the horizon, they're pitch black. The rain will start soon. When it does, I hope my headache will end. In the meantime, I take our compact umbrella out of the glove box, go into a nondescript professional building, and climb the carpeted stairs to the second floor. At the end of a short corridor, I see a sign on the door: K. L. Piclow, LLB, Barrister and Solicitor. Below it, another sign saying Please Enter. I turn the knob and straight in front of me I see his secretary intently peering at her monitor. I clear my throat and she immediately looks up, smiles, and comes around her desk. Recalling why I'm there the smile turns to sorrow and she expresses her sympathy. I'm sure Henri used to flatter her just like he did all the other women in town.

Gently squeezing my arm she guides me to Piclow's private office and opens the door. Piclow points to the chair and I sit down. Our conversation is banal, stilted. Henri hadn't had much use for lawyers, and he probably told Piclow as much in a jesting manner that thinly disguised his opinion. We review Henri's simple will, and then I leave. The rain begins just after I get into my car. I turn on the wipers and drive to Henri's apartment. It only takes a few minutes; our tiny village only has one stoplight.

I pull up in front of the red-brick building and get out of my car. Why Henri had kept his apartment after going into the hospice was puzzling to people who didn't know him well. Those of us who did were not surprised. Henri always had to have a place of his own. *"Mon château,"* he said.

Henri's apartment is as I remembered it: a TV in the corner of the living room, an easy chair, an end table, and a pull-out sofa bed. Four inexpensive chairs, a radio, and a yellowed table in the kitchen. In the bedroom, a single cot, a clock, and a dresser. Too austere for me, but Henri said the décor suited him fine. He wasn't much interested in worldly goods.

Henri's mementos are in his bedroom dresser. From the bottom drawer, under some old undershirts, I retrieve a plain cardboard box, the kind picture frames come in. In it are a medal, a notebook, a letter, and two pictures. There are two people in the first picture: a pretty young blonde girl and Dieter—the young man in the portrait Henri had given me two days before. I flip the picture over. The first thing I notice is a scrawled, hand-written date: 1961. My heart starts pounding, increasing the pain coursing throughout my body. 1961 had been a bad year for me. Henri knew that. What possible good can come from revisiting it? I had never known Henri to be a cruel man. Yet here he has left a trail that unnerves me. I turn my attention from the picture to the folded letter. With shaking hands, I unfold the yellowed, two-page document and begin to read:

July 10, 1961

Valiantly in the line of duty, Ranger Dieter Franc died today ...

"What? What kind of sick joke is this? It can't be. Henri, why are you doing this to me?"

CHAPTER 2

Dieter Appears

A wake or dreaming? I don't know. I only know I'm not at Henri's, and this isn't my bed. The chrome side rails, both pulled high, remind me of the hospice where Henri had died. My throat is dry, and the sheets are scratchy. They smell of laundry soap and disinfectant. A pale pink curtain cages me in a space just large enough to house the bed, a chrome chair with a vinyl seat cover, and a metal table with a fake wooden top. On the table is a plastic cup with a lid and drinking straw. I take a sip and almost gag. The water is tepid and tastes of chlorine—disgusting.

Jackie comes in, pulling the curtain back far enough for me to see she's carrying flowers and a crystal vase. She looks at me, her head cocked to one side, her eyes puffy, weary, and red.

"Jackie, you look like I feel, but I'm glad to see you. Will you get me some decent water, please? And tell me what I'm doing here."

Jackie puts the flowers on the table beside the cup. After opening the curtain halfway, she goes into the bathroom with the vase. I can hear the water running, its distinct sound changing as it fills the container. Jackie comes back and arranges the flowers, blending the reds, whites, and yellows among the green ferns. I don't have a clue what the flowers are. Don't care much either.

"Jackie, never mind the damned bouquet, talk to me!"

From the other side of the bed, a male voice I don't recognize answers. "Josh, she can't hear you. You're not awake."

I turn in the direction of the voice. No one is there. "Who said that?"

"Hi, Josh. I'm Dieter Franc, Henri's ward. I'm the guy in the picture Henri gave you at the hospice. Remember?"

"Dieter? The guy who died the same day as my brother, Ronnie?" My throat constricts, my stomach muscles churn, and my blood pressure skyrockets. I close my eyes, bury my head in the pillow, and start deep breathing exercises.

"Josh, I already told you, you're not awake. The good news is, in the state you're in I can work some magic."

The pillow slowly starts moving away from my head. My heart rate lowers, and my muscles relax. I have to ask him, "Are you doing this?"

"Yep, no need for you to be any worse off. Reading that letter knocked you flat and you're going to stay out of touch for a bit. The fact Ronnie and I both died on July 10, 1961, was a coincidence you couldn't handle, even though Ronnie and I've been gone for nearly forty years. That's why you're here, where you need to be."

"Well, I don't want to be here. I don't need to be here."

"Yes, you do, so get used to it."

I turn the other way. Jackie is sitting in the chair, digging a paperback out of her bag. What the hell's going on? I shriek at her. "Jackie!"

"Josh, you're not listening. She can't hear you. As far as she knows, you're in a coma, so forget about her. Scream, shout, do whatever you want. It won't make any difference. And we've got you in a state better than any guru, medium, psychic healer, or doctor could induce with their promises and prescriptions."

I sit up in bed, grab the side rail and look in the direction of the voice. Still no one there. I shake the railing. Jackie pays no attention and just keeps reading her book. I grip the rail in both hands and try to lower it.

"You're fighting this way too hard, Josh. The sooner you accept where you are, the better. As long as you think you're awake, you're just going to upset yourself. You can't talk to Jackie. Even if you get out of bed, no one will notice. As far as Jackie or anyone else is concerned, you're lying on your side, completely out of it—period. Just let go, then you can see me."

"Let go? I'm lying here in a strange bed, out of touch, talking to a ghost sent by Henri. I can't see you, and I'm watching a wife who can't see me ... doesn't make any sense."

"You're right. It doesn't make any sense now, but it will. Henri knows what he's doing."

"Henri knows what he's doing? What are you talking about? Henri's dead."

"Yes, Henri's dead, I'm dead, and you ... well, you're somewhere in between. And that's how it's gonna be for a while."

"No, you can't do this to me. This can't be happening. Why can't I see you? What's going on here?"

Just then, dressed in a dark suit, my youngest brother, Paul, enters the room. Jackie stands. Paul puts his arms around her. They both have their heads turned towards me. Jackie sighs and moves closer to the bed. I can feel her hand on my face. Paul comes and stands beside her. I put my hands up, motioning for them to get closer. No reaction.

"Paul, Jackie, for chrissakes, why are you treating me as if I'm not here?"

The voice of this Dieter guy is now talking to me from inside my head. *"Poor Josh, here, but not here. Confusing isn't it? Well, you're just going to have to accept it for what it is. When you do, we can move on. I'll be back later."*

What the fuck? What's going on? How do I stop this nonsense? I can see, hear, move about, but nothing I do has any effect on the physical world around me. Somehow there's a mental me and a physical me, and the link between them is tenuous. My state of consciousness has no relationship to my body. Where in the hell am I?

Jackie stoops and picks up a tote bag from beside her purse. She takes out a picture and puts it on the table next to the cup. It's a photograph of our family, taken the previous summer.

Paul loosens his tie, takes off his jacket, and stands next to Jackie, his arm gently touching her elbow. "Josh wrote a nice eulogy for Henri. It's too bad he wasn't there to deliver it. Was the way I read it okay?"

"It was fine, Paul. Such a complex man, your brother. He's tough and ornery and aloof with practically the entire world, but when it comes to words on paper, it's like there's a whole other person. Sensitive, caring, sympathetic. Even more bizarre, his best writing comes out in eulogies. Remember when your father died?"

"Yeah, when I told him Dad died he just grunted and said, 'I'm the oldest, I'll do the eulogy. You look after everything else.' At the funeral home, Josh asked us all kinds of questions, then locked himself in the basement to write the funeral speech. When he read it, there wasn't a dry eye in the place. He never said a word about his memories of Dad. Even more bizarre he was surprised there was a headstone at the gravesite. Dad had it put there after Mom died more than twenty years ago. Josh never visited her grave. All he said at the cemetery after we carried the casket to the graveside was, 'Good, they're back together.'"

There's a pained expression on Paul's face. He walks to the window and looks outside. Jackie gives him a minute, then joins him. She puts an arm on his shoulder and responds.

"Josh referred to Henri as his father figure. After I met Henri, I could see why. He said when he had time he'd probably write an article about Henri and submit it to *Reader's Digest*'s series 'The Most Unforgettable Character I Have Ever Met.' He admired Henri more than anyone else on this planet. Henri had five of you living with him once your mother found out she had terminal cancer. And it was Henri who found a home for your sister, Annie."

"Poor Mom, only forty-five when she died and in and out of hospitals for four years before that. I was ten when she got sick. Our doctor told Josh that if Mom had had regular screening he could have saved her. He wasn't happy. He told Josh that, with eight kids, she hadn't acted very responsibly."

"I never met her. I only know Josh was at university when she went for treatment at St. Margaret's in Toronto. He told me he went to visit her one day. It was only a couple of subway stops from his place. I remember because Josh told me not to tell any of you what he learned. That was years ago. Since then I've noticed, and he's said more than once, you're Josh's favourite. I suspect you know the secret."

"Yes, I do. On one of our golfing getaways he told me. Mom had had two miscarriages before he was born. Imagine eleven pregnancies, so probably a shotgun wedding. But Mom didn't tell him that. She told him the name of the doctor who delivered him because Josh was trying to get a birth certificate. Years after Mom died, Aunt Lucille told Josh there was a specialist involved because of the prior stillbirths."

I want to break into the conversation. I don't like dirty laundry being dragged out. They both know it's hard for me and here they are discussing it in a hospital. If anyone hears their conversation, everyone in town will know about it. More secrets spread around to confirm what an abnormal family we are.

"Yes, Josh told me that story too. He also told me he didn't say much about his family all the time he was growing up. He figured everyone knew his parents were drunks. Besides, he moved out when he was eighteen and back then it was cool to be on your own."

"Josh is the only one who seemed to be scarred. Mom and Dad never beat us. There was always food around, even if it was canned meat or fish and Josh was the server. Yes, Eddie and Luke had their share of problems and Ronnie was only nine when he died, but the rest of us turned out okay."

"I think Henri had a lot to do with that."

"Yes, he did and you were there at the funeral. Josh wrote a great eulogy and the anecdotes everyone shared with us were priceless. Henri left a mark."

"Yes, yes he did. I'm glad the witch, Liz, wasn't there to spoil the service."

"None of us heard from Liz, after he died. Once she and Dad were married, she made it clear her two kids were welcome but the rest of us should get out. And Dad was not the kind of guy to say anything. I remember Eddie saying Dad was pussy whipped. None of us are much in for swearing but we agreed Liz was a bitch and we were better off living elsewhere."

"I never liked Liz, either. She made me feel unwelcome any time Josh insisted we take our boys there. The only time she had anything positive to say was when Josh was preparing your Dad's eulogy, three years ago now."

"Luke was the only brother who stayed with Mom once she got sick, back in 1971.Eddie, Willie, and Ben ate and slept at Henri's and friends' homes off and on almost as soon as Henri came to Bond's Hill back in 1964. He only lived a block away and he was such a caregiver. Dad was never one to cook or stay at home and look after kids."

I don't want to be reminded of those times. Do I have to listen to this crap? I've got enough shit on my plate. I don't need any more. What purpose does it serve?

Jackie and Paul come away from the window, looking at me for just a few seconds; the expressions on their faces telling me they want to be elsewhere. Paul stops at the foot of my bed. Jackie rests her hands on the rail beside my head and continues their conversation.

"Josh didn't talk about it often, but I know he wished your father was more like Henri. He said your father was a good husband but not much of a dad."

"Well, maybe Josh was looking for something the rest of us didn't need or feel was missing. He's pretty quiet when we have a family reunion. He'd rather cook the hamburgers and clean up afterwards."

"Oh, Paul, he's such a different person when he's with me and the kids. I don't know what it is, but when the four of us are together, it's as if another person enters his body. He's outgoing, fun, telling all of us how wonderful we are and how much we mean to him, wanting a family hug every night. Now look at him. Lying here completely out of it. I still don't understand. It's been four days. All the doctors will say is he's had some kind of traumatic shock, and we just have to wait."

"I don't know what happened, Jackie, haven't a clue. Walking into Henri's place, after you called me, finding Josh on the floor. I was shocked but relieved when I felt his pulse. An open drawer, and a letter and some pictures lying there beside him. I wonder if they had anything to do with his collapse?"

"I don't know, but the doctor ruled out epilepsy and heart problems. The doctors say they can't help him until he snaps out of it, and the best thing for us to do is be here as often as possible, talk to him, that sort of thing. I told them about his childhood, how Ronnie's death haunts him, and his Adult Children of Alcoholics meetings. The doctor just shrugged and said mental issues can sometimes cause a breakdown."

"Josh always seems so thick-skinned and self-assured. This is unlike him. No one saw this coming. I'll drop in as often as I can. In the meantime, take care of yourself. We'll look after your boys while you're here. It's the least we can do. I'm sure Josh is going to be all right."

Paul gives Jackie a farewell hug, and then Jackie and I are alone. I can't do a damned thing to tell her I'm present. How can I see her, be a witness to all that is around me, and still not be seen or heard?

Jackie picks up the picture from the table and stands next to the bed, looking at the family portrait as she talks. "I remember when we had this picture taken, Josh. This spring, just after the spiraea bloomed. So typical of you to want the photographer to do an outdoor backdrop, with lots of flowers around. Even though you say flowers are such a bother and you refuse to learn their names, you really are a garden person."

Jackie puts the picture down and presses her nose against the flowers in the vase, taking deep breaths and smiling as she inhales their scent.

I can't smell anything. This twilight zone I'm in is starting to get on my nerves. What do I have to do to get out?

The voice breaks in again. "You have to believe, Josh. You have to believe I'm here, that Henri sent me, and that you can be in two places at once."

I must be crazy, or this is the weirdest dream I've ever had. But unlike any other dream, this one isn't ending. I can't waken. "Okay, I guess I have to go with it. You're Dieter, Henri sent you, and I can be physically in one place and mentally in another. Both you and Henri are dead, I'm totally out of it, but somehow this is all normal. Now, show yourself."

"Not so fast, Josh. Saying the words is not the same as believing. Right now, you're still three-quarters locked up in that body on the bed. Until you can accept you're not dreaming, and your spirit is free to leave, we're not going anywhere and I'm invisible."

"I'm not sure I want to see you. I don't understand why you're here or what I've done to be trapped in this nightmare."

"Because it's time, Josh. I came because Henri wanted me to, for your sake. He said something about exorcising some demons you've long suppressed. I'm part of the rescue team. He knew you were scarred by Ronnie's death and other things. So here I am."

"I'm fine! We all have some rough edges and emotional wounds that leave their marks. Why do mine need any special attention, especially from a couple of ghosts?"

"Because it's unfinished business for Henri, Josh, and because you never really, honestly said goodbye to Ronnie or dealt with all that repressed emotion in a healthy way. Henri says Ronnie's death haunts you way too much. Henri was never one to leave a wrong untouched. He was troubled when he died. You know that. He talked to you about it."

23

"He told me to look after his things. He never said anything about Ronnie. All he did was give me your picture and tell me he left something for me to resolve."

"He knew better, Josh. You've got an emotional shell that a nuclear bomb can't pierce. He tried to get you to talk about Ronnie before he died. Just like you tried to get him to talk about me, remember? So you both refused to go where there was great pain. All Henri would tell you is he was hearing voices and music, having strange thoughts, and seeing the number twelve. Anyway, what's done is done, and here you are listening to me. Henri blew things wide open."

"I don't see why I have to play a part in Henri's unfinished business. I just want to go back to Jackie and my sons. Can't you and Henri just leave me alone?"

No sound, just silence.

Jackie backs away from the table and opens the curtain around my bed. The sun sits atop the horizon, sharing its red and orange hues with the clouds that surround it. Jackie stares out the window, motionless for two or three minutes. Then she returns to the chair, picks up her book, and slides it into her tote bag. "I've got to go now, Josh. Time to eat. I'll be back later."

"What about me? When can I leave? I don't want to stay here. I want to go too and never come back. Jackie, take me with you." Suddenly I'm beside her, in the doorway, looking out to the hallway.

"So, you made the leap of faith, Josh, thanks to Jackie. Good. Now we can get started."

I look back to the source of the voice. It's Dieter, the young man in the photo Henri showed me. He's standing there wearing a ranger uniform, his arms open, beckoning me to draw near.

I see my body on the bed, and Jackie on her way out. I want to go with her but, like iron near a magnet, I'm drawn to Dieter's side and incapable of doing anything but follow him.

∞

Dieter leads me into the bathroom and points at the mirror. I see two translucent figures: his and mine. Around him is a brilliant, wide aura, like you see in a religious painting. My silhouette is just that, with no glow and no expanded radiance. Before I can ask any questions, he takes me back to the main room. A pinkish aura surrounds my body. Dieter moves to the far side of the bed. He's back in human form.

"Please forgive me for being so commanding, Josh. I wanted you to see your life force in the mirror. Proof you can be in two places at the same time. Sort of."

I stare at my body on the bed. Pins and needles, hot flashes, and goose bumps envelop me as I remember. *This has happened before.*

Dieter jumps in. "Yep, it isn't the first time. I can now hear your thoughts and tap into your senses and memories so I know. This is your third out-of-body experience. Both prior events were brief, happened years ago, and scared the shit out of you. You're feeling that stress again, but I can do something about it." Dieter claps his hands. My heart rate slows. Deep breaths wash away my bodily tension. Instead of goose bumps, my skin feels like it's being massaged, like I'm in a Jacuzzi. I want to relax but ... "Stop right there, Josh. Stinking thinking kicks in automatically when you feel good because you're afraid it won't last, all that you learned about in ACOA but now that you're out of your body, I can shut off that switch quickly."

I'm speechless and unable to think. I see and hear the words, tranquil, peaceful, and calm, and that's how I feel.

Seeing my state of composure, Dieter puts his hands in front of him, over the bed, his index fingers pointing down. "Your body and your aura." He then points his right hand straight ahead directly at me. "Your life force, 'you' in another realm." He walks around the bed, cutting off my view of my body. "Where you are now, I'm totally in sync with your life force and can pretty much transfer anything I want

to you. What you see, hear, feel, taste, and smell is coming from me."
He opens his arms and embraces me, his mouth pressed up to my right
ear. He whispers, "No harm will come to you here, Josh." He steps
back. "Henri brought us together for a reason."

"Henri didn't have a mean bone in his body, and the way I feel right
now is proof of what you say. Still I'm having a tough time getting used
to this ... this situation."

"Understandable, but this time you're not alone outside your body
and we're in a place where we can access your suppressed emotions and
memories and leverage all the lessons I've learned on this side of the
life/death divide. I saw you wince because of the rose tint to your body.
It's the same colour that healer saw when you and Jackie went on that
psychic cruise to the Caribbean islands. You were able to eliminate the
pain by following his suggestions, which convinced you that western
medicine doesn't have all the answers. We think we can do something
about your current maladies."

"I don't have any maladies. I'm not on any drugs, and every time I
go for a checkup I get a clean bill of health."

Dieter shakes his head and points at my comatose form on the bed.
"The fact your body is lying there surrounded by a red aura proves
you're not well, Josh. The cause, however, is not physical, it's psycho-
logical. The counsellors you've seen since your first year at university
just don't understand or have access to the tools we have. Your life
force had to make that third leap from your body but now that you've
done it I can work on it."

"This could just be a dream and Jackie and I will have a good laugh
when I wake up and tell her about it."

"You won't wake up until we've completed our mission. If this were
a dream you could exit at any time."

I go to the bed and place my hands on my inert body. It's warm. I
can see it breathing. It's solid and feels like a human, but I can't pen-
etrate its shell or feel any kinship with it.

"Poke it prod it. Nothing will change, Josh. You're not in control and you've conceded Henri is trustworthy. But ... let me give you a further demonstration." Dieter moves to the far side of the bed ensuring I can see him and my detached body at the same time. He extends his arms, palms forward. After taking a deep breath he smiles, raises his eyebrows, and opens his eyes wide to peer at me intently.

My eyes close involuntarily. Inside my head I see and hear ocean waves gently washing up on a sandy beach. Energy like you feel during a lightning storm gently makes its way from the back of my head through my body. Against a blue background, a dark silhouette of my body appears, front view with my arms and legs spread, palms extended. From just above my navel, a golden circle emerges. It expands into a twelve-inch-wide pulsating ring that transforms into a wagon wheel with five golden spokes. The spoke intersecting the rim at the twelve o'clock position then turns purple and extends itself to the top of my head. The other four spokes turn green, then arc to individually connect my hands and feet.

It's a multimedia experience unlike any I'd ever had before. Addictive sounds, sights, sensations, and scents course through me, voraciously whetting my appetite for more. I open my eyes, move close to Dieter and spontaneously yell, "Bring it on!"

Dieter grins, embraces me, and whispers, "Impressive, eh." He motions for me to look at my body on the bed. The rose-tinted aura slowly transitions to amber. At the same pace, my psychedelic feelings return to normal. Dieter explains, "The energy you saw, the sensations you felt, they were all made doable when you extracted yourself from your body. The impossible is possible and the change in the colour of your bodily glow is proof."

"That emotional high was ... amazing. Why make it go away?"

"Because it's not part of your world. You're out of your body, which has an aura as long as you live. What we've done is separate your life force from your body and your aura."

"You dragged me in front of the mirror to see my life force?"

Dieter smiles and continues. "Very few humans can detach their life force from their body, let alone see auras. Mediums and psychic healers have that gift. Few people believe them, but everyone sure is happy when they get here and see it's something we all have. It's all that survives. I wanted to show you what that psychic, John Holland, saw when you and Jackie went on that Caribbean cruise."

"You know about that. No surprises for you."

"Like I said, now that you've opened up, not only can I read your thoughts, I can also tap into your memories. Anything you see, hear, smell, touch, or feel that triggers a memory is there for me. When I showed you your aura, you remembered that medium meeting in the main lounge of that cruise ship. Lisa Williams had just finished talking about communicating with spirits and turned the show over to John. After talking about his background, he mentioned he was a spiritual healer and used you to demonstrate his powers. He could see your aura. It was red then too, and he said it had to do with health problems, specifically your back, starting from an early age."

"Yes, and he was right. We were going down the dirt road from our country home to visit relatives. I was five. I fell out of the car trying to close a partially open door. I didn't have any problems at the time, but I started having back pains when I was ten. Sometimes they would last a month or two, then go away. It wasn't until John Holland recommended I see an acupuncturist, which I did, that the pains went away and never came back."

"So based on your prior out-of-body experiences and the proven power of acupuncture, you developed a respect for mediums and alternative medicine."

"Yes, but Jackie and I don't say too much to others."

"And I know why. Heck, the way you reacted to seeing your own aura tells me you find it incredulous. John Holland saw a red aura. If you had been able to see it, you would have seen it was a deeper red than the one around your body earlier. That's because you got your back fixed and your aura changed in hue."

"But it's pink, now. Is that good?"

"No, it isn't. But you're far healthier than Henri was at your age and we've just proved that fiddling with the life force can change the colour of your aura."

"But you did that. Who's to say my aura won't be rose-tinted when this is all over?"

"We'll have to wait and see but you're out of your body. I'm dialled in and have turned you on—all without drugs. Remember Lily Tomlin, the switchboard operator on *Laugh-In*? Well, I have access to all your emotions, and like a switchboard operator, I can unplug them, not in your brain, which is in your body, but from your mind, which is in your life force. All because of what happened in the hospice."

"What happened in the hospice?"7

"Henri told you he was hearing voices, having strange thoughts. They were coming from us on the other side, connecting to his life force. We learned some things we can now share with you."

I raise my arm to object.

Dieter interrupts before I can say anything. "Nope, not going to let you go there, Josh. I'm unplugging that circuit right now. The protest switch is OFF."

My arm drops then both arms open up.

"Good, now we have you in a receptive frame of mind and can carry on. You asked some questions about Henri's past and why he left you to take care of some things. Now you're going to get some answers." He slaps me on the back, smiles, waves, then disappears.

CHAPTER 3

Henri Meets My Family

I'm alone beside my motionless body in the hospital, indifferent to the separation. No doubt Dieter's doing. Everything begins to fade to a dull, grey mist. The silent, still air slowly begins to pulsate. I sway back and forth in tempo, enjoying the rhythm, sensing it's a brief interlude. I'm right.

Out of the mists in a sudden gust of wind, a single page from a newspaper is pushed against my leg. I reach down, pick it up, and notice the banner and the year: *Bond's Hill Bugle*, 1970. Bond's Hill was where we lived—Ronnie, me, and Henri. And 1970? I look more closely at the broadsheet. There is a small ad in the classified section: "Henri Deault—Plasterer," with a phone number and a description of his services. Son of a bitch.

The fog lifts. I'm back in Bond's Hill where I spent my childhood, in front of our house. It has cheap imitation-stone siding on it: grey, black, and pale orange. The porch at the front is small, with a tiny, slanted roof affixed to white pillars. Above the railing is a lattice front where morning glories will later entwine themselves. But now it's late spring; the grass is still ridding itself of its yellow winter blades.

I remember how loud it used to get, being just fifteen feet back from the sidewalk. Anyone walking by could hear the music and heated arguments that went on inside. But today all is quiet, as it often is before mid-afternoon. Thank God for that.

Okay, Dieter, Henri. Have it your way. I'll go with this, whatever this is.

Just then, a battered blue truck sharply and swiftly turns into our driveway. In a cacophony of squealing brakes, a backfiring engine, and flying gravel, the rusted and faded vehicle skids to a halt beside me. The motor runs on a few seconds after being shut off. I shake my head. But the driver can't see me.

I'm a silent, uninvited witness to an event I never attended.

The driver-side door opens with a high-pitched squeak. Henri jumps out. An empty tobacco pouch falls onto the driveway beside him. He ignores it.

A hand-rolled cigarette is stuck in the corner of his mouth. His white cap, slightly askew on his head, is spattered with grey and white plasterer's cement. His pants, work shoes, and shirt are much the same.

Despite his appearance, there is the look of the craftsmen in his gaze and gait. He goes up to the front door and knocks. A few seconds later, my sister, Annie, a blonde, curly haired twelve-year-old, appears and looks at him quizzically. Henri takes the cigarette out of his mouth and says, "Hi dare, sweetie. Is dis da Bencet place? Say, dat's a pretty top. I like pink; looks good on you. Is your dad 'ome?"

Annie beams and nods. "What's your name?" she asks.

Playing up his Belgian-French accent, Henri answers phonetically, "Ahn ree Dohhh," and points to the sign painted on the side of his truck. "But you call me Ahnree, okay?"

Annie nods her head. "I see, Ahnree. Okay." She watches as Henri takes a long drag on his cigarette and scrunches up her face when she notices the nicotine stains on his fingers. "My Dad will be right out I'm sure, Mister Ahnree Dohh. Bye!" Then she vanishes.

Henri laughs, turns to face the street, and flicks the remainder of his cigarette into the ditch in front of our house.

A moment later my father comes out, his unbuttoned short-sleeved green shirt barely hiding the white undershirt beneath. Henri tips his cap, and looks long and steadily at my father's face. "Good afternoon, you want plasterer, eh, cash money, good price?" he asks in a heavy accent that is almost unintelligible, except to people like me, who would later spend so much time with him.

Dad nods and smiles. Then they circle our house, Henri expertly assessing the material and labour he'll need to give our home a face-lift. Once they finish the tour, Henri asks two questions: "You help with labour, yes, save money, eh?" and "You have cold beer, maybe? Even better price."

Dad's face brightens at the mention of beer. He invites Henri inside. They enter from the small add-on porch that faces the driveway. I follow, scarcely noticing that I go through the wall beside them as they enter. It strikes me as odd that Henri takes off his shoes. As if that will make any difference in our house. Henri's socks will get filthy. In the kitchen, Mom is washing glasses and setting them out on a plastic tray to dry. Dad puts his arms around her, introduces Henri, and then grabs three glasses from the counter. "Time for a beer," he says, opening the fridge, which has more booze than food inside. "C'mon, hon, wrestling's on TV."

Mom and Dad fill their glasses, sit down on the couch, and invite Henri to sit on the worn armchair that my grandfather gave them. Henri drinks his beer straight from the bottle. "Fewer dishes to wash," he says.

My sister is nowhere to be seen, nor are any of my younger brothers. As if he knows I'm there and what I'm thinking, Henri asks my mother, "You have many children, yes?"

Mom, dressed in pedal pushers and a tight sweater that clings to her ample bosom, answers, "Yes. Eight now; seven boys, one girl." A faraway look in her eyes, she sighs and then takes a drink from her glass. It's almost empty.

Henri looks at her for a moment, finishes his drink, and stands up. "You need another beer, yes?" He goes to the kitchen and takes three bottles out of the fridge. Mom and Dad don't say a word, seemingly happy to be served by this stranger with oversized ears and long, thick sideburns.

He refills Mom's glass, Dad's too. "Eight children, eh? I saw one, your daughter, *oui*? And boys, you have seven boys *now?*" He looks to see if there are any pictures in the room. There are four: two religious paintings and two black and whites. The first black and white is Mom and Dad's wedding picture. The second is a baby picture. Henri picks it up. It's a photo of my drowned brother, Ronnie, in a white shirt that buttons up the back. He's in a white diaper, sitting on a white blanket. He's smiling; a big smile, as if he's about to laugh. He's no more than ten months old. What little hair he has is curled up at the ends, above his ears, like the hair on Cupid in Valentine's cards.

I sob and fight back the tears as I always do when I see this picture. A hollow emptiness collapses my gut. Remorse, regret, and guilt wash over me. I withdraw and slip into the default catatonic state that keeps me from breaking, safe in a mental straight jacket of detachment. I don't know how long I'm there; long enough to stifle the pain, pushing it away, getting back under control. Dieter does nothing to speed up the process.

Henri looks at Mom and notices the pained expression on her face. He puts the picture back on the stereo cabinet. The cabinet, despite the plastic covering, still reveals bubbled and cracked varnish caused by a fire the year before. An overnight guest, a so-called uncle, had gone to sleep on the couch with a lit cigarette in his hand. I remember thinking that we were lucky. We all could have died in that fire.

Henri sits back down and points his beer bottle at the wedding photo. "Nice picture. Very pretty, very young, eh? When you get married?"

Saying it as if he has to make a point, Dad answers, "After the war, 1947. Three years before our oldest, Josh, was born."

33

"Josh is one of your sons, eh? Then he must be married, too, *oui*?"

Mom answers, laughingly, "Oh no, he's a student, goes to a university in Toronto. He just finished his first year."

Henri nods and raises his eyebrows. "Is he working somewhere, maybe? If not, he can work for me, help me do your house. Save money. Make money. What you tink?"

Dad answers, "You'll have to ask him. He works as a busboy at a restaurant, but they don't pay him much."

Henri purses his lips. "Which restaurant? Maybe I can visit, see him working. He's working now?"

Mom replies, "Yes, he is, at that yellow-roofed restaurant on the highway. It's on the left side opposite that discount gas station. An Oriental couple run it. One of them is always at the cash register, they won't let anyone else near the money." The tone of her voice makes it obvious she doesn't approve. Henri ignores her and carries on.

"Your son, Josh, what's he look like? You have picture?"

"No, no we don't," Dad says, "but it's not a big restaurant and they only have one busboy. They make him wear a white overcoat. Josh is tall, taller than me, black hair, blue eyes. He's got long hair; hasn't cut it since he left high school."

"Good, I'll go there later, see him work. If I like what I see, I'll call him, okay? I finish my beer; now I leave."

Mom and Dad both protest, "No, have another beer, watch some wrestling with us."

Henri declines, but he doesn't move. "You have six more boys and a daughter. Maybe they need jobs too? I need someone to clean house, walk dog."

Mom and Dad aren't at all bothered by Henri's questions. Dad gets up and goes to the fridge. He comes back with three more drinks and asks, "You married, Henri?' Dad pronounces the "H" rather emphatically.

Henri makes no effort to correct him. "Hahhh," is all he says.

Mom and Dad look at each other. I wish I could intervene. I wish I could ask Henri to tell them—tell me—why he never married. Then I remember why Henri induced my coma. Something happened in the hospice that made him regret his silence.

Henri picks up the bottle from the end table. "Molson Export, good beer, but no more for me, *monsieur*. I 'ave other people to see. Good day." Dad follows him, protesting that he should stay. Henri opens the door, saying before it closes behind him, "I'll call later. I'll tell you when I can start da job."

Dad hesitates for a moment and then goes to the porch where Henri is putting on his shoes. "Please, stay. Have that other beer. Our daughter, Annie, is outside. I'll bring her in. You can talk to her about the housecleaning. She may be interested."

Henri opens the door, tips his hat to my father, and says, "I'll talk to 'er some other time, *monsieur*, maybe tomorrow. Maybe I drop by and see Josh, too."

"Well, all right, Henri, but Josh goes to work at one o'clock."

"Fine, 'ave a nice day, Monsieur Bencet." My mother has come to the door, her glass in one hand, a half-finished cigarette in the other. "You too, Madame Bencet."

"The name's Mary. He's Gord. Goodbye, Henri." With a flourish of her cigarette in his direction, my mother goes back to the living room.

After watching the truck drive away, my father joins her. I follow.

"He's an odd one, that Henri. What do you think, Gord?"

Dad sits down on the couch and lights a cigarette. Mom pours beer into his glass, waiting for his answer. "He's new in town but Barry, the guy who built our garage, says he's good."

"What about his offer to have Annie and the boys work for him?"

"He told us he needs a labourer and someone else to walk his dog and clean his house. Seems pretty clear to me."

"He didn't really say he was a bachelor. He didn't answer that question. Do you suppose he's hiding something?"

"Even if he is, so what? Nothing stays a secret long in this town. Somebody will find out, and if there's anything juicy, it'll get around. The midgets are wrestling next." Dad butts out his cigarette, coughs once, and then turns up the volume on the TV.

I never liked wrestling, or confrontation of any sort. Time for me to leave. I know what is coming next—maybe not the exact chain of events but enough.

I look at the baby picture of Ronnie one more time before I go, remembering it came from Grandma Bencet. Mom and Dad never had a camera and never bought any school photos. If I hadn't become close to Grandma after Grandpa died earlier that year, I wouldn't have any pictures of Ronnie and me or the rest of the family either. It was Grandma Bencet who took the photos and kept them and the negatives in a shoe box.

I head for the back yard. Happy that my new abilities don't entirely depend on Dieter's presence, I go out the back wall. As I pass through, I can see a mouse scurrying down the thin insulation. Another reason I want to get the hell out of there.

The first thing I see is our well, which was later abandoned. The sun, casting mid-afternoon shadows, is behind, accenting its ash-grey wooden handle, muting the pump, pipe, and cover below. It will be another two years before the town installs water and waste systems. In the meantime, we draw water from the well and rely on an outhouse and chemical toilet for human waste. The chemical toilet is nothing more than a seat cover bolted to a round enclosure that contains a twenty-five-gallon metal pail.

It was my job to empty the pail in the outhouse—carrying it the fifty feet from the back door to the weathered clapboard privy hidden behind our garage. It always made me sick, disgusted, and embarrassed. Sometimes the pail was full, too heavy to lift. I had to use a smaller bucket and make several trips, gagging and crying, thinking it wasn't right. Everyone else had flush toilets.

I don't feel like seeing my brothers or sister anymore. I walk instead to the garage. The door is locked. Good. If Dieter isn't coming for me, I'll be in the one place no one can disturb me. I slide effortlessly through the giant double doors, rarely opened in the years since they were hung. Except for a heavy-duty overhead hoist, all the garage holds are some old tires, a few tools on a workbench, our lawn mower, and other garden tools. And the stacks of empty beer cases.

I look out the back window trying to avoid seeing the outhouse against the fence line. I wonder why Dieter brought me back in time to this crappy house, which I never considered my home. I sense a presence behind me and turn around.

CHAPTER 4

Turning Point

It's Dieter, but he's not in a ranger uniform. He's wearing a black T-shirt, blue jeans, and sandals. His arms are folded, his eyes look at me expectantly. "You don't know why you're here?"

"To remember how shitty my life was." I glare at him then turn away.

He spins me around and puts his hands on my shoulders. "You can turn your back but you can't run away, Josh. I didn't bring you here to remember the shitty parts. You do that well enough. I brought you to this time and place so you can begin to see your past and Henri differently." Sensing I'm about to push him away, he steps back.

I say to him, "All I see is this empty garage, the shithouse behind it and the poor man's house I grew up in."

"Ronnie told us you would say that."

I put my hands on my hips and spit out, "How would you know what Ronnie knows?"

Dieter holds up a folded letter and lets it go. It floats in the air and stops in front of me, at eye level. It's the yellowed dispatch I found in the cardboard box in Henri's dresser.

That's what put me in this coma.

Dieter snaps his fingers and the letter slowly vanishes. At the point it disappears, I hear the faint tinkle of a bell. I look at Dieter, who is no longer sorrowful. He's now sympathetic.

"Ronnie and I died on the same day in 1961, Josh. I've known him longer than you have."

"What? What are you saying?"

"There's another dimension. Ronnie and I've been in it a long time, and now Henri's here. We know you very well, better than you know yourself and Ronnie asked for our help."

"Well, I don't know you, and I don't know why you're here."

"I told you. You're not well. You buried your past, like Henri. He learned before he died that was a mistake and wanted you to know why. But right now he's got other business to attend."

"What?"

"Henri made a difference in my life, short as it was. And having discovered there's a way to do more—and Ronnie's too young for this sort of thing—here I am."

"That's why he asked me if he'd done enough?"

"Yep, and the way you reacted convinced him he could do more."

"Well, you certainly picked a strange way to do it."

"You'll see it differently later. I told you I can read your thoughts, feel your emotions, and access your memories. You're completely transparent, even experiences you've suppressed or distorted are clear to me. I know what you're thinking and feeling right now. You're wondering why Henri refused to talk about me and the daggers in your eyes and clenched fists tell me you want to sever the link between us."

"I'm forty-nine years old. I'm a successful businessman. I've been married almost twenty years and have two boys who were never exposed to the crap I had to put up with until I was a teenager: the shit, the cigarettes, the crying babies, and the booze. I rose above all that. Everyone who's heard my story is impressed."

"Don't give me that crap, Josh. You wouldn't be here if that were true. Even when you were still in your body in the hospital, you heard the conversation between Jackie and Paul. The doctors told Jackie they couldn't find anything wrong with you, physically. Jackie told them about the emotional issues you still carried being raised in a dysfunctional family and losing a brother. The first thing I did when you left your body was to show you the colour of your aura. You know why it's red. As Jackie said, you're still carrying a heavy load from your years in Bond's Hill, even though you left at age eighteen." Dieter pauses and holds up the 1970 newspaper I had seen earlier. "You're here now so you can begin shedding that weight. Henri learned some things you've forgotten."

"Like what?"

"Why this garage was built. Why the picture of Ronnie was on the stereo cabinet."

"That didn't come up in Henri's conversation with my parents."

"No, but like you, your parents wondered whether Henri was married and he didn't answer."

"I don't get it."

"You father said nothing juicy remains secret for long in Bond's Hill."

"We still don't know whether Henri ever married."

"No, but it didn't take long for Henri to get all the juice on the Bencet family. Henri buried his past, just like you did, Josh. The difference is that he shared none of his with anyone in Bond's Hill and the little he shared with me I took to my grave." He lowers his head and softly adds, "And what you shared of your past didn't make the pain go away."

Dieter points a finger at the garage window and it transforms into a short video clip. It's Henri with his arms around my youngest brothers, suitcases in hand, leaving our home after Mom died. Dieter puts his arm around me and whispers, "You often wonder how different your life would be if Henri had shown up when you were their age. We can't change your past, but we can open it up and let you see it differently."

The video clip ends with Dad waving goodbye, a beer bottle in his other hand. Before I can say anything, Dieter has us back in the hospital. Once again, he goes to the other side of the bed and peers down at my body. "In your world, one body, one brain, one person. All alone. A gap between you and others, impossible for you to close. Mediums and psychics can connect to others, but no credible scientific magazine recognizes vital energy, astral projection, clairvoyance, or telepathy."

"Then it's all hooey."

"Can't be. You and I are here together. Henri, Ronnie, and I stumbled on a way for us to connect. I'm inside your head. Nothing in your world—none of the words, pictures, or sounds, and none of your senses—can adequately describe how things work in my world. It's another dimension, and even though some of your physicists thought they stumbled on it in the 1920s, it's still not and will probably never be accepted."

"If it won't be accepted, why are you telling me about it? Why should I give a damn?"

The image disappears, replaced by another: Henri in a white robe, holding up a sign that reads "Eureka!" Inside my head I hear Henri saying, *I found it!*

"No, he didn't find the meaning of life, Josh. That's obvious, almost immediately when you get to our side, to AfterL. What Henri found was a way for him and Ronnie and me to share it with you—to deep-six your demons."

"AfterL? You're in a place called AfterL?"

"Yep, and we're all AfterLings, but we're very different from humans." Above him a circle appears, a blue surround with a purple centre that pulsates to music, which I recognize as Beethoven's Ninth Symphony, from the first movement.

"Beautiful, isn't it, Josh?"

"Looks like one of those electrical spheres you see in a Frankenstein movie. What is it?"

"Without getting into the details, it's how an AfterLing looks shortly after formation."

"AfterL, meaning 'afterlife.' Cute, I get it. But how does knowing this get rid of the demons you think possess me?"

"Patience, Josh. We've just opened a portal wider than Edgar Cayce or the Oracle at Delphi ever peeked through. I'm inside your head. You're outside your body. We're together between the world you know and the one Ronnie and I've been in for four decades. Think about how wondrous that is. Not only is there life after death but you and I are on a bridge between the two."

"You said that psychics and mediums have made contact. How many people believe them? Why will anyone believe me? How do I know this isn't just a weird dream?"

Dieter picks up the photo on the bedside table. "Jackie, Jess, Josh Jr. Your family. You say they're what gives your life meaning. We're offering you a way to make your life, and your life with them, and others, much better." He sets the picture down and goes to the other side of the bed. "Shortly after we met I said I could access memories you recalled. Remember?"

"Yes, I do. I don't like it much but you reminded me Henri has my best interests at heart."

"Good. I also said I knew about your prior out-of-body experiences."

"Then you know they were sudden, short-lived, and disturbing."

"How do you feel right now?"

"I'm getting used to it and I think you have something to do with that."

"I do. It started when Jackie entered your room at the hospital. You couldn't talk to her and none of the things you did to get her attention had any effect. You were frustrated and upset and I intervened. I can mess with your life force, then sense and suppress any negative emotions that surface. Permit me to show you how it works. I think you'll like it."

Dieter raises his arms and the aura I'd seen before reappears. It slowly moves towards me and then for just for a few seconds, it's all

I can see. I feel like Dieter and I are united. The sense of attachment is brief, but the impact is overwhelming. Briefly, I'm not alone and detached, but bonded and entwined at a level of intimacy and ecstasy I'd never experienced. As it diminishes, the blue aura returns to encircle Dieter before disappearing.

"You just had a teeny tiny taste of what it's like to join my world. Because you and I merged, I could sense the emotional impact it had on you. Much different from your last experience, which I know you never shared with anyone."

"No, and I doubt I ever will."

Dieter raises his arms to shoulder height. I recognize the posture. The Gallic shrug. Henri would assume that pose whenever I thrust a vitriolic comment his way. Did Dieter pick it up from Henri? He folds his arms and carries on. "Like I said, there isn't anything you can hide from me. For you that last experience began very positively. You felt yourself starting to do what I just did, join with another. You were willing but she blocked you."

"I don't want to talk about it."

"We'll see. When Henri is with you, you may change your mind." Dieter claps his hands, and then we're out in the country, on a small stone bridge over a slow-flowing river. I see a welcome sign on one side.

CHAPTER 5

Their Universe

Dieter gives me a radiant smile. "You liked that little meld I did with you, eh?"

"Yes, yes, I did. I felt like I did at my wedding, and when Jess and Josh Jr. were born, only better."

"That's what I was hoping to hear, Josh, that it felt better. Now you know why, and I can tell you more about AfterL."

"Even if this is just a dream, it's a wondrous dream!"

Dieter winks and changes his clothes. He's wearing a fancy suit complete with silk ascot, sapphire tie pin, and diamond cufflinks. He turns towards the welcome sign, puts his arm around me, and steers me in that direction. "We can't step off the bridge, Josh. You're still alive, but I wanted to leave this image with you. Before I tell you more, let's get comfortable. Let's go to the bar at the Château Frontenac. Henri was there when he emigrated from Belgium."

Now we're in their wine and cheese bar, overlooking the St. Lawrence River. Stuffed geese are suspended from the ceiling. They honk at us and flap their wings when we sit down. Dieter points his index finger at the geese, and they break free from their wire harnesses and fly out the windows. "I had to let them out, Josh."

"Just like you'll let me go at some point?"

Two mugs of beer pop out of nowhere. Dieter passes one to me and proposes a toast, "To wondrous journeys and safe returns." After taking a sip, he sighs, wipes his lips, and then frowns. "I think the bar is a distraction. Let's get rid of it. I don't much care for sitting on a stool either."

I find myself sitting in a leather armchair facing Dieter in an identical chair. The bar rises from the floor and vanishes through the roof. From the vacated space come panelled walls. Once the bar has entirely disappeared, three giant whiteboards appear. The AfterLing image I'd seen earlier floats in from the window beside us and attaches itself to the centre whiteboard.

"I gave you a sample of how it feels to connect with another life force a minute ago, Josh. You thought it was better than sex and becoming a parent. Imagine how it feels to join with eleven others."

"Eleven others?"

"It's a fundamental number, Josh. Just like pink, blue, and purple are basic colours and music is a universal language."

The blue surround on the AfterLing image pulsates and quadruples in size to the da-da-da-da notes from Beethoven's Ninth Symphony. Dieter raises his mug and proposes another toast, "To light, music, and metaphysics!"

I put down my mug and fold my arms. "Metaphysics?"

Dieter points at the AfterL image on the screen. It has twelve segments with lightning bolts flashing around and between them.

"Looks like a sparky spider's web."

"Yep, and if you count the strands and concentric waves, there are twelve of them too."

"I still don't get the connection to metaphysics."

"Mind and matter, body and soul, life forces and auras—the basics and what lies beneath them, tying them all together. That's what metaphysics is, Josh, and although we don't have all the answers, we've managed to outdo anyone on your side of the divide." Dieter looks down at my mug, and it rises off the table and floats in front of me. He raises his eyebrows and gives me an expectant look.

I grab the mug. "To body and soul, mind, and matter, and the meaning of life."

"Bravo, Josh." Dieter takes a drink, smacks his lips, sets his glass down, leans forward, rests his elbows on the armchair, and looks at me intently. "I didn't want to die at age twenty-two, Josh. You saw the picture of me and my fiancée, Dorie. I had the job I wanted, the woman I wanted, the life I wanted. Everyone left behind was devastated, sad, and mourning, wishing they could bring me back. That's what sucks about life as you know it. It ends and nobody really knows what comes next."

I study Dieter's face. There is an intensity that tells me he's making a crucial point. "Life as I know it ends, Dieter, but you're here to tell me that it's the beginning of something more wondrous, something that Henri felt compelled to share with me, through you."

Dieter finishes his drink and snaps his fingers. Over his empty glass, a stream of beer appears and fills his mug. "Once Ronnie and I hooked up with Henri in the hospice, it didn't take him long to decide that we had to get to you."

"Why?"

"We think we can undo the damage caused by Ronnie's death and change how you feel and what you remember about your childhood. Henri wants you to know everything you need to know to see your past and live your future differently. His resolve on some things has already gone through a fundamental change."

"And why's that?"

"Because seeing is believing. No room for cynicism and skepticism here, Josh."

Dieter makes the beer mug in my hand vibrate. He smiles when he sees the look on my face. "Sensing is also believing, Josh. Your beer's getting warm; let me get you a refill."

Out of nowhere, a young blonde waitress approaches. She takes the glass from my hand and gives me another. When she leans over, I see the name Alice stitched on her blouse. As she turns away, I hear Arlo Guthrie sing out.

You can get anything you want ...

Before Guthrie can sing anything more, Alice disappears and all is quiet. I gaze intently at Dieter. The look on his face tells me he's enjoying himself and expects me to be the one to break the silence. "Okay, I get it. It's not about my experiences and memories and sense of who I am. You can mess around with my life force."

"You're catching on. The thing is, you're in a coma, and everything that goes on 'til you wake up is like a dream; all your senses will be working but the sensations have nothing to do with what's going on in the physical world around you. Just like in a dream, you're not in control."

I put down my mug, wiggle my fingers, and pull on my earlobes. "I'm in control of some things."

"Ahh the problems with words and interpreting them." Dieter stands up and walks to the back of his wing chair, facing me. I find myself mirroring his actions, standing, and then going behind my wing chair. Dieter crosses his arms, and I do the same. Next, he claps his hands, and instantly he's back in his chair. Straight away, I'm sitting in my chair.

"Okay, self and sense of self are different here."

Dieter nods and points at the whiteboard. "Practically everything humans use to identify themselves is meaningless here, because AfterL is a spiritual world—no bodies, no matter, no substance."

The image on the screen disappears. Dieter finishes his drink and puts his mug on the table. He peers at me intently. I feel compelled to respond. "You had to bring me to the Château-Frontenac to tell me this?"

Dieters sighs, raises his eyes skyward, leans forward in his chair, then in a kindly voice says, "You can be a bit of a shit, Josh. Let's do the math. Henri was here in Québec in 1947, the same year your parents married. He was twenty-seven. What was your life like when you were twenty-seven?"

"Let's not go there."

"We will, we must, but not yet. And if you had a choice wouldn't you rather have been here?" Seeing the contrite look on my face, Dieter sits back in his chair and continues. "Henri wanted you far away from Bond's Hill in a place he made some critical decisions about his future. Just like you did when you were twenty-seven. Remember, Henri came to Ontario when you were twenty. He knows more about your life than you ever told him. Hell, after he moved from Timmins to your little village, his apartment was a five-minute walk from your house. We took you back to 1970 so you could witness his introduction to your family. It wasn't long after that your mother was diagnosed with cancer and Henri started taking care of your siblings. He knows your brothers and sister better than you do."

"I'm sorry, Dieter. Thinking back on those years is hard for me."

"We know. Those were hard years for Henri, too. I know a little bit more than you but not much of what he'd been through in Europe, why he left Belgium, and what his life was like growing up on a small farm outside Bastogne. Henri wanted you far away in a place that meant something to him to begin our journey."

"Why isn't Henri here?"

"He's still a baby AfterLing. His group has some things to work out before he can see you. But don't worry, once that's done he'll join us."

"And in the meantime?"

"I'm gonna be your guide on a journey through Henri's past. There are some parallels he thinks you should know. Since this hotel is where he made some decisions about his future, it seemed fitting. You gotta admit we have a magnificent view of the St. Lawrence."

"Yes, but we're not here to sightsee."

"No, no, we're not but you have to lighten up, Josh. I can't do what I have to do if I'm busy cranking back your antsy mode. Stand by the window, chill, and check out that ship."

Dieter points to the window and a telescope appears out of nowhere. "You've been on some memorable cruises with Jackie, but not up the St. Lawrence. Tell me what you see."

I glare at him. He shakes his head and raises his arm. Above me, myriad strings attach themselves to my arms and legs, lifting me from my chair. Powerless to resist, I'm forced to the window. When I get there he claps his hands. The strings disappear and I'm back in control. He grins and points to the telescope. I resign myself to cooperate. As I bend down the telescope repositions itself. At least Dieter is making it easy. Being considerate, just like Henri. I peer through the eyepiece and almost immediately back away. It's an up-close view of a small group of men standing by the rail.

Dieter laughs and explains, "Fancy telescope, eh? What you see is Henri and some of the guys he met in Antwerp. They came to Canada with him in 1947. Some got off in Québec City. Henri was one of them. It was his first stop."

"That's why you brought me here?"

"Yes, look at them again, watch their faces."

"They're crying."

"Yes, tears of joy. After they cleared immigration they came here, looked out that window, and thanked God they were alive and away from it all. That's the last time Henri cried tears of joy, the last time he cried tears of any kind."

"Why are you telling me this?"

"You'll find out later. Henri's tied up with AfterLing stuff right now. Before he died, however, he shared a few things that got him wondering. Remember when he asked you if he had done enough?"

"Yes, I do."

"Well, he's revisiting that thought and one of the reasons you and I are here is to see why the doubt."

"Both of us?"

"Yes, when I was in the hospice he said we both needed to witness some scenes from his past. He said he was tight-lipped with both of us throughout his life and because of my time in AfterL I could be the tour guide. I'm enjoying it so far. How about you?"

"The antsy mode reference you made stung. I'm not used to someone half my age making such comments."

"Josh, I was born ten years before you were but you have no idea how old I am *now*. Earthly years have no relevance here. You'll get that before we're through. Just accept that I enjoy being twenty-two, looking exactly like I did in the photo Henri gave you."

"Okay, I'll take your word for it and show more respect."

"No need. I'm impervious to your mood swings, but I'm going to mirror some of them so you can see how you look and we'll go from there. Please come back and sit down."

"Since you can make me a puppet or feel any emotion you choose to transfer, what choice do I have?"

"Good point. I'm glad we have your attention. Have another beer."

"Okay, but can you give me a little more on what's coming?"

"Sure, a little bit but 'show and tell' is the default mode on this journey. That's why we took you back to Bond's Hill to the first meeting Henri had with your family. As Henri instructed, I left you there to see how you reacted."

"So there're going to be more surprise temporal trips, some of them unescorted?"

"I don't know, maybe. That's up to Henri."

"So you're a stranger as far as some of this goes?"

"Questions, questions. Henri was buried yesterday, Earth time. It's not as if he's written a play and asked me to be both director and actor on his stage."

"Well, he was a caring man. I'll try and bite my tongue."

"Not necessary. Probably best you don't. Henri said something about an emotional well he wanted us to dig."

"Hmmm, intriguing, a magical mystery tour, eh? Okay, what did he tell you to share with me?"

"His past in Belgium, some of his time in Timmins with me, and some of yours. The scenes from your past are still being reviewed. As I get direction. I'll let you know." Dieter takes a drink, smacks his lips, and wipes his chin before continuing. "Just so you know, since I've been in AfterL longer than I was on Earth, I'll be exercising some control. I missed out on all the fun and games most people enjoyed in the '60s and Henri has given me an opportunity to *live it*, so to speak." He makes a quotes sign with his fingers when he says, 'live it'.

"Okay, but don't expect me to go on any LSD rides with you."

"I'd say something clever but Henri wants me to save that line for him. Rest assured, there won't be any acid trips or nude baths near Yasgur's farm at the Woodstock Rock Festival." Dieter puts his mug on the table and gives me a look that reminds of an undertaker at the entrance to a funeral parlour. "No Josh, quite the opposite but still a serious moment. Part of this journey is about me. There are some circumstances about my history that are similar to yours. Henri wants me to take you to Timmins to see for yourself."

"Did he say why?"

"Yes, we had some issues to deal with and now he thinks his way of dealing with them at the time was wrong, not bad, but judged as wanting once he found out about AfterL."

"A moral to the story. Okay I can accept that. Henri was not one to give bad advice or show a bad example as far as I could see."

"All the more reason he wanted to reach out to you, while there's still time."

"Why me? I never lived with him. I learned plenty when I worked for him and he pretty much saw my younger brothers through to adulthood."

"It will all become clear but none of them remember much about Ronnie. You and Henri were their caretakers. You're different from them and you know it."

"How?"

"I know you know the reasons but one overshadows the rest—you suffered much more. There was no one there to look after you."

I fold my arms across my chest and open my mouth to speak. I can't talk. Dieter has shut down my voice box.

"Before you carry on with the twenty questions, let's cut to the chase. You want to know the bottom line. Here it is. We were *both* ashamed and embarrassed during our early years, as you'll see. That had an impact on Henri and he has no regrets, but in the hospice after meeting us, he agreed to and, I quote, 'orchestrate a reunion.'"

"Hmmm. Henri always did like music. When we last met, my last minutes with him, he mentioned Beethoven. I don't see how that relates to you and me."

"You will but that's not essential. It's about our early years. I was much older than Ronnie when I died, but I had some trauma to deal with, just like you. You'll learn all about that shortly, but it had to do with my father and some of the guys in Timmins. Henri didn't spend much time on my Dad or those guys. He just listened to me. I knew he understood, but the message was clear. He expected me to get over it—to move on. I remember what he said after I unpacked at his apartment. He said it with such passion, such conviction, that he never had to repeat it."

"What did he say?"

"Make a man on you, Dieter. Don't sweep it under the rug. Make it so you don't need one."

"That's an odd expression."

"He said it was a rough translation from a French expression you can hear in the bars in Timmins."

"I see. So, did you?"

"Frankly, I never really understood it. I knew Henri loved me, would do anything to help me be warm, safe, and comfortable. After I went to live with him, there was no problem we couldn't solve, no topic we couldn't discuss—except my past or most of his. I felt like I had the world by the tail and Henri was as much a friend as a father. He was always there for me, Josh—"

The shrill sound of a train whistle interrupts our conversation. On the wall, a giant banner appears:

"There is no future in the past but it often explains the present."

Dieter looks as puzzled as I feel. Henri's distinct voice fills the room. "When Dieter told me about AfterL at the hospice, I realized my past haunted me. Hiding it didn't make it go away. It was always there affecting what I did and said. Now I understand."

Dieter puts his hand on his chin and nods several times. "Henri was my most admired person. I was so darned happy when he took me in, but as he just said, he wouldn't let me dwell on my past because he wouldn't talk about his own. He obviously couldn't go there because it was too traumatic. Like me, when he got to AfterL, his mind and soul, all his values, beliefs, memories, and experiences blended in with eleven others. That immediate bonding and expanded perspective fundamentally altered his self-perception. He knew he had to deal with the past and that's why."

"Aha. Now I get it. You can't go forward in AfterL until you've gone backward on Earth and got rid of the shit still roiling around in your mind."

"You got it, Josh."

Dieter sees that I'm still coming to grips with his world and invites me to probe deeper.

"If there's a welcoming ceremony and you bond with eleven others as part of the whole ritual, how is it Ronnie and you were in the hospice with Henri a day or two before he died?"

Dieter smiles and then responds. "Our contact with Henri had nothing to do with the AfterL orientation. I told you the gap between our two worlds can be closed. Psychics and mediums bridge it on your side. We AfterLings can do it when those we want to contact are asleep, in a delirium, a coma, or some other unusual state. In short, when they're unconscious. Henri told you he was having strange dreams, hearing unusual sounds and voices. He was comatose or asleep, and Ronnie and I came visiting."

The banner rustles and then transforms into a cat of nine tails. It cracks three times then disappears.

"Was that Henri?"

"Yeah, he says it would be easier if I took you back to the hospice and let you sit in."

CHAPTER 6

Contact

We're back in the room where Henri had spent his last days. He's lying in bed, eyes closed, motionless from the neck down. His lips are moving, and he's shaking his head from side to side. Instinctively I back away, I don't want to be here. As quickly as this reaction erupts, Dieter shuts it down. I'm back in a calm state, a dispassionate observer in an inquisitive mood. He's not letting me lose it.

"What we're gonna do, Josh, is hook you up to what is going on in Henri's brain. Think of it as a mind share. You're going to see everything as if you were Henri. Don't worry, it's all good—just a dream."

It's as if all my senses dim, and I'm inside Henri's head, intimately witnessing what he only hinted at during my last visit, August 10, 1999. Dieter asks me to report what's happening. I don't think it's necessary, but I'm told I have no choice. Okay.

Everything is in darkness for a split second. Then the baby picture of my brother Ronnie appears, suspended in space. It's the picture Henri saw in Bond's Hill the day he met my parents and Annie.

I hear the voice of a young boy. "Henri, Henri Deault? Can you hear me?"

"Uh, what? Who's there? Show yourself."

"In a minute. Do you recognize this picture?"

"Yes, the only kid's picture on display the day I met Gord and Mary Bencet. It's Ronnie Bencet."

I want to jump in, but as quickly as the thought arises, Dieter crushes it, compelling me to experience and report this scene without any means to suspend, alter, or interfere with it.

The childish voice continues. "You remember?"

"Sure, I asked Josh who was in the photo when I picked him up for work one day. He said it was his brother, Ronnie, a year younger than him, who drowned at age nine."

"On July 10, 1961."

"Yes, that's why I remembered the name. I lost someone dear to me that same day."

"I know. I met him. Dieter Franc."

"What? How could you? Why are you here?"

The baby in the photo becomes three-dimensional, then quickly ages. His T-shirt expands with him; the diaper and baby shoes are replaced by pale green shorts and black-and-white sneakers. A white light against the dark background illuminates Henri's hospice bedroom.

The young boy sits at the foot of the bed. "I'm Ronnie Bencet, here to ask a favour."

As if a grenade goes off in my chest, my heart shatters, and my head explodes. I sob and stare at Ronnie, my chest heaving. Dieter embraces me, cradles my head in his hands, and says, "Take your time, Josh." Then he gently places a warm cloth under my eyes, and whispers, "Let them flow."

Five minutes, ten minutes pass. Dieter has Henri and Ronnie in freeze frame and I'm out of the mind meld with Henri. The warm cloth and the gentle, caring caresses dry my tears and calm me. Exhaling a last deep breath, I step back and say, "I didn't see that coming. Now I remember that's how he looked the day he died."

Dieter takes the cloth from me, smiles, and stands behind Ronnie. He puts his hands on Ronnie's shoulders. "It's all good, Josh. Those tears, at the end, they were tears of joy, and you're gonna have more.

Ronnie's on a mission, and trust me, it will be very clear." Moving towards Henri, Dieter motions for me to follow. "Now, let's get you back in the mind meld so you can experience the exchange between these two guys.

I'm back inside Henri, listening in as he makes the connection between Ronnie and me and says, "Josh's dead brother. This must be a dream."

"I've tried to get a message to Josh for years, but he's shut me out. You haven't, maybe because of who you are and where you are. Pleased to meet you, Henri Deault."

"I'm dying. Can't get out of here. What could I possibly do for you?"

Ronnie pulls a picture out of his back pocket, jumps off the bed, and comes to stand near its head. "Mr. Deault, did Josh ever show you this picture? It's me and him, our last summer together. It's a picture Grandma Bencet gave him long after I was gone."

"No, he never talked about you. I sense it was a sore spot."

"Dieter told me he was a sore spot for you too, after he died."

"Everyone dies, some sooner than others. No sense of going back or reliving the pain."

"I wasn't in any pain, Mr. Deault. I enjoyed my time with Josh. I'm still enjoying myself, but I'd enjoy it more if Josh let go of his pain."

"How do you know Josh's in pain? He seems to enjoy life."

"He's forgotten mine." Ronnie has a wistful smile on his face. He slides off the bed and puts the picture back in his pocket. He goes to the other side of the bed and stands midway between its head and foot, toying with the side rail. "I want him to remember our good times."

"What's that got to do with me?"

"I'm not sure, yet. Dieter tried to contact you many times after he died. Didn't work. I had the same problem with Josh. But Dieter knew you had a soft spot for kids. He suggested I try to get in your head. Maybe that was enough, 'cause here I am." Ronnie gets back on the bed and pulls out another picture. It's a picture of three people.

Henri responds. "That's the last picture of Dieter and me, the day he and Dorie got engaged. They were going to marry that September. Why're you showing me that?"

"The only picture you had on display was Dieter in his ranger outfit. You hid this picture in a drawer in your apartment after he died. He wondered why. It was such a joyful day."

"I had my reasons. If Dieter is a ghost, and has been dropping in on me, I'm surprised he doesn't know why."

"There're some things we can't do. That's one of them. You're gonna learn all about that soon, but me and Dieter are really excited I'm here sitting on your bed, talking to you."

"I've had worse dreams." Henri holds out his hand, and Ronnie gives him the picture. Dorie is in the middle, a diamond ring front and centre; Dieter on her right, Henri on the left, everyone smiling. "That was May 1961. I took them out for dinner to celebrate."

Ronnie slides off the bed and claps his hands. Dieter appears in the same clothes I see in the photo. He stands next to Henri and says, "You bought a bottle of Champagne, and that's the only night I saw you drink anything other than beer."

"Dieter, *tabernac*, what're you doing here?"

Dieter turns to Ronnie, picks him up, and dances around the room for a few seconds. "We did it, Ronnie, we slipped into his head, finally, before it's too late!"

Dieter lowers Ronnie to the ground. They join hands and dance around the foot of the bed repeating several times, "Let what I see encircle me."

One of Henri's favourite sayings.

After their refrain, Ronnie and Dieter part. Ronnie jumps on the bed, gives Henri a big hug, and then vanishes.

"What in hell's going on here?"

"Hell and *tabernac*. Those are the first words you have to say to me after all these years?" Dieter sits on the bed and grabs Henri's right arm, sliding down from the elbow to firmly grip his hand.

I feel Henri tightly clutching Dieter's arm.

"Nearly forty years and never once did I dream about you. Now here I am on my deathbed and you show up, not looking a day older."

"I tried many times, Henri. Couldn't get through. Just like when I asked you about your past, you shut me out, and you didn't want me talking about my drinking father."

"Best all that grief was buried."

"That's what you thought, but it's not true. You'll see when you get here."

"Well, if I'll find out different, why show up now?"

"To help Ronnie get through to Josh, who's carrying a weight, probably not as big as yours, but still ... a load we can eliminate."

"Like I told you when you moved in with me, men bury their past and move on."

Dieter puts his arms around Henri, his cheek against Henri's. "It's not true. It's there. It's a wall. It keeps people out. I think that's why you never married or told me about your family or life in Belgium."

"Not gonna tell you now either, but I'm glad to see you." Henri puts his arms around Dieter, and the two of them are silent, caught in the moment.

Ronnie reappears, standing at the foot of the bed, smiling. After a few seconds, he taps on the bedrail. "Henri, are you gonna help me?"

The two men gently pull away from each other and look at Ronnie. Dieter is the first to speak. "Henri and I have eternity to get closer, closer than Henri ever imagined." He turns to face Henri again, staring at him intently. "Then I'll learn all your secrets, all the things behind your Berlin Wall."

"Like I said it, hasn't stopped me from having a good time."

Ronnie and Dieter look at each other. Ronnie moves from the foot of the bed and stands next to Dieter, facing Henri. "You don't want to talk about it. Dieter told me you probably wouldn't. That's okay. Soon, it won't matter."

Dieter stands aside. Ronnie floats up in the air, swivelling and turning so he's in a horizontal position, ninety degrees relative to Henri. He rests his head on his hand, a pleading look on his face. "I want to talk to my brother, Josh. Will you help me, Mr. Deault?"

Henri gives Dieter a bewildered look. Dieter moves away from the bed and slowly begins pacing back and forth. "For over thirty-eight of your years, Henri, I've tried to get in your dreams and couldn't. Somehow, now you're dying, Ronnie got through and here we are. Ronnie, leave us alone for a few minutes okay?"

Ronnie nods, changes into a cowboy outfit—the Lone Ranger—and disappears.

Dieter returns to Henri's bedside. "I still don't know how Ronnie did it—got in your head and opened the way for me. I think it has something to do with his innocence and your condition."

"If you don't know how, and I'm dying, what makes Ronnie think I can get him in touch with Josh?"

"Josh admires you and what you did for others, especially his brothers. Ronnie knows that. He also knows how much his death affected Josh. Ever since Ronnie died, Josh has stunted his emotional growth. He can only get so close to people, then he backs off."

"He got close enough to marry twice and make the second one stick."

Dieter snaps his fingers and the boyhood picture of Ronnie and Josh reappears. "Ronnie told you this picture was given to Josh long after his death. You also know the only picture in their family home was a picture of Ronnie as a baby."

"So?"

"Their parents were alcoholics, Henri. You know that. It got worse after Ronnie died. They turned to each other and the booze and spent little time sober with their kids. Josh had no one to comfort him or turn to. Most of the people that dropped in on them were also drunkards. Even relatives stayed away."

"I know that, which is why I did what I did after I met the Bencets."

"Exactly, which is why Ronnie and I hooked up. By then it was too late for Josh. No one was there to support his continuing emotional growth."

Henri takes the picture from Dieter. "I remember the day Josh told me about Ronnie. I knew it was a sore spot, and he wasn't going to say any more."

"Just like you wouldn't say anything about me when Josh asked."

"Apparently the barriers we raised didn't stop you and Ronnie from trying to break through. A remarkable young boy. Why did he persevere?"

"Josh was the one he knew best and loved most, which is why Ronnie focused on Josh's life after he died. Ronnie only had nine years in your world. He won't get any older here, in AfterL. He has a young boy's memories and experiences. They were happy years because he and Josh were so close. After he drowned, he tried to get in touch with Josh but couldn't. He had one option, as all of us AfterLings do. It's kinda neat. We can 'check-in' on people we cared for when we were alive. It's like having a giant videotape library—"

"You've been checking in on me too?"

"Often, Henri. Like Ronnie, I can scan for noteworthy events that have happened since my death. That's why we're here."

"Ronnie knows about my past?"

"Just our time together. You'll learn more about that soon. After you die, you can follow the lives of the surviving Bencet family members—Josh, Eddie, Willie, Luke, Ben, Annie, Matt, and Paul—anyone you loved going forward. Nothing from the past except shared memories and experiences."

"Why not?"

"That's the way it is in AfterL. It's a barrier that comes down after you die. That will all be explained to you."

"Okay, obviously Ronnie wasn't happy with what he saw."

"No he wasn't, and he got excited when you entered his family's lives, the way you stepped in when his mother got sick and became such a major influence."

"On five of them. Eddie got married a year after their mother Mary died, and Luke, being gay, headed to Toronto once Mary was laid to rest. Gord kept to the bottle, shacked up, then remarried someone who didn't want them around. As for Josh, he'd already moved out and wasn't letting anyone get close."

Despite Dieter's control of my emotions, I'm still capable of thought. I don't want to hear any more. I know how screwed up our family and Mom and Dad's friends were. That's why I moved out when I was eighteen. I want out of here. The word OK flashes in front of me, even though I'm still seeing the world through Henri's eyes.

Dieter takes the picture away from Henri and grabs his hand. "Let's go someplace more to your liking."

Seconds later, we're beside a river. It's midsummer, and we're sitting on opposite sides of a picnic table. I'm still seeing and hearing everything through Henri's eyes. Dieter is looking at the river.

"This is one of my favourite memories with you, Henri. After I moved in, we came here on weekends to enjoy the water and our time together. I especially liked your sandwiches and cookies."

Egg-salad sandwiches, peanut-butter cookies, and soft-drink bottles appear on the table along with a mirror, which Dieter hands to Henri.

In the mirror, I see a much younger Henri, wearing his signature plasterer's cap and white T-shirt.

"When you get to AfterL, Henri, you can choose whatever appearance you want, even some other body."

"I think I'm gonna like this place you call AfterL."

"You'll be here soon, and you can explore anything you want, go anywhere you want. I brought you here, back to Timmins, to the Mattagami River, because it's one of the first places I shared with

Ronnie. Ironic that our fondest memories of people we loved were associated with water."

"The fact that he drowned wasn't an issue?"

"No, cause of death has no emotional significance in AfterL. It's just one of the things that determines which AfterLing group you join. Josh doesn't know that, but it's one of the reasons why Ronnie's so intent on paying him a visit."

"And he thinks I can help?"

"It's what you did when you weren't working, Henri—help others. My death didn't stop you, even if you never told anyone why you were so community-minded."

"I wasn't in it for recognition."

"No, and soon I'm going to know what turned your crank."

"I never thought I needed to explain myself. Are you saying I'll have no choice once I'm out of here?"

"More like you will reveal all. No choice, and Ronnie and I think you'll do us this favour. Being on your deathbed shouldn't stop you."

"Appealing to my heart strings, eh?"

Dieter nods, picks up a sandwich, and takes a bite, followed by a gulp of soda. After he's finished, he burps. Henri laughs, grabs a sandwich, and takes a mouthful.

"This is much better than the stale bread and tasteless stuff they serve me in the hospice. They won't even give me a soft drink. If my bed was a coffin, you'd think I was already in a funeral parlour."

Dieter jumps up on the picnic table, drink in hand. He raises the bottle, does a 360-degree turn, and shouts, "Let what I see encircle me." He finishes, takes another drink, leaves the table, and gives Henri a big hug. "You're gonna be pleasantly surprised at how appropriate that expression is in AfterL."

"And you got Ronnie hooked on it, too."

Dieter looks across the Mattagami, his back to Henri for a moment. When he turns around, Dieter has a paint brush and palette in hand.

He dips the brush then rotates it, writing on air as he turns 'Let what I see encircle me. He smiles and softly says to Henri, "You used to bring me here to paint, and before I put brush to canvas, you'd use that expression."

"Yes, they were good times, Dieter."

"And things are going to get incredibly better for you."

"So you say, but it's just a dream."

"You're wrong, but that's okay, Henri. Are you gonna help Ronnie?"

"Why me?"

"I've had thirty-eight years to explore a gazillion things related to 'why.' Sometimes there's no answer, other than 'because.' It's because Ronnie hooked up with me after he found out you were his living connection to Josh and gave me a look like the one he gave you a few minutes ago. He's still a young boy with a brother who's hurting."

"He coulda sold Bibles to atheists if he'd lived longer."

Dieter laughs and shakes his head. "The religious thing still plays on you, eh?"

"Given you're here and don't have a halo or wings, I get the feeling AfterL isn't covered in any book of prayer."

"No, but stay tuned. All will be revealed."

"Okay, but I'm going to die soon. What can I do?"

Dieter smiles and claps his hands, and Ronnie reappears, still in a cowboy suit. The two of them sit next to Henri, one on each side. They put their arms around him and in unison, ask him, "How's this feel?"

"Like I'm in a cocoon, in the midst of a wonderful transformation."

Dieter and Ronnie rise from the table and do cartwheels. Henri stands on the table, raises his right arm and says, "Let what I see encircle me!"

Ronnie somersaults onto the table, gives Henri a hug, changes into a Superboy outfit, and then flies off into the stratosphere.

Dieter does a handstand, springs onto the table, and puts his arm around Henri.

"Nearly forty years and Ronnie's still a carefree, young spirit. He will remain that way."

"Why?"

"Because he won't age. He'll always have a young boy's mind and spirit. He never had any hormonal or hurtful memories or behaviours in his brain; there was nothing to transfer over to AfterL. He brought no traumatic experiences with him and can't understand anyone else's 'cause they were never part of his earthly existence."

"Not even his own death?"

"At Morgan's Creek where he drowned? Nope, once he was near death, beyond revival, a portal opened and several ghosts, young boys and girls his age, were there motioning for him to follow them. The trauma never registered for any of them. As far as they were concerned, it was a good thing and time to move on, to leave the physical, temporal world and enter an endless metaphysical one."

"You said Ronnie was able to check in on Josh. Doesn't Ronnie understand Josh's trauma?"

"Nope, what he sees is that Josh misses him and doesn't remember their good times. Ronnie still believed in Santa Claus and the Tooth Fairy. 'Good and bad,' 'sad and happy' have very circumscribed meanings in his AfterL universe. Any pairings he makes to older AfterLings is bound by that."

"Which explains the Lone Ranger and Superboy outfits."

"Partially. The outfits relate to good times Ronnie had with Josh. I suspect Ronnie will wear them when we hook him up with Josh. In the meantime, Ronnie's here fighting evil, saving fair maidens, and living happily ever after."

"Except for the times he checks in on Josh."

"Which is why we're here. You get a last shot at doing a good deed for someone that you and Ronnie both love."

"Josh hasn't let Ronnie in before, Dieter. You say that your being here with me is proof enough we can do it?"

"Only one way to find out."

"I'm on my deathbed, not on your side."

"I've had some time to research encounters humans claim they've had with an alternate universe. It's either when they were revived from a seemingly fatal situation, in a dream or in a coma. None of them describe AfterL. Josh isn't near death. Ronnie hasn't got through to him so far, which leaves one option."

"A coma? You think we can put him in a coma?"

"It's worth a shot."

"How can we do that?"

"Short-circuit his brain cells. Present him with a coincidence he can't handle."

Over the river, dark clouds form, followed by thunder and lightning. Dieter jumps on the table and lightning bolts flow up to the heavens from his fingertips. The thunder reaches a crescendo, blocking all other sounds. The lightning ascending from Dieter and descending from the clouds unite into a pulsating, all-encompassing light show.

∞

Before the display blinds and deafens me, we're back in the hospice. Henri is lying in his bed, sleeping. Dieter and I are leaning against the window. Outside, a storm like the one we left behind in Timmins is in full force. Dieter turns, and with a flick of his hands, the tempest rolls away as if it were a giant wave being pulled back into the ocean, leaving a setting sun to accentuate the raindrops falling from the trees and pooling in the parking lot.

"How about that, Josh? Now you have a glimpse of what it's like in AfterL, sharing in another life as if it were your own."

"Weird, Dieter, it feels weird, especially since it seems you can suspend my emotions and control the weather."

"It's cool, Josh. You won't think it's weird, later. Now you know what happened and why I'm here."

"So do I get to hook up with Ronnie now?"

"Not yet. We have to wait for Henri to finish crossing over, and join an AfterLing community. All the crap he's carrying around has to get cleansed."

"Cleansed?"

"We don't know the traumatic events in Henri's past, Josh. Why did he say, 'Make a man on you' and expect that to solve all problems? Yes, right up until that stroke hospitalized him, he was a caring, giving man but as far as we know he never had his own sweetheart, never his own kids."

"Come again? Why do we have to know that now?"

"Remember what I said about Ronnie's innocence and his AfterLing world. He doesn't experience nor can he understand trauma. I just had turned twenty-two, three months before I entered AfterL. Unlike Ronnie, I had a rough childhood. I came from a broken home. I lost Dorie and had no kids. These weren't things that became non-events the day I died. I had to purge all that as the price of admission to AfterL. Until Henri does the same, he can't share his past with you or me."

"So the trauma limits his ability to share his past?"

"Yep, just like it probably killed his will to marry and have kids of his own."

"Hmm, sounds like something the church would say; you have to confess your sins."

"Trauma and sin aren't the same thing, Josh. I doubt Henri has any skeletons in his closet, though I'm thinking we'll know that soon enough. Now let's leave Henri here, the way he was after he hooked up with Ronnie and me and bought into our plan to short your circuits and get us connected."

"Before we leave, can you tell me where we're going?"

"Back to the Château Frontenac."

"It means nothing to me or Ronnie."

"You've forgotten your good times with Ronnie, and I'm gonna turn things over to Henri soon. We know already that he's fond of the Frontenac."

Before I can say anything further, we're back in the Château. We're facing the St. Lawrence River, opposite from the wall where Dieter did his show and tell on AfterL. The suspended stuffed Canada geese honk at us. Dieter waves, and they break free from their wires. I laugh as they circle the room, swoop down above us, and fly away. I can hear their fluttering wings and feel the draft as they leave us in our leather chairs. Two cold beers appear on the table between us.

I look at the beer and images of my boyhood kitchen appear in my mind's eye. Dieter somehow senses this and the beer disappears.

"Still haunted by images you can't suppress, eh Josh? I'm not surprised. You're still alive, and from the dark recesses of your mind, unpleasant memories, and feelings still surface. It's another reason why you need to spend time with Ronnie. We may not be able to get all that shit shovelled, but we think we can dig up all the good stuff he knows is buried beneath it."

A glass of red wine appears on the table beside me. Dieter smiles mischievously, waiting for my reaction. "No, wine wasn't part of my problem growing up, and it was kinda neat going to wine and cheese parties when I got to university."

Dieter has some Camembert appear on the table. A bottle of Merlot and a glass magically show up on his table. Wine floats up from the top of the bottle and arcs into his glass, half filling it. "Gravity doesn't apply here, Josh."

"It seems a great deal of the world I know doesn't apply here."

Dieter raises his glass and proposes a toast. "To a fine man, Henri Deault."

We clink glasses and sip our wine—a smooth fruity red. After he sets down his glass, Dieter leans closer to me. "There isn't anything you know about Henri that I don't, but there is much about the man before he moved to Bond's Hill that he never shared with you. I know a lot about his time in Timmins, and while we're waiting for him to come clean in AfterL, let me share that past with you. It's part of Henri's story and you've expressed an interest in it several times."

CHAPTER 7

Dieter's Childhood

I push back my chair, cross my arms, and hiss. "I've got a job and family back in Bond's Hill. I'm not going to drop everything because Henri has a story to share."

Dieter smiles and gives me a knowing look. "What did you tell Jackie when you went to those first ACOA meetings?"

I sigh, move my chair closer to him, and say sheepishly. "I should have remembered. You and Ronnie know a lot about me."

"Well, we didn't grab a bag of popcorn and watch your intimate moments, but we can access many of your thoughts and conversations. It was precisely because of some of the talks you had with Jackie that we are paying you this visit. You told Jackie you remembered little about Ronnie, and until your Grandma Bencet gave you the picture I showed you earlier, you couldn't remember what he looked like, except as a baby or corpse. You also told Jackie how thankful you were that Henri raised your brothers and that you'd love to know and write his life story. We're giving you what you wanted and more. What you do with it is up to you."

"Okay, I should be more grateful. I just hope that, when I recover, you'll leave me alone."

"That's been part of your problem, Josh. Too much solitude. After you spend some time with Ronnie and Henri, you may change your mind."

He has a point. He sees me nod and signals that it's time to move on by rotating our chairs to face away from the river.

A giant screen rolls down from the ceiling and the room's lights dim. In the centre, a picture of Henri appears, looking to be in his late-twenties. He has a full head of dark hair and isn't wearing glasses. He's smiling, lips parted, teeth showing. His eyes match his grin. He looks mischievous and self-assured. Not handsome, but comfortable with his looks—big ears, beaked nose, and all.

"You didn't know Henri then, Josh. This is what he looked like when I first met him, not long after he came to Timmins from Montréal. Because Henri is now in AfterL cleansing his soul, my AfterLing community can connect to times in his past that don't have any traumatic elements. You and I are gonna watch him in the local bar with my Uncle Gilbert, my dad's younger brother. Watch how Henri makes his acquaintance. You're gonna hear the conversation in English but the original was in French."

The photo of Henri fades and the words *Timmins, July 1948,* briefly appear. As these words dissolve, the hotel's rear parking lot is on screen. Henri is heading towards the men's entrance. He enters the bar. A young man is sitting next to the jukebox. Below him, the name Gilbert Franc shows up for a few seconds. Henri walks over to study the music selections. He looks over at Gilbert. "Do they have any good French songs in this Wurlitzer?"

Gilbert snorts and rolls his eyes before saying, "Ha, this is not Québec, *monsieur.* You want French songs you go to Iroquois Falls or come to a party in our neighbourhood. And how did you know I wasn't an Anglais?"

"I saw you getting out of your car when I pulled in. I noticed the Montréal Canadiens decal on your bumper. It made me think maybe you were one of us. In this province, I've yet to meet a Frenchmen who supported the Leafs." Henri holds out his hand and says, "I'm Henri

Deault, fairly new in town and hoping to make some friends—some friends who speak my language. Can I buy you a beer?"

"I'm Gilbert, Gilbert Franc, and yes, you can, *merci*." He firmly shakes Henri's hand and returns to the bar.

"Let me put a nickel in this old music machine first, Gilbert. Are you a country and western fan?"

"*Oui, monsieur*. In this town there isn't much choice. Your accent, it's not Québécois. Where're you from?"

Henri raises his left hand, signalling for the bartender, and waits for the song "Your Cheating Heart" to begin playing. Then he sits next to Gilbert and replies, "From Belgium, the French part. I came to Canada, to Montréal via Québec City, after the war. But big cities? Not for me. Lots of pretty girls, but I'm a country boy and towns the size of Timmins are fine by me."

"Why leave Belgium?"

"I wanted to put an ocean between me and a woman I knew there. Bartender, two drafts, please."

When the glasses are set in front of them, Henri raises his glass and says to Gilbert, "To the bachelor life."

Gilbert hesitates before picking up his drink. Henri quickly adds, "Good for me, but not for all."

Gilbert smiles, clinks Henri's glass, takes a sip then asks, "What'd she do to you, that woman in Belgium?"

"I promised I'd leave that story on the dock in Antwerp, Gilbert. Maybe I carried some of it around for a while after leaving Europe, but in Montréal, with so many young, agreeable women around, I got lovin' enough." Henri emits a lustful growl and raises his thumbs.

Gilbert raises his eyebrows. "This is a mining town, mostly men. Dames here have plenty to choose from." Gilbert has a disdainful look on his face when he says *dames*.

Henri draws his head back and quickly replies. "Dames, *monsieur*? I'm not talking about dames. Dames you pay for. I'm talking about women and ladies. Satisfying a man isn't the first thing a lady or woman thinks about. It takes more than a smile and money to get them to open their legs."

"I don't expect any lady to open her legs for me until Père Lacroix, our priest, blesses us and I put a gold ring on her finger!" Gilbert has a self-righteous look on his face.

"Ah, Gilbert, you are talking about rare *ladies*, virgins with pure hearts and chaste thoughts. I had the same plan, years ago—not now. How old are you?"

"I'm twenty-two."

"Five years younger than me." Henri stares off into the distance, a wistful look on his face. He shakes his head, sighs, and then continues, "You were lucky, Gilbert; no bombs, no Germans, no war being waged around you."

"Why would the war make you bitter towards women?" Gilbert raises his arms shoulder high, an *I don't get it* look on his face.

Henri reaches over and puts his left hand lightly on Gilbert. He then shakes his head and answers, "Oh, that wasn't the war. That came after. I lost my trust and faith in church and state before the war. As for the ladies? There was only one—one who I thought was going to be mine forever. I'm done with ladies, but I still like women very much. Ladies, priests, and government ... no more for me, thank you." Henri laughs and finishes his beer. Keeping the empty glass raised, he says to Gilbert, "I don't drink much, but how about one more? May I buy you another?"

"*Monsieur*, please, let me have the honour. I don't think we've finished our conversation."

When Henri doesn't object, Gilbert raises his hand. The bartender holds up two glasses, Gilbert nods, swivels his bar stool back towards Henri, and holds up his right index finger. "Do you tell women you're a confirmed bachelor?" Before Henri has a chance to answer, he raises another finger and asks, "Don't some people think you're a bit odd?"

"I guess you haven't met any yet, Gilbert, but there are women who want to have some fun before they get married. Those are the women I chase. They'd run the other way if they thought I was trying to rope 'em in and stick a ring on their finger. As for me being odd? I tell people I'm *eccentric,* and there are just as many single eccentrics as there are married ones. I'm just the only one they've met. The rest of them live in caves, out of sight."

Henri rolls his eyes and laughs. Gilbert grins and shakes his head, offering Henri his hand again. "Monsieur," he says, "you sure are different than anyone else I've met. I don't know that any of the young women you're looking for live here, but if they do, then they're probably Anglaise." He and Henri vigorously shake hands for a few more seconds before they raise their glasses and say, simultaneously, "To the Anglaises!"

The scene freezes with Henri and Gilbert caught in infectious smiles.

I can see from the look on his face that Dieter, the AfterLing, is enjoying himself. "So, Henri is making a new friend here in Timmins, and it happens to be your uncle?"

"Yep, Josh, from an early age, Uncle Gilbert was the one everyone trusted. He didn't mind a drink or two, but he was always the one the family relied on. He seemed to have a sixth sense for trouble and would suddenly appear to deal with it. Ronnie tells me you have some of that in you."

"Not that much. If someone asked or if I happened to be there, I wouldn't run away. But I don't go looking for problems to fix. I appreciate what Ronnie told you. I was his older, and bigger brother but ... I wasn't like your uncle Gilbert or Henri."

"Ah, yes, not a white knight. There are few of them around. I had my Uncle Gilbert, then Henri."

"You had your Uncle Gilbert, then Henri? What happened to your uncle?"

"The labour problems and mining industry cutbacks forced him away two years after Henri came to town. He went west, to Manitoba, then Alberta. After that, he headed south, to Colorado. He got a job, married there, and never came back. He told me when he left that I was in good hands. He wasn't worried, and he said I shouldn't be either."

As I sip my wine, the screen image of Henri and Gilbert dissolves. It's replaced by text:

"First Encounter—1948."

Dieter snaps his fingers and two footstools pop up in front of us. Dieter sits back, puts up his feet, and motions for me to do the same. "Henri met my uncle first, and it was outside that same bar that he met me a few days later. I was nine years old then."

"The same age as Ronnie when he died."

"Another coincidence, Josh. One of many we'll see before we're through. Now sit back and watch the show."

Beside my glass of wine, a box of popcorn appears. Dieter looks at me expectantly. I take a handful and pass him the container. He smiles, as the screen changes. The text is replaced by a blue-and-white licence plate mounted on a car. The scene slowly pans out from the plate to show the rear of a green 1943 two-door Ford.

Panning out even farther, I see the Ford is in a parking lot behind a building. Under its flat-top roof, the words "Timmins Hotel" are painted in large, white letters against a black background. To the left, above an entranceway, is a smaller sign: "Men." At the opposite end of the hotel is another sign, with a circular light fixture above it. This one reads "Ladies and Escorts." It reminds me of the King's Arms in Bond's Hill, a bar in which my parents had spent countless hours over many years.

Judging from the sun's position, it's about 7 p.m., mid-July. The parking lot is half full. The green Ford is in the first row, closest to the hotel entrance, suggesting it arrived early. A large black crow caws raucously nearby. Another crow, perhaps its mate, dives down from an adjacent tree, landing behind the Ford. It flaps and hops about before jabbing at a half-eaten sandwich, then safely retreats skyward to its verdant shelter.

A young boy peers briefly out the oblong rear window of the car at the same time the skittish bird clamps its beak on the sandwich. It's Dieter. From where I sit, I can see the back of his head; the colour and style of his hair are very distinct. He has blond hair, more white than yellow, close-cropped at the sides and a little longer on top—a home cut, like the ones Dad used to give me and my brothers. The kids at school called it a *bowl job*. I look away but the schoolyard taunts come vividly back, stinging as they did then. The scene transitions.

Instead of observing the car from the rear, I can now see into the back seat where the young Dieter sits, reading a Marvel comic— *Captain America*. Close up, I can see Dieter has fine hair, straight and shiny, radiating out from his crown in a monk-like style. His nose is thin but straight with a clearly defined central ridge that gives it a chiseled look. His ears, too, look sculpted, the tips a little pointed, elfin-like. He looks up as he turns the page of his comic. It's as if he's staring at me.

I snap my head back and grab tightly onto the arms of my chair. Dieter laughs, saying I'm pretty skittish for a spirit. I shoot back that it isn't easy to block a reflex; I don't have much experience being a ghost.

Young Dieter raises his arms, stretching and yawning. When his mouth is at its widest, so are his eyes. I can see he has straight teeth and, for his age, a strong, powerful jaw line. His face is a bit thin, like the rest of him. Perhaps malnourished? His eyes are not as blue as Ronnie's, more steel blue than sky blue. What I notice next are his lashes, long and curly, the kind most women envy and end up having to paste on to get the same effect.

Dieter asks me what I think. I say that as a boy he was good-looking, albeit skinny. He tells me the half-eaten sandwich the bird had taken away was his, adding "There's only so much stale bread and dried bologna anyone can stomach, Josh, hungry or not. It's as bad as shrivelled up hot dogs on rock-hard buns."

He knows what it was like for me, but before I have time to reminisce, the young Dieter pushes the driver's seat down with his feet, then leans forward to open the window two or three inches. He checks to see that the door is locked while poking around up front. I can see he's wearing a wrinkled white T-shirt, blue jeans, no socks, and old, dirty running shoes. He sticks his left hand out the window, waving it back and forth in a fanning motion. He then pulls the seat back and repeats his routine on the passenger side.

"It was no different for me back then than it was for you, Josh, when you were my age; the smell of booze, stale cigarettes, and the musty odour of dirty, unkempt fabric in your dad's old Hillman. You opened the windows, too." He directs my attention back to the '43 Ford.

Young Dieter picks up a rubber ball and an old brown baseball glove from the floor. He plays catch, bouncing the ball off the side rear window and back of the seat. He hums to himself while he plays. After a few minutes, he puts the ball in the glove, sets it on top of the comic, and leans against the armrest on the left side of the car, head supported by his hand. For a few moments all is quiet. Only the occasional sound of sparrows and chickadees furtively flitting in and out of nearby hedges disturbs the silence. Dieter begins breathing irregularly, inhaling through his mouth. The rhythm alters, becomes hesitant and sharp. Tears roll down his cheeks. He wipes them away on his arm.

A truck rumbles into the parking lot at that exact moment; a 1940 GMC in even worse shape than the old car in which Dieter sits crying. Behind the wheel is Henri Deault.

"He left Montréal in the spring of 1949, Josh, two years in Canada then. He came here and got a job as a plasterer's helper' same job he had in Québec. Now watch what happens."

Henri cranks hard right on the spinner mounted on his steering wheel and comes to a squealing, gravel-digging halt. The squeaking door opens even before Henri has shut off the ignition, and the rust-eaten half ton lurches forward when he pops the clutch and jumps out.

He looks at his face in the side mirror for a moment, adjusting his cap and scraping some plaster dust off his cheeks and ears.

Satisfied with his appearance, Henri rolls up his sleeves, pulls three unfiltered Export Plain cigarettes out of his shirt pocket, sticks one behind each ear and makes his way towards the hotel, flipping the third fag up in the air, catching it between his teeth. He stops to light it just as he reaches the car in which Dieter sits crying.

Preoccupied with the fine art of lighting a wooden match with his thumbnail, Henri doesn't seem to notice Dieter at first, but just as he raises the lit match to his lips, he hesitates, cocks his head, and appears to hear the sobs and sighs. He leans over, peering inside the Ford, lights his cigarette, and sucks on it hard, taking in a deep lungful of smoke. Seeing the front windows are partially open, he looks in at Dieter from the driver's side. He turns sideways to exhale, puts his arm on top of the car, and gazes at Dieter.

"Run out of smokes, boy? I got a couple extra here if you need a puff." Henri takes a cigarette out from behind his ear and sticks it through the window.

"Don't smoke and won't talk to strangers either!" answers Dieter, taking a big swallow to arrest his sorrow-filled sobs.

Henri laughs, a little laugh, like Dieter has said something funny. He puts the cigarette back. "Seems to me only one of them things you said is true, young man, and I'd guess you don't smoke. How about a handkerchief? Looks like you could use one." Henri reaches into his back pocket, pulls out a wrinkled piece of white cotton, and places it on the window's edge.

Dieter looks up at Henri, a puzzled expression on his face. He seems unsure what to do but shows no signs of fear or suspicion.

"Don't want no dirty nose-wipe, mister. Just want to go home." As Dieter completes his sentence, the tears began to flow and once again he is crying, sobbing, unable to show a brave front to this stranger kindly looking in on him.

"Well, there. Unless you got an invisible chauffeur, seems to me you need to hop in the front seat and drive yourself on home!"

"Can't do that. Have to wait for my parents."

Henri takes another puff of his cigarette and nods as he slowly exhales the smoke through his nostrils. "Quite right to wait for them. Guess you don't drink either, though if you wanted to be sociable, I suppose you could probably sit with them, listen to the music maybe."

"Not old enough," is Dieter's wistful reply.

"Ah, I see!" says Henri, in sympathy. "Well, is there anything else I can do for you?"

Dieter shakes his head and says nothing.

Henri pushes his cigarette down close to the joint of his fingers, takes another long puff and starts walking towards the men's entrance to the hotel. While still in range for Dieter to hear, Henri says, "Watch my truck for me then. Make sure no one bangs it up, or if they do, get their licence number. If you're still here when I'm finished, I'll give you a little something for taking care of it."

The scene shifts to the bar. A quick pan of the men's section shows it's crowded. I notice a calendar on the wall. The single page on display says it's Thursday.

The screen momentarily shows a table farthest from the men's entrance, closest to the ladies and escort door. Henri approaches from the opposite corner. When he arrives, he puts his hands on the back of an empty wooden chair and leans towards the couple seated in front of him. The man has a long-sleeved red-and-black checkered shirt. His pants are thick, dark blue in colour. The woman sitting next to him is wearing a white skirt and tight red sweater, her cleavage protruding from the low V-neck. On their table are two half-empty beer glasses, an ashtray full of cigarette butts, and a plastic-covered menu.

"Bonjour, m'sieur, madame. Pardonnez-moi. Je m'appelle Henri Deault. J'ai une question."

I don't need this translated, but Henri quickly switches to English when he sees the puzzled look on the woman's face. He continues, "Sorry about the French."

Waving his arm in the air, in a heavy French accent, the man at the table responds. *"Mon ami, je comprends ...* but my wife, she's Anglaise, a pretty Anglaise *n'est-ce pas?"* He caresses her arm, running his hand up behind her head.

She brushes him away, her lips tightly sealed, her eyes narrow.

"Yes, you are a lucky man, *m'sieur.* Such a lovely lady. I hope I can find someone as pretty. But to attract such a beauty ... you have to be Prince Charming *n'est-ce pas?"*

Looking pleased by Henri's comments, the man gives Henri the thumbs up, stands, shakes Henri's hand, and asks him to join them. He adds, in a heavy French accent, "I'm André, André Franc, dis's my wife, Annie. Can I buy you a beer, Henri?"

"Ah non, m'sieur. I just finished work." Henri points at his clothes and continues. "I was coming for a couple o' quick ones, but when I was parking, I saw something and thought I'd better come in and find the owner of the green '43 Ford. Is it your car?"

"Yes, it is. What's da problem?" Annie and André look at each other, guilty looks on their faces.

"When I was parking, I saw some boys with baseball bats around your car. They took off when they saw me coming, but I figured they were up to no good. I ran after them but lost them around the corner. I'm not sure, but they coulda done some damage. Now that I've told you, I'm gonna go take a closer look and let you know if I find any dents."

Before the Francs have a chance to say anything more, Henri heads for the exit. Back in the parking lot, Henri takes a two-dollar bill out of his pocket and a piece of string out of the back of his truck, then snaps a branch off a nearby bush. He wraps the two-dollar bill around the branch, ties it with the string, then goes to the car where Dieter is still sitting in the back seat. He slips the branch into the opening in the front window.

"Hey there, young man. You did a superb job looking after my truck. Take this, but don't tell anybody. I only gave the last boy a dollar, and I don't want him to find out."

Dieter opens his eyes wide when he sees the two-dollar bill. Only hesitating for a second, he reaches forward, pulls off the string and puts the bill in his pocket. "Gee, thanks, mister! I can buy a lot of comics with this."

"You're very welcome. I'm Henri. What's your name?"

"I'm Dieter."

"Well, Dieter. You did such an excellent job; I'd like you to look after my truck regularly. Are you interested?"

The screen goes blank for a second, then back to the table in the hotel where Dieter's parents are sitting. Annie's beer glass is still half full. André is chugging the beer left in his glass. Annie says, "That man, Henri, will see our son sitting in the back seat of our car and wonder what kind of parents we are."

"We've only been here thirty minutes," is André's reply. "But if it bodders you, den go and check on 'im."

Annie nods her head and heads out to the parking lot. Henri is on his way back to the hotel, and the two of them meet each other halfway.

Henri smiles at her, points back to the car, and remarks, "I take it that's your son in the car, madame. He told me he didn't see the men with the baseball bats, so I must have scared them off. Oh, and he's good-looking, like his mother."

Annie narrows her eyes a fraction of an inch and slightly inclines her head. She appears to be thinking about what to say. After a few seconds, she smiles and responds, "André is a jealous man, Henri. He wouldn't take kindly to hearing you say that—if you were an Anglais."

"Ahhh, then I have nothing to worry about. That's probably why you're out here alone."

"You're probably right. You French men expect each other to openly flirt with the ladies." Annie frowns, then carries on. "I do wonder about those boys you saw. I don't understand why they would be interested in bashing our car."

"I could have been wrong, madame. If they'd seen the boy, then probably they woulda moved on. Besides good-looking, your son is very smart, I think, and well-behaved. He told me his parents warned him about talking to strangers."

"Yes, we, André and me, are very lucky. The good Lord so far has only given us one child, but he's definitely a blessing."

"Then maybe you will introduce us?"

Annie looks at Henri suspiciously. Seeing the look on her face, he quickly responds, "I have no brothers, just two sisters, back in Belgium." There is a wistful look on Henri's face as he says this. He continues, "I was just thinking that, if you introduced me to Dieter, he wouldn't worry if I said hello, and maybe I could look after him when you come here."

Annie moves her head from side to side a few times then replies, "We don't leave him alone very often, and we don't know you at all. Why should I?"

"It was a suggestion, madame. I meant no harm. Please forgive me." Henri takes off his cap and lowers his head.

Annie walks to the car and motions for Dieter to roll down his window. She points at Henri and asks, "Dieter, did that man over there talk to you?"

"Yes, Mama, he asked me if I wanted a cigarette! I told him I didn't smoke, and I didn't talk to strangers. Then he said, 'Please look after my truck.' He was only gone a few minutes, then he came back and gave me two dollars! He said his name was Henri, and he wanted me to watch his truck regular." Dieter pulls the money from his pocket and waves it in the air. Then he continues. "He's funny, Mama. I like him. Can I look after his truck? Can I, Mama, please?"

Henri coughs. Annie turns to look in his direction. He bows, puts his hat back on his head, and then gets in his truck. Annie moves to the driver-side window, looks up at Henri, and says, "You impressed my son, Henri. He seems to think you're a good man. He doesn't normally take to strangers. Maybe the money had something to do with it. I don't know. But you did scare off those boys and come tell us. We live over on High Street, number twenty-three. If you're in the neighbourhood and see our car in the driveway, stop by and you and André can talk."

Annie heads back to the hotel. After she is out of sight, Henri waves goodbye to Dieter, and then drives away, only going a block from the hotel and parking on a side street. He gets out of his truck and walks back to the far side of the inn, away from the green Ford where Dieter is sitting. Slipping behind the bushes on the edge of the hotel property, he sits down, resting his back against a fence post.

"Look at that, Josh. Henri is in his mid-twenties and already he's being a guardian angel. My parents won't be coming out of the hotel for another hour. Henri won't leave until they do."

The scene fades away, closing in around Henri humming in the parking lot. I stare at the cameo image of Henri—bittersweet emotions engulf me.

"Thinking about your family, eh Josh? After Ronnie died, you felt alone; didn't have any friends or anyone like Henri to watch over you. You never did get close to any of your brothers until years later."

"Is this why I'm seeing your past?"

Dieter sighs and makes the box of popcorn disappear. He stands and walks away from me. I watch as he leans against the window, peering at the St. Lawrence below. He takes another big sigh and returns, sits in his chair, and leans towards me. "All this is uncharted territory, Josh. I'm here because your little brother asked for help. Because of what I know of AfterL and what Henri knows about helping others—"

"Sorry, Dieter. I was having an immature moment."

"Which is typical for us ACOAs. Apology accepted."

"Booze was a big part of your early years, and despite your Uncle Gilbert and Henri, there were scars."

"Yes, you know them all: shame, embarrassment, feeling victimized ... They never really went away, until I got to AfterL. Now I look at my past very differently."

"And you're here to change how I feel about my past."

"Like I said, we're in virgin territory. Ronnie wants to share the memories that you seem to have forgotten. Henri and I are here to fill in some blanks that may help you better understand Henri's past, and how it shaped his character. Okay, another glass of wine and back to Timmins."

Alice reappears with a carafe of wine and fills my glass. She smiles and in Henri's voice says, "Dieter was as much a part of my family as you and your siblings, Josh. Best you get to know him as well as I did." She winks, then vanishes.

I shake my head, still feeling my way in this surreal world. The screen shows a countdown sequence from ten to one, like you see in old black and white movies. Next up, I see a title screen: "Dieter and Me."

"You heard what Alice/Henri had to say, Josh. We're family, and all the secrets are coming out. Back to Timmins and my early years with Henri."

"From what you've already shared, Henri's been a charmer all his life. It only took him a few minutes to impress your mother. But wasn't your father suspicious? What did he say when he found out Henri had your home address and an open invitation to visit anytime?"

"Henri had brains as well as charm, Josh. Timmins isn't a big town. Most of the French-speaking folks live in the same neighbourhoods and drink in the same bars. It didn't take Henri long to find out who was who and how to gain their trust. Back to Ontario."

Before whisking us away, Dieter invites me to raise my glass. It's in my hand when our comfy chairs are replaced by lawn chairs on a flat, grassy surface. The screen that we had at the Château Frontenac is with us.

∞

"We're on the Mattagami River just outside Timmins, Josh. It's a family reunion. All my relatives are here. They don't know it, but Henri is nearby on an afternoon hiking trip with a co-worker and two girls."

On the screen, I see water running slowly over rocks and sand in the river. It's banked on one side, with a wide sandy beach on the other. There are some fifteen to twenty adults and children along the shore and grassy area, with another ten people in the water. About two-thirds of those at the reunion are children of various ages. The men away from the water are standing in a circle, drinking beer. Many of them are smoking cigars and cigarettes. One of them, a shorter man, is wearing a flat cap and a grey vest over a long-sleeved blue shirt and filling a squat, bulldog pipe with tobacco. His grizzled face and sparse grey hair make me think he is Dieter's grandfather. The quick offer of a match from the other men confirms my suspicion. Inside my head I hear the word *patron* in Henri's voice.

Among the women close to the picnic tables and fire pit, I see a plump, smiling older woman in a long white dress and thick, dark, full-length apron. The other women appear deferential. Dieter mouths the words, "My Grandmother Franc." I surmise that most of the other people in sight are Dieter's aunts, uncles, and cousins. His Uncle Gilbert is standing next to Dieter's father, André. Gilbert is wearing a beret, and checkered short-sleeved shirt. All the buttons are undone. I can see that around his neck is a gold chain with a cross suspended from it. His blue bathing suit has white stripes along its sides.

The only other adults I recognize are Dieter's parents, Annie and André. They're both in dark bathing suits. Annie looks stunning in her one piece. Except for the white accent that draws attention to her bosom, her swimsuit is black. She's in white sandals and a white bathing cap with a covering of rubber flower petals. Like all the men in the park, I try to be discreet in admiring her figure.

Dieter laughs. "It's okay, Josh. From an early age, I noticed my mother had that effect on men. The milkman, the postman, every male over the age of puberty admired her. Dad was proud that he'd won her heart ... but ... he was also very protective. All the men in town knew to keep their distance."

"I can see why, Dieter. Your father looks like the scrappy type." I notice that André is wiry and fit. Half the men there are his brothers-in-law, but even so, he is watching them, narrowing his eyelids, clenching his fist, and taking a long drag on his cigarette whenever any of them looks towards Annie. Before I can ask AfterLing Dieter where he is in the scene, I see him break away from the men and join the other children playing in the water. Two of the boys splash water on him, laughing and shouting as Dieter joins in the fray. Soon, they turn their attention to the younger boys making sandcastles near the shore. One of the mothers standing nearby quickly steps in before the older boys can undo any of the construction.

Dieter motions the older boys to follow him out of the river to the picnic table. After drying themselves, they each have a glass of lemonade and then discuss what they are going to do next. One of them picks up a net and says, "Let's go hunting for minnows." The other boys agree and start back towards the water. Before following them upriver, Dieter sidles over to his mother and says, "Mom, we're goin' fishin'."

Annie nods her assent, tousles his hair, kisses him on the forehead, and gently shoos him away, saying, "Don't go too far away."

Dieter promises to stay nearby, then runs after the other boys, a paper cup in his hand "to hold the minnows."

The scene fades to black, and when it reopens, I see the banked side of the river. The shoreline is grey rock, and as the scene expands to reveal the terrain higher up, I see grass, fallen trunks, and free-standing deciduous trees of many types, mostly beech, maple, and ash. Panning out and climbing skyward, I see the beach, the river, and the forest from above. About a quarter of a mile from the family picnic, on the opposite shore in the forest, a circle appears on the screen. Beside me, Dieter takes a deep breath. I wrap my hands around the arms of my lawn chair and keep my eyes on the display. The camera pans in below the forest canopy. I hear laughter and singing. Two couples are visible, first from above and then from the side. They are part way through the song: *Auprès de ma Blonde*, a song Henri often sang when we were working together. He told me it was an extremely popular song dating back to the seventeenth century to the time of Louis XIV.

I recognize Henri's voice. He's waving his right arm back and forth, like a band leader, enjoying the music. The two girls and the other young man following behind are marching in time to the melody. When the song is finished, Henri turns around, raises his arm high in the air, and says, "Enough of song, my friends. Let's go down to the river."

The screen in front of me splits into three panels. One shows Henri and his companions descending the rock-strewn hillside toward the river. The second panel shows Dieter and his friends running along the bank on the opposite shore. In front of them is a small stream flowing into the river. It is about six feet wide and shallow, with tall cattails on the bank opposite the boys. One of the boys shouts, "Come on, guys, we'll probably find some minnows here."

In the third panel are three bears: a mother black bear with her cubs. They are moving towards the boys, hidden by the cattails and rushes. The cubs suddenly dart out in front of their mother and run towards the stream. As they make their way through the marshland, the boys are startled. One of them shouts, "Bears!" and they all begin running back towards the picnic area. One of them, a younger boy, races towards the river, slips, and falls, hitting his head on a boulder protruding through the water.

Young Dieter hears the cry just before his younger companion loses his balance. Dieter turns just in time to see him topple backwards into the Mattagami.

I stand and turn away. My heart is in my throat, choking me. In my mind's eye, I see a bloated body in a casket. Tears erupt and I shout, "No more, Dieter, no more!"

As at the hospice, Dieter embraces me, soothes me. After I calm down he asks me to turn around. The screens collapse into one, Ronnie in a bathing suit. His smile and sparkling eyes reach inside me, relax me. The funeral parlour image in my mind's eye disappears. Ronnie winks, gives two thumbs up, and mouths the words *I love you, Josh.* Then he grins and runs fervently to the river, vanishing as he nears the river's edge.

Dieter slowly releases me, gently wipes away my tears, hugs me once more and in a soothing voice whispers in my ear, "He always loved the water, Josh. It's gonna take some time but we're doing a makeover of your memories. What you just saw is a harbinger of things to come." After assuring himself that I feel, understand, and accept this, he returns to his chair and the three screens reappear. The moment with Ronnie has completely changed my mood. No longer apprehensive, I sit down eager for the story to continue.

Henri and his companions are close enough to hear the commotion and see what is unfolding. Henri quickly jumps into the river and swims to the other side. He raises his arms in front of the bears and says, "Go away!" He stares at the mother bear. She slowly backs away and her cubs follow. Henri then picks the young boy out of the water and gently lays him on the ground, face up. He puts his ear close to the boy's mouth, then checks for a pulse. Feeling none, he starts CPR, tilting the boy's head and lifting his chin.

Within two minutes the boy begins breathing. Henri then picks him up and holds him in his arms. Recognizing Dieter, Henri says, "Where are the adults? Run ahead with my friends and tell them we're coming."

Dieter nods his head, points in the direction of the campsite, and heads off, with Henri's friends quickly overtaking him. Gilbert sees them coming and runs to meet them. Once he is apprised of the situation, he races to his truck, drives it close to the river, and opens the passenger door. Seeing that Henri has the boy in his arms, Gilbert races towards them, motioning the boy's mother to get in the truck with them. Gilbert reverses, spitting sand and grass underneath his rear tires. Once he is on the gravel road, he slams into first gear and races away from the river.

Beside me, Dieter the AfterLing levitates from his chair and dispels the scene at the Mattagami. I wipe away the tears in my eyes, clap my hands, and shout, "Well done, Henri!"

Inside my head I hear Henri slowly, softly say, "I was able to save one drowning child, Josh."

Ronnie reappears in my mind's eye. He smiles, claps his hands then gives me a high five. I laugh, and return the gesture. Dieter joins us. It's a golden moment, a fusion that fills me with joy. Henri, Dieter, and Ronnie—there to celebrate an event I knew nothing about until now. Warmth spreads through me, compelling me to say, "I love you, thank you!" I'm seeing a side of Henri I'd never known, grateful for the revelations, looking forward to more. I sense Henri and Ronnie leave, sensing I'm enjoying my time with Dieter. Afterling Dieter continues.

"It didn't take long for the story to be on the front page of the *Timmins Daily Press* with a picture of Henri, my Uncle Gilbert, and my cousin Clément, the little boy Henri saved."

"Why didn't Henri have a copy of that with the other things he left for me."

"Well, Josh. Henri wasn't much for being in the spotlight. Clément's parents were the ones who contacted the reporter and told the story. My Uncle Gilbert had to really work hard to talk Henri into posing for the photo. For the rest of the time Henri lived in Timmins, people would tip their hats, give a thumbs up, or bow with their hands clasped in front of them when they saw Henri. He was a local hero."

"Typical Henri. Always so private and modest. I wonder if it has anything to do with his own childhood."

"We're going to find out. Before that, more about Henri and my family."

"Why?"

"There's some relevant stuff from my puberty years that ties to Henri's time in Belgium and some of your own adolescent years."

Our lawn chairs disappear, and with a snap of his fingers, Dieter transports us to a different park setting in Timmins, one with a walkway and bridge. "We're in town now, Josh."

CHAPTER 8

A Common Thread

Dieter grins and then starts walking up the pathway, motioning for me to follow. The pathway rises sharply and a large granite rock, surrounded by poplar and fir trees, looms on our right. He scrambles up its side, stopping on a ledge and waiting for me to join him. When I'm next to him, he says, "I'm just around the corner, twelve years old. I want you to follow me home, then to Henri's."

Before I can say anything, he vanishes. Not the first time I'm alone. Is this their way of giving me time to think about what I've just experienced, to allow my brain back in my comatose body to store these mental events for later recall?

I do as asked and round the corner. Young Dieter leans against a stained rock, drawing in a notebook. I walk close to see what he's sketching. It's the park below us with the Mattagami and the waterside bridge, trees, and park benches already penciled in. He's working on waterfowl now—a Canada goose.

Inside my head, I hear Henri's voice. "This is how Dieter spent many of his afternoons. His Uncle Gilbert told me about his talent, and after I saw it for myself, I got Dieter that sketchbook he's using."

"Are you going to show yourself, Henri?" I whirl around, hoping to see him.

Nothing, a void. I sigh, take a deep breath, bow my head, and close my eyes.

Henri continues, "Not now. What you're going to see speaks for itself. If you have questions, AfterLing Dieter will answer them."

"So why doesn't he stay with me?"

"You need to be alone for this part of the journey, Josh."

As if I'm a puppet on a string again, an outside force raises my head and arms. They lock in that pose. Am I about to deliver a speech or talk to God? What's going on? A big gong appears above me. Beside it a short stick covered with a round leather pad strikes the disk. Its vibrations are deep, sonorous, and soothing. The sight and sound soon vanish. My arms fall to my side and a sense of peace mixed with curiosity compels me to continue. I'm okay being in a different time and place now, trusting Henri.

I watch Dieter. He puts his sketchbook away and descends the rocky slope to the park. When he crosses the bridge, I see his mother, Annie, waving at him. He quickens his pace, and once he is at her side, she holds out her hand. Dieter reaches inside his folder and hands her his sketchbook.

She flips to the page he was working on earlier and smiles. "Oh, Dieter, this is wonderful! We must let Henri show what you've done to Miss Benton, that lady who gave him the sketchbook."

"Sure, Mom. Can I go with Henri?"

"That's a good idea. Maybe Miss Benton will have some pointers for you. I'll tell your father. He'll want to talk to Henri."

"Yeah, Dad's kinda funny that way."

"He's just a proud papa."

Dieter smiles and gives his mother a hug. She tousles his hair and kisses his forehead. In a joking voice, Dieter says, "Mom, not on the street, some of my friends might be watching."

From the other side of the road, a middle-aged woman shouts, "Annie! Annie, come quick! There's been a—" She stops when Annie gives her a warning look and tilts her head towards Dieter.

The woman puts her hand to her mouth, but before she can say anything else, Dieter finishes her sentence. "... fight or a pushing match, and your husband's in trouble. Mom, Mrs. Rochès, don't try to hide things from me." Dieter takes the sketchbook from Annie, puts it in his folder, and storms away.

I can't move. I'm left to hear what Mrs. Rochès has to tell Annie.

I listen in on a conversation that I know will be like dozens I've heard before in Bond's Hill when I lived there. After work, many men go to the local bar. One of them says or does something that provokes an argument. Soon a fight breaks out. The bouncer tries to break it up, and the bartender calls the police.

Mrs. Rochès continues. "Oh, Annie, it was awful. My Charlie was there and saw the whole thing. It was in the men's lounge. Charlie and André were just sitting down at the bar to have a beer. At a table behind them, four other miners, Anglais, were playing cards—poker, Charlie said. Eddie Smith, who had his back to André, held up the queen of hearts, kissed it, and said something about you, Annie, something like he wished he had you in his hands instead of that card. The other men all raised their glasses. Well, André got up from his stool, grabbed the back of Eddie's chair, spun it around, and kicked Eddie in the chest."

Annie shook her head, gently grasped Mrs. Rochès' arm, and interjected. "Please, Mrs. Rochès, I don't need to hear anymore. André is short-tempered and protective, especially when Anglais are involved. Was anyone badly hurt?"

"No, the bouncer and Charlie managed to get between them before any chairs or bones were broken. By the time the police arrived, they were just shouting at each other—André in French—which I'm sure none of the Anglais understood. The police took André to the station."

"It's a good thing half the local police are *Canadien*. Otherwise we'd have more problems here than we do. I'll go see to André, Mrs. Rochès. Thank you for letting me know, and thank Charlie too."

Annie leaves Algonquin Boulevard and walks three blocks south to the police station. I'm compelled to go with her. At the reception desk, a burly policeman addresses Annie as she approaches. It's obvious from his accent and the name on his shirt, Thaddée Brun, that he's French Canadian.

"Sorry we meet again under dese circumstances, Madame Franc. I guess you heard de news. It wasn't too bad dis time. André 'as cooled down. You can take 'im 'ome now. I'll be right back."

Thaddée rises from his chair, plucks a key from the board behind him, and disappears down a hallway to the back of the police station. Minutes later, he returns with André and talks with him in a quiet voice. I can't hear what he's saying, but André seems pleased. When they are back in the reception area, they shake hands and wink at each other. Thaddée presses a button that lowers the turnstile, and Annie hugs André as he joins her in the reception area. She then looks closely at his face and arms. Seeing no bruises, she hugs him again, holds his hand, and leads him out of the building.

I shake my head and mutter, "I don't get it. How did Annie, like so many of the women back home, end up with a barroom brawler for a husband?" No one answers. A headset appears in front of me, motioning me to follow Annie and André. I put on the headset and find myself listening to their conversation. André's is the first voice I hear.

"Dose Anglais, Annie. Dey tink dey can say dose tings and expect me to do notting? Hah. Dey are jealous, sure. Dey don't like it when a Frenchie marries an Anglaise, 'specially one as pretty as you. But there wasn't one of dem dat was good enough for you."

"Yes, André, I chose you, but sometimes I wonder. You weren't there with Mrs. Roches. You didn't see the look on Dieter's face. Honestly, André, it breaks my heart when our son looks so hurt and embarrassed. No matter what I say, he keeps asking me why ... why you do these things?"

"It's bad enough dat our son doesn't speak good French, I won't 'ave 'im tink de Anglais can treat us like dirt or show no respec."

"André, it isn't just a French–English thing. Even Dieter knows that. If you wanted him to speak good French, then you should have married someone else." She lets go of his hand.

"You are not a typical Anglaise, Annie. Even when we were young, you would play wit us frogs. You were building bridges. Dat's what I saw. Dat's why I married you." He grasps her hand.

She puts her other hand on his face, cradles his chin, and asks, "Then why aren't you building bridges too, André? Even when I build a bridge, you insist there is a toll gate that prevents you from crossing. And the beer doesn't help."

"I've never missed a day's work, and I don't 'ave a problem." He brushes her hand away, a defiant look on his face.

"You keep telling me that, André, but many others don't see it the way you do. At your work, you've been lucky. Today, if it weren't for Thaddée Brun, you could have spent the night locked up. No way would they have let you out to get to work by 6 a.m. tomorrow. On the weekends, your brother Gilbert is there to make sure you don't get in trouble, and sober up by Sunday afternoon."

André puts his arms around Annie, and says, "*Oui, chérie*, I 'ave a good brudder and a great wife. Now let's go home, fluff the pillows, and pump my pipe." As he finishes his sentence, his hands slide down and squeeze Annie's rear. She laughs, puts her hands behind his head, and whispers, "Dieter's home."

André replies, "I'm sure you can fix dat."

I murmur to myself, "She says he's a boozer, and two minutes later she's not only ready for the bedroom but she's going to banish Dieter."

Inside my head, I hear Dieter reply. "Josh, really. You heard what Andre said, 'Annie builds bridges.' They'll be home in a few minutes. Go and listen in."

Instantly, I'm in front of a white, clapboard bungalow with a gravel driveway and white picket fence on the right. On the left is a thick hedge separating the Franc property from the neighbour's lot. The entrance to the Franc residence has an outer, aluminum-framed glass door with a stained wooden door behind it. I feel myself being dragged through the wall to a couch in the living room. Young Dieter is sitting there, reading a comic book. Annie and André enter.

André says, "Allo, Dieter. Give your papa a hug. Doze Anglais won't disrespec' your mudder again. I taught dem."

Dieter sets his comic book aside and stands. He has a look of surprise and then uncertainty on his face. He shifts his eyes from his father to his mother, who is smiling at him. Annie holds her husband's hand when she expands on André's comment. "Yes, Dieter, your father did the right thing. Come here, let's have a family hug."

Dieter shakes his head and takes a step back before answering. "Why did Mrs. Roches look so excited, Momma? What did Papa do?"

Annie puts her arms around André and presses her cheek against his when she replies. "He defended me, Dieter. One of the men said something nasty. Your father didn't let him away with it."

André smiles, picks Annie up in his arms, whirls her around, and puts her down next to Dieter. He puts one arm around Dieter, the other around Annie. He pats his son's neck and in a steely voice says, "I protec your mother. I protec you. Dat is what's right."

Annie sees Dieter's sketchbook on the table and slips away from André to get it. She opens it to the page Dieter showed her earlier. "Look, André, isn't this the best drawing he's ever done? I think it's time he showed his work to Mrs. Benton."

André seizes on his wife's suggestion, takes the sketchbook from Annie's hand, and holds it out to Dieter. "Yes, I agree. Dieter, why don't you go see Henri? Maybe he can arrange a meeting. He only lives three blocks away, in that apartment building where your Uncle Gilbert used to live."

Dieter takes the sketchbook and looks to his mother. She nods and then fishes some coins from her purse. "Here, on your way back, buy some bread, please." Dieter puts the money in his pocket and heads for the door.

As soon as Dieter closes it, André sweeps Annie into his arms and carries her to the bedroom. Annie laughs, André throws her on the bed, and I'm whisked away to an apartment building.

The 1940 GMC pickup I saw before pulls into the parking lot beside me. Once it stops, Henri Deault steps out, retrieves his plaster-spattered clothes from the bed of his truck, and then makes his way toward me. At the same time, Dieter rounds the corner, waves his sketchbook at Henri, and joins him on the stone path that leads to the entrance.

"Hi, Henri. Mom and Dad sent me. I think they wanted to be alone."

Henri grins, removes his peaked plaster cap, and beckons Dieter to his side. "I thought maybe you came to wash my truck, make some money. I see you have the sketchbook Mrs. Benton gave me. Have you made some drawings in it?"

"Yes, but I don't think that's why I'm here. Dad did something bad at the hotel." Dieter has a tone of anger in his voice. "Mrs. Roches was shouting from across the road. Mom stopped her. She didn't want me to hear. I went home. When Mom and Dad got there, they made it sound okay. It's not okay. Dad drinks, then gets in trouble. Some of the other kids, the ones I want to hang out with, make fun of him. They call him a boozer. From what I see, it's true. He's always drinking. What am I supposed to say? Mom doesn't even make a fuss."

"Let's talk when we get inside."

I wish I had someone to talk to when I was Dieter's age.

Henri unlocks the main door and holds it open for Dieter. Once inside, they go down the hall about fifty feet, where Henri uses his key to enter apartment 17A. I follow them.

It's a small, one-bedroom apartment, sparsely furnished and decorated. Straight ahead, the hall opens to an L-shaped living room. On the left through an archway, I can see into a kitchen area with a narrow walkway between the partition wall and the counter, with the sink and appliances on the opposite side. The walls throughout are painted in what Jackie, my wife, called "builder's beige," a colour she deplores. Knowing how little Henri cared for furnishings and décor, I'm not surprised.

"The living room is straight ahead, Dieter. You want a drink?"

Henri goes into the kitchen, opens the fridge, and grabs two bottles of Coca-Cola. After opening them, he sets his hat on a nail and joins Dieter in the living room via the other doorway from the kitchen. Along the way, he passes a grey, vinyl-topped, steel-legged table with two matching chairs. There are several stains on the vinyl top. The seat cushion on one of the chairs has been ripped. Black tape, the kind you see on hockey sticks, has been affixed to it.

Dieter is sitting in a worn, threadbare, cloth-covered armchair. Henri sets the soft drinks on the rectangular coffee table in front of Dieter. Seeing that Dieter is squinting from the sunlight coming through the windows, Henri closes one of the dark-blue curtains and then stands in front of the open curtain. Conspicuous in the distance is the Sacred Heart of Jesus Catholic Church. It looks like a grain elevator, the kind you see on the prairies. The sun reflects off the golden cross high atop its white, stuccoed spire. The bells start ringing.

Henri grunts, stretches his arms, then hums the refrain from *Frère Jacques*. "Recognize that song, Dieter? The bells in that church remind me of it."

"Sure, everybody knows that song. I know it in English and French." Dieter has a look of pride on his face. Henri grins.

"Let's sing the French version. I'll start, you join in. But first, let's wet our whistles." Henri picks up the bottles, hands one to Dieter, then proposes a toast. "To Father John, wherever he is." He takes a drink, waits for Dieter to finish, and then begins to sing.

When Henri begins to repeat the verse, he raises his voice and moves his arms and legs to the tempo. There's a twinkle in his eye. I see how Dieter responds, and I'm drawn into the moment. I sing along too, fighting back a lump in my throat. I'd almost forgotten how much Henri loved music.

I miss you, Henri.

The bells in the church stop ringing long before we stop singing. Caught up in the melody and the moment, we carry on.

This will be a lasting memory.

As if knowing it's time, Henri slows the tempo and lowers his voice until his whispers fade into silence. He turns to the window, raises his bottle, and says, *"Merci, pour la musique."* Dieter gives him a quizzical look and Henri asks, "How do you feel right now?"

"Happier than I did," is Dieter's response.

Henri nods and carries on. "Yes, sunshine, music, and chiming bells have that effect on me too, especially when other people are around and they sing along and sway with the beat. Thanks for joining in, Dieter. You have rhythm. I bet you got that from your family. I noticed your mom and dad dancing at the Legion a few times. They seemed to be enjoying themselves, and even won a few dance contests."

"Yeah, my Dad and Mom like music. Sometimes we sing and dance together. I remember the weekend you saved my cousin Clément from drowning. After Uncle Gilbert came back and said Clément was okay, we celebrated. Grandpa Franc got out his fiddle, Uncle Gilbert played accordion, and we had a great time." Dieter is smiling when he says this, but when he is finished, he sighs.

Henri notices and asks, "Why the glum look?"

"Because Dad drank too much, like always. He started slurring his words, stepping on our feet, losing his balance. Mom had to make him sit down. He finally passed out, and Uncle Gilbert took him home."

"So nobody was hurt and the party carried on?"

"Yes, but nobody else passed out or embarrassed their family."

"Ah ha, so you were embarrassed?"

"Yes, but Mom carried on as if nothing happened. When I told her I was ashamed, all she said was that Dad was good to us, and we should be grateful."

"I can see they're happy together, Dieter. Your father doesn't strike me as a violent man. Is he good to you?"

"That doesn't matter."

"Hmmm?" Henri's leaves the room, returning a minute later with a faded envelope. He asks Dieter, "Do you read French?"

"Yes."

Henri hands him the envelope. I look over Dieter's shoulder as he reads the envelope and then the faded note inside.

While he reads, Henri continues, "My gramma, Mémère Camille, gave that envelope to me just before I left Belgium. I had been through some rough times, and I was upset and angry. She told me not to open it and tapped on the words written on the envelope.

Dieter holds up the envelope and reads out, "*Ne pas ouvrir en colère.* I think that means don't open in anger."

"Yes, another translation is 'Don't open while angry.' When Mémère gave me that envelope, she told me to wait until I was in Canada and pick a sunny day, when I was in a good mood—open to advice. So I waited until I settled in Montréal. I went to Mount Royal on a Sunday afternoon. I looked up at the Goddess of Liberty above the Sir George-Étienne Cartier monument. I was happy I was also grateful. I was surrounded by happy *Canadiens*. Montréal hadn't been bombed like Antwerp and other Belgian cities. In Belgium, everyone was angry, bitter, sad ... So many people killed." Henri sighs, shakes his head, and then carries on. "It was horrible, but in Montréal, my past was fading behind me—a new world and new country lay before me. I opened the envelope."

Dieter reads out the words on the note: *"vous ne pouvez pas gérer logiquement l'émotion."* There is a hint of uncertainty in his voice as he translates, "Do not manage emotion with logic."

Henri responds, "That's pretty good. One of my English friends in Montréal suggested a better version, doesn't sound so Germanic: You can't deal logically with emotion."

"Why are you sharing this with me, Henri? I'm only twelve."

"Because you seem to be a bright young man. I thought that when I first met you a few years ago in the hotel parking lot."

"So? Your grandma gave you that note when you were much older than me, and she told you not to open it until you were happy and in a different country."

"Hmmm ... you *are* very bright. I was thinking, maybe if Mémère gave me that note when I was your age, and explained it to me, I wouldn't have spent so long being angry."

"I'm not angry. I'm just upset."

"Angry, upset, they're both emotions, Dieter."

"So is happiness."

"Ah, but it is quite different. Look at your mother. Wouldn't you say she is a happy person?"

"Yes."

"And weren't you happy when we were singing?"

"Yes."

"And what about when you are drawing?"

"I'm happy then."

"Okay, let's have a look at your drawings, and we'll come back to Mémère later."

Dieter jumps up from the chair and retrieves his sketchbook from the coffee table. When he sees Henri settle himself on the couch, he hesitates for a few seconds and then stands in front of him. He holds out the sketchbook.

Henri smiles and folds his arms. "You know what the word 'perspective' means, Dieter?"

"Yeah, it's how you look at something."

"Good. Where I come from, artists usually look at their works from the same perspective as their audience. It's easier for them to talk about it." Henri unfolds his arms, motions for Dieter to move to his left, and then stands beside him. "Now you can show me your drawings."

"I'd rather be sitting down."

"So would I. But you don't want to sit next to me on the couch, do you?"

"No."

"I think I know why." Henri goes to the window and looks out at the church. I go and stand next to him. The sun is still shining on the Cross but less intensely. Henri takes a deep breath and then asks Dieter to join him. He points at the church and asks, "Do you go to that Catholic Church, Dieter? I know your Uncle Gilbert does." Henri says the words *Catholic Church* in a scornful, bitter voice. Dieter picks up on it and asks,

"Aren't you Catholic, Henri?"

"I used to be a very devout Catholic."

"What happened?"

"I'm going to tell you. It's a secret I haven't told anyone else. Then maybe we can sit on the sofa and look at your art." He takes the sketchbook from Dieter, places it back on the coffee table, and sits on the chair. He motions for Dieter to sit on the couch.

CHAPTER 9

Innocence Lost

Henri places his hands on his knees, lowers his head, and begins speaking in a monotone, as if in a trance or under hypnosis. "Back in Belgium when I was a young lad, I wanted to be an altar boy. Be in front of everyone, wear special clothes, light candles—that all seemed so wonderful. I imagined myself beside the priest, Father Magloire. I thought I'd be the envy of all the Catholic boys in our parish."

Henri sighs. "I remember when I told my mother. I was seven. It was after my First Communion, at the big family celebration. She gave me a big hug and said she was thrilled and proud. I would be so much closer to God. She told Mémère Camille and Tante Marie. Before long, every adult there, including Father Magloire, knew."

"You were seven?"

"Yes. In our parish, children could take First Communion at age seven, after two years' Sunday school and home lessons. It's the age of reason." Henri snorts—the tone of bitterness evident in his voice. He pauses for a moment before he asks, "When did you take First Communion?"

"When I was ten. That was Mom's decision. She was Anglican before she married Dad, and she said seven was too young."

"Another reason I like your mother."

"Did you become an altar boy at seven?"

"Yes, Father Magloire was very eager for me to join *his chosen boys*." When he says these last three words, Henri makes a quotation marks gesture with his fingers.

Dieter has a puzzled look on his face.

Henri takes a deep breath, then continues. "Father Magloire told my mother that surely it was part of God's plan. Boys wanted to become altar boys because God had spoken to them ... had chosen them."

"So it was a big deal?"

"Indeed, for years, my mother and Mémère Camille would proudly introduce me as *petit Henri, our altar boy*. For a long time, it was a big deal for me too."

"Then what happened?"

"The Devil showed up when I reached puberty. You know what puberty is, Dieter?"

"It's growing up. Girls get boobs, boys get boners." Dieter smiles. He seems pleased with his answer.

"Boobs and boners, I like that. I doubt you got that from your father."

"No, but I told him my weenie gets hard sometimes. He laughed and said that was a good sign. I was growing up."

"A good sign? How strange. Father Magloire said the same thing to me." Henri has a pained expression on his face. He gets up from his chair and excuses himself. He tells Dieter he'll be right back. He goes into the bathroom. We can hear him turn on the tap in the sink. Three minutes later, he's back in the living room and stands in front of the window. His eyes appear a bit puffy. He shakes his head, then faces Dieter. "Sorry about that. Some memories came back. I had to flush them."

Henri turns his back on young Dieter and picks up where he left off. "Father Magloire said a boner was a wondrous thing, a gift from God to Adam. Without a boner, Adam couldn't help Eve make babies."

Henri shakes his head, then carries on. "Father Magloire then asked me what my Dad told me about sex. Because we lived on a farm and bred and raised animals, my Dad said it was pretty much the same, and that I'd figure out the rest, preferably after I married one of the local farm girls."

Henri turns from the window, crooks one leg to rest against the wall, and looks up, as if he's trying to see beyond the ceiling, perhaps to the end of the universe.

Dieter fidgets on the couch. He waits several seconds for Henri to resume. When this doesn't happen, he says, "Dad said he'd tell me more about sex when I got older. For the time being, he said I should keep my willy in my pants."

The break in the silence gets Henri's attention; he lowers his head and leg and stands tall in front of the window, facing Dieter. Behind him, the sky is still bright, no clouds, late afternoon, but Henri's face is clear, not hidden in shadow. He flashes a tiny, knowing smile at Dieter then asks. "Has your Dad said anything more?"

"Well, a few weeks ago, on a weekend, near dawn, still dark ... I went to the bathroom to pee. I turned on the light, opened my pyjamas, and saw a long, pale yellow thing in the toilet bowl. It looked like a skin shed by a snake. I was so frightened I ran outside. On my way back from the bushes, Dad asked me where I'd been. When I told him where and the reason why, he laughed, grabbed my hand, and took me into the bathroom. He pointed into the toilet bowl and said the thing in there wasn't a snakeskin; it was a *caoutchouc*, a condom. He said that, if I couldn't keep my willy in my pants, I should have a condom in my pocket. He then flushed the toilet and went back to bed."

"So did you figure out what he was saying?"

"I didn't ask him to explain. It was Saturday morning. He'd been partying most of the night. If I hadn't slammed the screen door, he probably wouldn't've got up to check what was going on." The exasperation in Dieter's voice ends, and in a conspiratorial tone he carries on. "My friends told me more about condoms that Sunday, after church."

Henri raises his eyebrows, opening his eyes wide.

Seeing the inviting look, Dieter continues. "We were sitting on one of the high banks of the Mattagami River around the bend, where no one in the park could see us. There were three of us: me, Dan, and Elie. When I told them about the condom, Elie got up, then knelt between Dan and me and put his arms around our shoulders. He said he knew all about condoms. His older brother, Jacques, who was married, had taken him to the local drugstore for an ice cream one day that summer and asked for some condoms. On the way back to the car, Elie asked what condoms were. Jacques said they were 'willy covers for whoopee sessions.' Me and Dan didn't know what he was talking about. 'Whoopie is the same as jiggie-jig,' he said. 'A girl and boy take down their pants and roll around together, in bed, in a car, or on the grass—it doesn't matter where. A condom keeps the seeds, sperm, from getting out. If the seeds get out, then the girl could get pregnant and have a baby.'

"I knew then why I didn't have any brothers or sisters. My dad used *caoutchoucs*."

Young Dieter has a proud expression on his face for a moment, then he looks disgusted.

Henri probes. "What happened then? Did Elie have more to say?"

"No, but Dan did. He said that his older brother, George, asked him if he'd had any boners yet. Dan said he had, and one night, he woke up because his willy was spitting yucky, cream-coloured stuff inside his pyjamas. He said it felt good for a few seconds, but when he was fully awake, he knew it wasn't pee and thought he'd be in trouble if he told his mom. So he rinsed his pyjamas and put them in the bottom of the laundry basket under other dirty clothes."

Dieter's shoulders are hunched and his hands are underneath his legs, as if he's trying to hide them.

Henri reacts. "It's okay, Dieter, I think I know where you're going. Dan was sleeping, had no control, and just like a full bladder makes you pee, a hard willy makes you squirt seed. It's natural, but parents find it hard to talk about. Dan had an older brother who explained it to him. You don't have an older brother, neither do I, so you learned about boners from your friends. I learned about them from Father Magloire." Henri scoffs, moves away from the window, and sits on the chair. Leaning forward, he continues, saying softly, "I wish I had friends like yours."

"No, you don't! What Dan told us and what he asked us to do next was disgusting."

Henri says nothing. Seeing the look on young Dieter's face, I wonder how his ghostly counterpart is taking this. I look at AfterL Dieter. I can't read his expression.

He looks at me, smiles, and says, "Remember, Josh, I have no trauma. Revisiting these scenes is pain-free for me. If anything, they confirm what I've said about earthly reality; it sucks compared to AfterL. I'm an objective, dispassionate observer. Having eleven other souls know the earthly Henri I knew was truly inspiring. It still is, almost forty years later. Now listen up. Henri is about to offer my young, earthly doppelgänger an epiphany."

Henri retrieves the sketchbook from the table and makes sure Dieter is watching him before he begins speaking. "Remember our earlier conversation? I asked you about perspective? It not only has to do with drawings. It also has to do with behaviour; how two people can see the same thing but describe and react to it differently. One of my favourite examples is about two farm boys and two horses. Do you know that story?"

"No, I don't." The expression on Dieter's face changes. He now looks curious.

Henri carries on. "It's Christmas morning. One young boy, Joe, about your age, wakes up and under the tree is an envelope with his name on it. He opens it. Inside is a card that says, 'I'm in the barn.' He runs out of the house, and in the barn he sees a saddled pony and a sign: 'I'm yours, Joe, Merry Christmas.' Joe is so excited that he runs over to the pony, puts his arms around his neck, and then turns to see if his parents followed him to the barn. There they are, smiling, enjoying the moment."

Henri pauses, checks to see if Dieter is following, and then continues. "The other young boy, John, in a different family, also on Christmas morning, sees an envelope under the tree with his name on it. The same message is inside. John reads it, shakes his head, then slowly puts on his coat, hat, snow boots, and mitts, and plods his way to the barn. When he sees the pony, he shakes his head and says, 'Horse shit. Wonderful. Pig shit, cow shit, and now horse shit for me to clean up. Just lovely.'"

Seeing no more needs to be said, Henri opens Dieter's sketch book, stopping at a page with a doe and fawn beside a stream. "I don't see any deer shit in this picture, Dieter. Now tell me what Dan said and did when you were talking about condoms and boners on the banks of the Mattagami."

"Dan's older brother, George, said it was lover's nuts, or blue balls, that made Dan squirt semen while he slept. Lover's nuts make your weenie hurt, and the older you get, the more you suffer. George said he and his friends found a way to relieve it. George took Dan into their garage to show him. After bolting the door, he got two rags from a box on the shelf—'so we don't make a mess,' he said—and then led Dan to the couch next to their wood stove. He took off his pants, told Dan to do the same, and then he lowered his undies and sat on the couch."

Henri slowly nods every time Dieter completes a sentence. Henri's facial expression is constant. Open and non-judgmental.

It seems to have a hypnotic effect; Dieter's words come out more gradually, more calmly as he continues. "Dan dropped his boxers and sat next to George on the couch. George then put his left hand around Dan's willy, squeezing and pumping it slowly. Dan said it felt really good, and in no time, he had a boner. George's weenie was already big. George said he was going to get lover's nuts if Dan didn't jerk him off. Dan grabbed George's penis. He said it felt kinda weird but not bad weird. Then George used his right hand to rub and gently squeeze Dan's balls. That felt really good, so Dan followed George's lead. George started panting, and between breaths, told Dan gently squeezing each other's balls would help both of them get their rocks off."

I'm reminded of my own adolescence and several memories I'd suppressed suddenly return. Before I get too far in their recall, I feel Dieter take control and neutralize the feelings of disgrace and disgust that accompanied my repressed recollections. At the same time, I hear him say inside my head, "*You were just a boy, Josh. This and other memories now being unlocked can do you no harm.*"

Dieter pauses the scene and stands silently beside me. Somehow he knows I don't need words or more interventions in my mind. All I need is time for my earthly brain to process these latest revelations, without shame, embarrassment, or revulsion. As these thoughts churn, the story of the two boys and their ponies serves as a key, a Rosetta stone, allowing me to understand and integrate things very differently in my sense of self, of who I am and who I will be when I recover.

Somehow these moments of musing better prepare me for the journey ahead. Dieter crosses his arms, evidently pleased. I hear "Ode to Joy," then the refrain from Bizet's *Carmen*. With a twinkle in his eye, Dieter says, "Hoity toity music. Who'd a thunk a ranger from Timmins would mix them in a scene about masturbation and puberty?"

Once I stop laughing and shaking my head, in my mind's eye I see Elie and Dieter, wide-eyed, listening to Dan, unlocking a door, starting to make sense of puberty. Their innocence is touching. The picture softly fades along with my nostalgic feeling. I expect the exchange between Henri and young Dieter to resume. Instead Dieter says, "I think you can handle the real thing now Josh, so let's go to the Mattagami and join the earthly me and see and hear firsthand what happened next."

Dieter snaps his hands, and suddenly I'm seated in front of him in a canoe. The canoe levitates from the floor in Henri's apartment.

Using his paddle, Dieter turns the canoe ninety degrees, and with long strokes, propels us through the walls and across the streets to the Mattagami. Once we're in the water, he paddles past the site where his family had their picnic, past the cattails and shallow waters where Henri had rescued Dieter's cousin, around the bend where Elie, Dan, and young Dieter can be seen high on the left bank. The canoe stops and transforms into a couch, which rises slowly on the air. A rug and two foot stools ascend with us. Seconds later, we're facing the boys. Dieter tells me Elie is the one in the middle. Clearly, Dan is the boy on the right.

Elie is of medium build, has brown eyes, straight dark-black hair, and a dark complexion. He is wearing running shoes, a blue T-shirt, black shorts, and a straw hat. A Mickey Mouse watch is strapped around his right wrist and a fishing pole fashioned out of a tree branch lies at his side. The shape of his eyebrows, cheekbones, and eyelids remind me of a panda bear. I want to give him a hug.

Dan is the most athletic-looking of the three. He has curly hair, blue eyes, and sunburned skin. His plaid shirt is unbuttoned, open to reveal a cross suspended on a gold chain. White underpants protrude above his cut-off jeans. He's wearing a blue baseball cap with NY in white letters above the peak. Sandals cover his large, wide feet.

I put my left elbow on the arm of the couch, rest my legs on a foot stool, and follow the conversation among the three boys.

Dieter reminds me this is a conversation in process. Dan is describing his initiation into puberty by his older brother, George.

Dan: "And we did. It didn't take long. George said it was because I was a virgin." He pauses and checks to see if his companions are following.

Dieter is squirming, looking like he wants to be somewhere else.

Elie's eyes are looking up to his right. His brow furrowed.

Elie: "I thought only girls could be virgins."

Dan: "George said it also meant untouched and pure. I wasn't pure anymore."

Elie: "So Dieter. What about you? Are you pure?"

Dieter: "I guess so. What about wet dreams? Do they count?"

Dan: "George says they don't cause you're asleep. You have to be awake."

Dieter: "Then I'm a virgin."

Elie: "Me too!"

Elie holds out his hand. Dieter strikes it gently. Next they give each other a high five, slap their knees three times, and then repeat the high five, hooting in time to the contact. I sense this is a ritual—their unique way of bonding.

Dan holds up the cross around his neck.

Dan: "Hey, I'm still a virgin as far as the girls are concerned."

Dieter and Elie see the hurt look on Dan's face and repeat the ritual, including him this time. When it's over, they're all smiling. Elie puts his arms around his companions and tugs at their hats.

Elie: "I wonder when we'll lose our virginity with the girls?"

Dan: "Not before I get married."

Dieter: "Same here."

Elie: "I think I'll follow my older brother's advice—get some experience so my wife gets the benefit of my know-how."

Dieter and Dan stare at him.

I turn my attention away from the boys and look across the couch at the AfterLing Dieter. He suspends the scene in front of us, shrugs his shoulders, and holds up his hands, palms pointing upward. Even though he has a *What can I say?* look on his face, he answers, "I know, that sounds like something Henri would say. But he would never have said that to me. You remember your own puberty, Josh, the uncertainty and confusion?"

"Yes, but why're you bringing that up?"

"The tone of your voice and the look on your face tell me you don't want to talk about it." Dieter is now smiling at me—sympathetic, not mocking.

I take a deep breath, exhale, and open up. "It was an awkward time for me too, Dieter. Hell, I haven't even talked to my own kids about puberty. Even my wife, Jackie, didn't get much help when she was a teen."

"Which is why sex is absent from AfterL. Here joys are mental, spiritual, communal, and cumulative. An orgasm is such a fleeting physical and personal thing. Besides, few societies accept sex education as their responsibility. Most kids learn from each other; the blind leading the blind."

"That's what you're sharing with me now."

"Uh-huh and Henri's already hinted at some of his first lessons."

"Yes, with a priest." I grimace and shake my head.

Dieter raises his eyebrows and says, "You think my first lessons pale in comparison?"

"From what I've seen so far, Dieter, there's no abuse. You were one of three young innocents trying to understand something adults avoided. Henri's lessons came from an adult, someone he admired and trusted. He was abused."

Dieter sighs and responds. "You don't mean that Josh. You suspected this was a traumatic day for me. Dan and Elie made me feel inferior. You sensed that. That's why you looked over at me—to confirm."

"You brought me here for a reason. Like I said, though, you were with friends trying to understand puberty. I sense it was awkward and a bit embarrassing but you felt something more, right?"

Dieter nods, looks at me intently, and then replies. "I was traumatized, but until *Ben Casey* aired in the sixties, trauma was something associated with major stresses like war and fire. Coping with alcoholic parents or puberty didn't fit. Trauma, fear, phobia—you name it—all gone in AfterL."

"But when you were alive, a young boy with only your friends to rely on, sex education wasn't easy."

"Not the puberty part with my friends. It got better after I met Henri. Now can we get back to 1951?" Without waiting for a reply, Dieter points to the boys on the bank. Their conversation resumes.

Dan: "George told me you can get sick fooling around with girls who aren't virgins."

Elie: (*laughing*) "Then I'll get my experience with virgins."

Dan: "That won't solve the problem with blue balls, Elie. George told me that, now that I've had wet dreams, I'm gonna have to do something about the pain during the day, several times a week. You won't be that good with the girls."

Elie: "I'm gonna try, but you're probably right. Can we do what you and George did?"

Dieter: "Wait a minute? Who said anything about that? Somebody could come by and think (*trembling*) we were—"

Elie: "Hey, I'm game. If it's not for you, be our watchdog."

Dieter: "I'm outta here."

Dan and Elie laugh and hoot. As Dieter runs away, Elie shouts, "Don't be such a pansy!"

I turn to Dieter, my eyes wide. He smiles lifts his eyebrows, shrugs, and then twirls one hand in the air like a crane helper signalling the operator to raise the hoist.

∞

The scene on the Mattagami recedes. Our couch splits and transforms into two armchairs that recline beside each other, miles above the earth. It's dark, except for the twinkling of stars, the glow of a full moon, and a lonely comet streaking across the sky.

Bathed in lunar light, Dieter says, "I've always enjoyed the night sky, Josh. In AfterL, we can pick any star, any comet, any planet, and in a heartbeat, travel there. That comet you see, that's Halley's. It didn't appear in the lifetimes of any of us in A Magnificent Mind., my AfterLing group of twelve, so when Halley showed up in 1986, we went for a ride." Dieter has a serene look on his face as he slowly returns us to Earth. "I imagine how Neil Armstrong must have felt peering from the moon in 1969, except his field of vision couldn't compare to ours." As we get closer, *Also sprach Zarathustra* begins playing. Dieter has bass drums appear before him, and he plays along. As the song reaches its end, and we near Timmins, our chairs transform into a two-seat ultralight that Dieter lands in a field close to Henri's apartment. When we're back on the ground, and I've recovered from my amazement, Dieter, showing no emotion, replays Elie's last words from the Mattagami: "Don't be such a pansy."

A black-and-white picture of Dieter, Dan, and Elie holding fish and smiling for the camera appears in an oval frame in front of me. I grab it, remembering similar photos from my own past. The images of Dan and Elie fade, and the fish in Dieter's hand turns into a sketchbook.

Dieter shows me a pencil drawing of Elie and Dan waving goodbye. "That was the beginning of the end of our friendship. Over the next few weeks, Dan and Elie started treating me differently. In the yard before school, if one of them was around I could talk to him, but when the other showed up, the two of them would put their arms around each other and walk away. At recess and after school it was the same. They avoided me."

"You didn't make any other friends?"

"Don't look so sad, Josh. I was in the school band. I had my sketchbook. The music and art were enough to attract company."

Dieter grins. Behind him, several black-and-white photos of his school band and art club appear, with circles around the girls. The pictures fade away, replaced by images of me in my high-school yearbooks in theater scenes and pages with my poems and short stories highlighted.

"I get your point, Dieter. Neither of us were jocks, so we spent our time with our hobbies and the girls once we left grade school."

"Yep, and Henri helped me make sense of puberty."

"How so?"

"Let's go back into Henri's apartment and you'll see. We'll pick up where we left off that day Mom sent me to show Henri my sketches."

The ultralight disappears and Dieter takes me through the walls back to Henri's living room.

CHAPTER 10

Henri Clears the Confusion

Young Dieter is sitting on the couch. Henri is standing in front of him, the sketchbook open to the picture of a doe and fawn by the stream. Henri closes the book, finishes his drink, and asks Dieter if he wants another. Dieter shakes his head. Henri takes the two empties and goes into the kitchen. From the hallway, I can see him put the Coke bottles on the counter next to some dirty plates and cups. I notice the plates haven't been rinsed; streaks of peanut butter, jam, and egg yolk lie underneath toast crumbs and bacon bits. As if he senses we're watching, Henri puts the plates and cups in the sink. While the sink is filling with hot water, he gets another Coke from the fridge and pulls a bag of cookies out of the cupboard over the fridge. He then rinses a plate, dries it, and fills it with cookies. While he is busy in the kitchen, Dieter leafs through his sketchbook.

When Henri returns to the living room, AfterLing Dieter motions for me to join him on the floor, and the two of us sit, leaning against the outside wall. We watch Henri set the plate on the table, take a swig from the bottle, and then sit next to young Dieter. When Henri burps—a deep, from-the-belly belch—Dieter looks at him, a look of astonishment on his face.

"Haven't you heard a burp before?"

"Yes, but only from some of the boys at school."

"So adults don't burp?"

"None I know. It's disgusting."

"I guess you think the same thing about farts."

Young Dieter grimaces and vigorously shakes his head.

Henri laughs, then stands facing Dieter. Lifting the tail of his shirt shoulder high with his right hand, he cups his left hand in his right armpit and begins flapping, vigorously. A variety of fart-like sounds echo through the apartment. Dieter puts his hands over his ears and tells Henri to stop. Laughing, tucking in his shirt, Henri grabs a cookie, and sits facing Dieter. The sun shining through the window basks the room in an orange glow.

From my vantage point, four feet from his side, I can clearly see Henri in profile. His hairline is already receding, foreshadowing the frontal and mid-region baldness he has when I meet him some thirteen years later. His aquiline nose, strong jaw line, and ruddy complexion give him a hale, hearty look. There is a confidence in the way he holds his head that reassures me. How many people get the opportunity to peel away the veil surrounding a loved one's past? A warm glow radiates from my chest.

Henri takes a bite of his cookie, holds the remaining bit in front of him, and addresses it as much as Dieter as he resumes talking. "Take this cookie; raisins, eggs, oatmeal, baking flour, sugar, shortening. I could get real hung up thinking about the eggs. After all, they come from a chicken's arse, the same hole used for pee and poop. I could worry about the shells. Maybe they were covered in shit and some of that shit got into the bowl when the cook cracked the eggs and dumped the yolks and white into the batter. But I don't—and you know why?"

Hesitating for only a second, Dieter responds in an excited, *I get it* voice. "It's like the pony story you told me. You're the boy who sees the pony and doesn't worry about the pile of poop."

"*Oui!* Yes, Dieter. That's me. When I left Montréal to come here, the guys I worked with had a nickname for me: *L'heureux.* You know what that means in English?"

117

"It means 'happy.' They called you Henri, the Happy One."

"Good answer, young man. You know why?"

Dieter doesn't answer. Instead he has an expectant look on his face.

Pausing only for a moment, Henri downs the last of his cookie and grabs another. He breaks it in two and stuffs both pieces in his mouth. Between bites, he carries on his conversation. "Because I was happy! By choice."

Henri raises his chin, puts a hand on each side of his mouth, and as he swallows the cookie bits, he lowers his hands and rubs his tummy, making an 'mmm ... mmm' sound in time with the circles he makes round his stomach. Dieter smiles and reaches for a cookie. Henri gives two thumbs up, then forms the letter V from the index and middle finger on his right hand. After Dieter bites into his cookie, Henri continues. "See what my happiness did? It spread ... to you. You saw me relishing my cookie, and now you're enjoying yours. No worries about poop, right?"

Dieter nods his head, finishes his cookie, and opens up, as if Henri has unlocked a door. "You talk to me different than anybody else, Henri. You make me feel like ... like I'm a somebody. The only other person who comes close is Mom, but ... well, you know, she's my Mom. And when I tell her I'm embarrassed by my Dad's drinking, she says is he's a good man and takes care of us."

Henri pauses a few seconds before answering. He slowly gets up from the chair and sits on the couch, his back against the armrest at the opposite end from where Dieter is sitting. As if he's ticking each item off a list with his right hand, Henri responds. "Drinking, pooping, farting, and burping. Have I got them all—the things that bother you?"

"What Elie and Dan said—that was the most disgusting!"

"Ahhh, I see. Elie's brother, Jacques, bought condoms and told Elie what they were for. Dan's brother, George, went quite a bit further in showing what you can do with a willy."

Dieter furrows his brow for a few seconds, opens his mouth, closes it, pauses a bit longer, and then says in a hesitant, somewhat perplexed voice. "It doesn't sound so disgusting the way you say it."

"This whole conversation started with me asking you about puberty, Dieter. You said it was about boners and boobs. You, Elie, and Dan probably didn't know much more than that a few months ago. Then you saw a condom in the toilet and asked your Dad what it was. Elie asked his older brother, Jacques, in a drugstore. As for Dan, well, it was his older brother George who maybe went too far."

Henri gets up from the couch and stands looking out the window. Somehow I know he's looking at the church. After a few seconds, he returns to his chair, picks up his Coke bottle, takes a drink, and then sets it gently back down on the table. He leans forward, his hands clasped in front of him as he continues sharing his thoughts. "If I was your older brother, I think I would've done things differently than George or Jacques did with Dan and Elie. It seems Dan and Elie wanted to go down a path that disgusted you, and without meaning to, I put you back on it. I'm sorry for that."

The contrite look on Henri's face and the tone in his voice have the desired effect. Dieter nods. Reassured, Henri continues. "Let's see if I can put things right."

Before he can continue, the alarm in the nearby fire hall interrupts him. He and Dieter run to the window. The siren from the fire truck suddenly adds to the raucous sound. I want to see what's going on too, but AfterLing Dieter tells me to stay put. Once the alarm is turned off and the fire truck has sped away, Henri and Dieter turn away from the window. Henri looks at his watch and says, "It's six o'clock. Do you have to go home soon?"

"I don't want to. Dad is probably having more beer, and I don't like to be around when he's drinking. I usually grab my sketchbook and go to the park by the Mattagami. Mom knows I'm here."

"I think you better call, and if your mom's okay, maybe we can eat out. All I have is breakfast stuff and no clean plates."

"I'm almost thirteen. I don't need to call my mom. We can eat out, but I'm not hungry right now—the Coke and cookies."

Henri shrugs his shoulders. "I'll make a deal. When we finish here, we'll check in at your place, and then we'll go for a bite to eat, okay?"

"Okay."

Henri goes to the kitchen and drags one of the metal chairs into the living room. He puts it in front of Dieter, about six feet away, the back of the chair facing Dieter. Sitting on it backwards, arms folded over the top, Henri smiles and explains, "My dad, *mon père*, used to sit this way when we were in the shed 'having a talk.'"

Dieter raises his eyebrows and opens his eyes wide. Henri smiles and continues, "I don't have any brothers, just two younger sisters, twins Lise and Chantal, in Belgium. Anyway, *mon père*, would sometimes say, teeth clenched, 'Henri, let's go for a woodshed chat.' It was always after hearing me say something he didn't like, often in front of my sisters and mother. I remember the first chat very well. I was a couple of years younger than you. We lived on a farm with no indoor plumbing. No hot and cold water taps. We had a well and three hand pumps. One was over the well. Another was in the barn. We'd fill a bucket with water from that pump to feed our pigs, chickens, and cows. That's why I'm so muscular; from carrying all that water."

Henri raises his arms and flexes his biceps. "What'cha think? Me, instead of Steve Reeves, Mr. Universe 1950?"

Dieter laughs and shakes his head.

Henri lowers his arms and resumes his pose behind the chair. "Our third pump was on the back porch. I used it to fill the pail so we could boil water. *Mon père* had me fill the pots on Saturday night, so we were all clean for church on Sunday. Lise and Chantal were first to bathe. I wasn't allowed in the room until they—and after them, *ma mère*—had finished. By then the water was lukewarm and soapy. *Ma mère* called *mon père* and me in to skim off a couple of buckets and add clean, hot water. Lise and Chantal, in their bathrobes, were standing by the wood stove drying their hair. When I was stooping to put my bucket in the tub, I saw a small bloody streak on the rim. I looked at *ma mère* and *mon père* and said, 'I'm not bathing in this—it's all bloody!' I dropped my bucket, but before I could move any further, *mon père* said it was time for a woodshed chat. Our first. He grabbed my arm and off we went."

Unexpectedly, as if the last words were a cue, I feel myself being pulled out of Henri's apartment. Dieter, the AfterLing, sets me down in the parking lot where a worn seven-by-nine-foot Persian carpet, a roll of paper, and a telescope lie on the gravel. Dieter snaps his fingers and a purple vest appears over his white T-shirt. His blue jeans become baggy white pants and a wide black belt, and pointed black shoes complete his new wardrobe.

From the look on his face, I see he expects me to guess who he is. A quick look at the intricate patterns on the carpet makes it easy. I say, "Aladdin."

Dieter nods, and a lamp appears in his left hand. He rubs it three times and a genie pops out of the spout and hovers above us, arms folded, awaiting Dieter's command. Dieter unfurls the roll of paper. I see it's a map of Europe. After motioning for me to join him on the carpet, Dieter picks up the telescope, and in a very authoritative but gentle voice, says, "Genie, Belgium please, year 1931, date August 11th, time 8:30 p.m. Latitude 50 degrees north, longitude 5.71 degrees east. Hover about a hundred feet from ground level and await further instructions."

Quickly, I lie on the carpet, tightly grasping the tassels on top and the fringe on the right. Dieter laughs. I look over. He is sitting yoga-style left of centre on the carpet, arms folded just like the genie. He explains, "I, we, my AfterLing group, we're the genie, Josh. Call it teleportation, telekinesis, or a magic-carpet ride, but we can be at the Deault farm outside Bastogne in a nanosecond. We don't need to worry about time, speed, altitude—any of that stuff that restricts you living creatures. But—instant gratification, immediate understanding, no sightseeing—how boring would that be?"

"Ode to Joy" sounds out once again. The genie grabs the telescope Dieter tosses to him, and midair it changes into a baton. Behind and above us, dressed in long blue, white, and purple gowns, a chorus appears. A full orchestra materializes in front of our carpet in the parking lot. Dieter stands. The sublime look on his face envelops me. Sheepishly, I let go of the carpet and go to his side. Even though the lyrics are in German, I can't help but hum along and sway with the music.

The carpet slowly lifts off, and once we're about 3,000 feet in the air, the band, the chorus, and the genie all disappear with the music. Below, I can clearly see Timmins and the Mattagami River. Even more evident is where the fire truck sped to from the station beside Henri's apartment, a house three blocks away, on the street where Dieter lived. Before I can say anything, Dieter puts his index finger vertically over his mouth, and then as he waves his finger in the air, he says, "We'll come back here after Henri has us witness his woodshed chat. I know you never had one and neither did I. I'm looking forward to it. Hold your questions about that fire. They'll be answered later. Let's enjoy the ride and hear the lesson Henri is about to learn from his dad, Jean. I just learned that Jean stuttered. We'll dispense with that."

Our carpet expands and two reclining chairs pop up. Dieter motions me to sit. After I'm in the chair, it reclines. Dieter waves his arms and suddenly the carpet is upside down! I gasp, clutch my throat, my heartbeat quickens. Dieter laughs, dances around the carpet, waves his arms. The carpet and chairs, and Dieter and I all spin around several times slowly, then stop, again in an upside-down position. I'm still gasping, clinging tightly to the chair, my legs tucked under the footrest. I'm fearful of falling, unable to believe we are suspended here. As he wiggles his fingers at me, I watch as thin, white, vaporous waves emanate from Dieter towards me. The waves split as they near my head; half to the right, half to the left, then swirl around in my ears. After a few seconds, I feel relaxed, as if sitting upside down over Timmins is perfectly natural.

"Your human sense of balance, Josh, can't handle an upside-down world. That's why I had those waves messing about in your head; your ears, your eyes ... all the muscles and joints that help you know where you are in space. Totally unnecessary when mind and soul dispense with all that baggage. Now while we're travelling, you can enjoy the view and appreciate what we AfterLings can do with thought alone, to defy gravity and explore Mother Earth—the whole universe from the convenience of a comfy recliner. So you're not completely disoriented, I've got the carpet pointed east 'cause we're headed to Belgium. Now lie back and check out the scenery."

∞

Our carpet remains upside down but tilts to about a forty-five-degree angle. Now I can clearly see both the Earth and the horizon in the distance. The bright sun forces me to squint. Before I can say anything, Dieter has a giant circular screen appear to dim the intense solar rays. Silently, we begin moving slowly towards Europe. White boundary markers appear below and signs, like you'd see along a highway, identify our whereabouts. The signs are transparent, hardly blocking anything from our view.

The first sign shows Timmins, with its geocode in brackets underneath: [48.4758° N, 81.3305° W]. Dieter comments: "I'll get rid of the latitude and longitude stuff shortly, but I wanted to make a point about travel for us AfterLings. We don't need any navigational tools, just the memories and experiences within AfterL communities. It's enough that Henri lived in Belgium, crossed the ocean in a ship, and made his way to Timmins over land. Once Ronnie and I hooked up with him while he was in the hospice and after he crossed over, we tapped into his mind and had access to all that. Let me show you."

Bubbles, about three feet in diameter, start floating up in front of us. In the first one, I see Henri inside his truck, cigarette dangling out of his mouth, on the road into Timmins.

"In that bubble, what you see is an AfterLing community's view of a moment in time in Henri's life. This was after he left Montréal and was about to come into town."

Dieter reaches out and the bubble comes within arm's length. He grasps it in both hands then pushes it at me. I feel myself being pulled inside. I hear a popping sound and immediately I'm in Henri's truck, seeing what he must have seen that midsummer day in 1948. There is an open provincial map on the passenger seat. Empty coffee cups, soft drink bottles, squashed up sandwich bags, and candy wrappers litter the floor. A logging truck approaches from the other direction, its flatbed fully loaded. It passes by engine rattling, exhaust belching black smoke, and tires humming. The turbulence created in its wake flattens the grass roadside.

"You're getting a snippet of an AfterL experience, Josh. Pretty neat, eh?"

"It reminds me of *Star Trek*, Dieter, like what Spock might have felt when he did a Vulcan mind meld with someone."

"Not a bad analogy, Josh, but Spock's experience ended when he took his fingertips off the other person's head. Telepathy and consciousness apply in a one-on-one context. Here's how things are in AfterL:

"No us and them—only we on an endless journey"

"It could have been stated as:

"No you and me—only we on an endless journey

"It's hard for mortals to accept, but the word *individual* is irrelevant, almost meaningless, in AfterL. You start off as twelve and grow from there."

"Let me guess. When you entered AfterL, eleven other souls fused with yours and ever since the number of fusions has continued to increase. Your mind, your memories, and your experiences blended in and are an ever-smaller part of an expanding community."

"That's it, Josh! Because you're still human, Henri, Ronnie, and I can only make you a rich *observer* of AfterL. You can see, smell, feel, hear, taste anything in the AfterLing communities we have fused, but you're still an outsider."

"I get it. Everything shared with me comes with all the sights, smells, sounds, and sensations that you AfterLings brought with you from your time on Earth. The really cool part is you can see it in many ways, from many perspectives."

"Right on. In AfterL, a community cannot only experience what is in its collective memory but it can also examine it from an almost unimaginable number of perspectives. You can't do that."

"So that bubble I entered was a quasi-AfterL way of seeing and being Henri at a point in time and place, which begs the question, Dieter, where exactly is AfterL?"

"Josh, that may be a relevant question in your world, but it doesn't apply once you're here. What's most interesting—and Henri grasped this almost immediately here—is that it was a Belgian priest, over seventy years ago, who figured it out."

"Really?"

"Yep, Georges Lemaître, at the Catholic University in Louvain. He proposed the Big Bang theory."

"A Catholic priest?"

"Yep, Henri now has a very different view of the Church than the one left with him by Father Magloire."

Below us, a church briefly pulsates inside a circular golden halo. The opening baritone voice from "Ode to Joy" surrounds us as the carpet picks up speed and takes us away from Timmins. Bubbles start popping up below.

Dieter tells me what they are: "Signposts for places Henri lived in Canada. Pick one, stare at it for a few seconds, and watch what happens."

I look to my right where Lake Huron, Lake Erie, and Lake Ontario reflect the sun's rays and momentarily distract me.

Dieter whips the carpet to get my attention, then says, "I know it's beautiful, Josh, but you'll have eternity to feast your eyes on a gazillion breathtaking views. Please pick a bubble so we can get on with our journey, and I can finish my explanation of AfterL travel."

Directly in front of us, I see the boundary line separating Ontario from Québec. I extend my right arm, see a bubble directly in front of my index finger, and say "Pow!" The bubble bursts into a rectangular signpost. I can see what it says: "1968, Kinsall, Ontario. Teaching Josh—first day on the job."

The memory of that day leaps from my mind and manifests itself on the signpost, turning the memory into a movie. "I remember that day, Dieter. I was unloading the cement mixer from the back of Henri's truck. It slipped off the planks and crashed to the ground, just seconds after Henri told me I should be able to do it alone. The mixer tipped over on its side and no matter how hard I tried to get both tires on the ground, I couldn't do it."

The movie plays out exactly what I'm recalling. Next on the screen I see Henri coming around the corner of the house we were working on, toolbox in hand.

"I was sure Henri would chew me out, but all he did was set down his toolbox and come over and help me set the mixer back on its wheels. After it was righted, and we pushed it next to the sand pile, he just wiped his hands on his pants and said it was about time he replaced the wooden planks with some metal ramps."

"If you were part of an AfterL community, Josh, you could relive that day and enjoy the beer Henri had at your mid-afternoon break."

"I must say, Henri did love his beer, but I never saw him drunk."

Dieter gives me a knowing smile and then says, "Henri told you the same thing he said to everybody in Timmins when they offered him another drink."

Dieter joins me in repeating Henri's words. "That's verrrry kind of you, but I'm high on life. Another beer would dilute it."

We give each other a high five as the scene below dissolves, and Dieter points to the east. I see we've crossed the Ontario border. Dieter points out the St. Lawrence where the outflow from the entire Great Lakes system feeds into its riverbed, near Kingston. Myriad bubbles appear off in the distance.

Dieter confirms my suspicions. "They all relate to Henri's past in Québec. I'm sure you'd like to pop inside one or two, but Henri tells me there's nothing you need to know about his time in *La Belle Province*. He did want to set up his own plastering business there, but big-city life just wasn't for him, which is why he came to Timmins. Just enjoy the view, and we'll fast forward across the Atlantic and slow down when we hit the coast at Penzance in southwestern England. As the crow flies from there to Calais, we'll be on a straight line to Antwerp, where Henri boarded a ship for Canada. The Port of Antwerp is the second largest in Europe, Josh. Given your French heritage, you might be interested in knowing Napoleon ordered its construction in 1811. Henri sailed from there in September 1946. Check out the number of bubbles here."

I see dozens of bubbles in and around Antwerp. Dieter explains: "Henri moved here from the family farm in 1945, after the war. He's going to bring you back here, soon."

"Henri is going to join us?"

"No, I'm gonna be here with you for a bit and then take you back to Timmins. Henri will take over from there. But Henri has been with me and Ronnie off and on since his last days in the hospice. He's shown up a few times already."

"Yeah, I know, but Henri was always so direct and conciliatory in life. Why all this scheming?"

"It's not scheming, Josh. Henri didn't enter AfterL as any kind of perfect soul. Besides, he's revealing much of his life even I didn't know or have access to before."

Dieter slows our carpet to a crawl. I can see from his face that he's as curious to learn Henri's story as I am. Suddenly a black cloud appears below us. It shimmers and the words "Not Now" in gigantic white letters rise up.

I begin to laugh, as does Dieter. "I know who's behind that interruption."

Dieter nods, makes the cloud vanish. "Henri! Until he crossed over and dealt with his trauma, my AfterLing community couldn't open the door to his memories and experiences—in AfterLing language: *his essence*. We only knew what he had told me during our time as living, breathing critters in Timmins. Now that he's finding his way in AfterL, he knows how much I want to explore his past."

Below us the bubbles begin to fade. Only one remains—near Bastogne. My reclining chair resets to the upright position then tosses me out, forcing me to stand. I look over to see what Dieter is doing. He, too, is standing. Our reclining chairs disappear. The carpet turns into a Roman chariot. We are shoulder to shoulder in the basket.

Dieter switches into a legionary uniform, complete with red-plumed helmet, breastplate, tunic, and belt. He explains, "I just learned Henri and I are both descended from Roman peasants. And I thought we were French. Anyway, our Roman ancestors always wished they could be wealthy landowners with gold-leaf chariots. Now we can live their dreams."

Pegasus suddenly appears in front of the chariot, reined to its yoke, his wings beating quietly in the air. Dieter looks over at me, a mischievous look on his face. A mirror appears between us and Pegasus' rump. As soon as I look in it, I too am in Roman garb: a white toga with a bright purple border and laurel wreath, like you'd see on a military commander on a victory lap in the Colosseum.

"What's with the wreath, Dieter?"

"That's Henri's doing. He'll explain it to you later. For now, just accept that you're getting first-class passage. Enjoy the ride."

Pulling on the reins, Dieter signals Pegasus to veer right from north northeast to a more southerly path. Within minutes, we're on the outskirts of Bastogne. Pegasus and the chariot vanish. Dieter dresses us in peasant clothing befitting Belgian farmers, and we make our way to the yard beside Henri's ancestral home. I follow Dieter to the woodshed. He makes himself comfortable on a stump that looks like it's been there for decades, probably used as a base for chopping wood. I jump up on a hay wagon and notice that no one is there besides the two of us.

Dieter explains, "They'll be here in a minute, Josh. Henri's father, Jean, is getting an old diary to bring with him."

Two minutes later, Jean opens the woodshed door and Henri enters. Daylight is beginning to fade. Jean pulls on a chain that activates an overhead light over a long worktable. The fixture is suspended from a rafter and begins to sway slowly back and forth, casting eerie shadows around the room. Jean motions for Henri to stand beside him as he opens the diary. Henri joins his father and places his elbows on the bench peering at the page Jean has chosen. I can't see the book from where I'm sitting. Dieter snaps his fingers and a copy of the diary, complete with a candle, hovers in front of me.

CHAPTER 11

Camille

"Henri talked about his paternal grandmother, Camille, earlier. This is her diary. She passed it along to Henri's father. You'll learn more about his family later."

I see the date in the diary: October 12, 1909. The candle above me magically powers up so the diary in front of me is vivid, clear, and in handwriting that would easily score an A-plus back when penmanship was on primary-school curricula. Before I can begin reading it, Jean begins talking. Dieter and I listen in.

Jean: "Your grandmother, Camille, is a remarkable woman, Henri. She gave this diary to me last year and said I'd find it useful for birds-and-bees discussions with you."

Henri: "Papa, we got pigs and cows and cats and dogs. I know where babies come from and how they get started. Besides, Father Magloire told all us altar boys about Jesus' mother, Mary and the Maclet Connection."

Jean: "It was the Immaculate Conception, and I doubt Father Magloire is an expert on (*chuckles*) female matters. Your mother was raised by her aunt and uncle, nice, God-fearing people, but not good at practical things for young boys and girls."

Henri: "Poor Mama, just three days old when she lost her mother, and her father left for Canada three months later."

130

Jean: *"Ben oui,* it's not a happy story. Her father went to Saskatchewan, was conscripted in 1917, and was never heard from again. We've been blessed with good health and your mother often turns to Mémère Deault for advice."

Henri: "I love Mémère Deault too, Papa. Every Sunday at church, she winks at me and blows me a kiss when I enter the nave with Father Magloire. And she was so happy last week when I told her I'd be the crucifer next year and get to carry the Cross. I'll only be eleven, and most altar boys have to be twelve to get that job!"

Jean: "Yes, Father Magloire says you're his favourite."

Henri: "Some of the other altar boys are jealous. Father Magloire told them I was a good Catholic, and if they were as God-fearing and obedient, they would be considered. He said he might even switch who did what during Sunday service."

Jean: "Sounds like our local priest is a good man. You will do well to take his advice."

Henri: "I do, Papa. I do."

Jean: "Well then, let's get back to the diary."

Dieter shrieks, stands away from the stump, and runs over to me on the hay wagon. On his way past Jean and Henri, a giant black screen as high as the woodshed appears, blocking our view.

"Why the yelp, Dieter? Jean hasn't even begun to discuss the birds and bees with Henri."

Dieter stares at me for a second, a puzzled look on his face. His frown then turns thoughtful. He nods, and slowly shakes his head side to side a few times. "You haven't heard what Henri said to me as a young boy in Timmins, Josh, 'cause Henri wanted you to come with me and see and hear firsthand what he shared. Just think about it for a moment. The Church, Father Magloire, my disgust with Elie and Dan ..."

"Omigod, Jean has no clue. And he's now innocently approving Father Magloire!"

"Exactly. Poor Henri. How could he possibly say anything bad about Father Magloire after this?"

"He couldn't, and he didn't. Here, he's a ten-year-old boy, and I'll bet Father Magloire has been the one getting his rocks off with Henri's help."

"Are we going to bear witness to any of that Dieter?"

"No way, Josh. Henri just wanted us to understand why he never told anyone about Father Magloire."

"But he did get past it. He became a great father figure."

"Yes, he did, for me and your younger brothers especially."

"We still don't know why."

"No, but we will. Let's see what more he wanted us to learn from this trip."

The black screen silently rolls up as if it were a blind. Dieter and I are side by side on the hay wagon. A copy of the diary Henri and Jean have floats before us, and the conversation continues.

Jean: "Mémère is proud that you serve God the way you do, but she's said more than once the Bible lacks a woman's touch."

Henri: "What do you mean, Papa?"

Jean: "Too much fighting and not enough nurturing."

Henri: "Every Sunday, after Father Magloire reads from the Gospel, he says, 'The Word of God.'"

Jean: "Mémère says there are surely words missing."

Henri: "Why are you telling me this, Papa?"

Jean: "Because you're old enough to learn things Father Magloire will never preach, and Mémère wants me to tell you. So that you're a better Christian in her eyes."

Henri: "Can't Mémère tell me herself?"

Jean: "Yes, but she won't. She made me promise to have this talk with you when the time came."

Henri: "Was the blood in the tub a sign, Papa? Father Magloire told me God left signs for girls and boys to know they're growing up."

Jean: "Hmmm, I never thought Father Magloire would discuss such things. He is indeed a fatherly priest."

Henri: "He said signs and wonders are in the Bible, and it was his job to help altar boys understand them."

Jean: "Did he say anything about girls?"

Henri: "Yes. He said they couldn't become nuns before they received their signs, and the signs everyone could see was their tops getting bigger."

Jean: "Sounds like Father Magloire has done some good. I must thank him."

Henri: "Oh, no, Papa, please don't. Father Magloire said things in the church were between God and us. He said it was like in the confessional. Because I'm an altar boy, I must keep secrets."

Jean: "Well then, I won't come between you and God, but I will share what Mémère has to say and yes, the blood in the tub is a sign. Now let's read this together."

Our copy enlarges in front of me. Dieter lies back, puts his hands behind his head, and explains. "Right now I'm melding with Henri and his AfterLing community, getting a bit of background. Camille was thirty-four years old in 1909 when she wrote these diary entries. For years, she was skeptical about the Bible, but her parents told her to keep her thoughts to herself. No good would come from attacking the church. She shared some of her thoughts with her husband, Louis, even before they were married. He too was reluctant to question church doctrine, although he did agree with many of her views; he just thought they were better off keeping their opinions to themselves."

"As I recall, Dieter, Catholic masses were all in Latin until the mid-sixties, when I was a teenager. That didn't make it any easier."

"That was after my time, Josh, but Mom and Dad just shrugged when I asked them about that."

"We both know what Henri thought about the church. Now we're getting to understand why."

"Yes and his grandmother played a part in that. She told Louis that God needed a mother, and Jesus should have had children."

"Wow! I've never heard that before."

"Me neither. Henri was a silent crusader. He picked his battles, and none of them were direct attacks on church or state. He would just roll his eyes, mutter a curse, and change the subject. I wonder if—"

Dieter raises his hand, and I stop talking. Seconds later, he explains. "Sorry about that. Henri was just reminding me that we're not here to solve world hunger or eliminate poverty. He told me that, after he left Belgium, he wasn't much interested in partnering with others. Now we're going to see some of the reasons why. A lot of it had to do with his grandma Camille, and this woodshed review of her diary."

"Right, is there more I need to know?"

"Well, we both just learned that Camille thought the Bible lacked a woman's touch and questioned its truthfulness. Like Henri, she was very much a discreet crusader. She shared her thoughts with very few people."

"Did she share them with Henri's mother?"

"No way! She realized Thérèse was rock solid in her faith, absolutely convinced the Bible was the Word of God. Besides, Camille's issue was with its dominant male slant."

"That's why she gave Louis her diary unabridged, so he could pass along her thoughts to his children?"

"Not to his children, Josh, just to her grandson, Henri. If Henri had any brothers she would have included them. He only had sisters. She said that, if she influenced just Louis, Jean, and Henri to get in touch with their feminine side, she would consider her mission accomplished."

"Interesting. Her diary then is a woman's view on religion."

"It's her interpretation of what a good Christian man in *her* family should teach *his* sons. She didn't have a quarrel with some of the New Testament verses, especially Mark and Matthew and Jesus' comments about children. She was a Christian, but like Mark Twain, she wasn't convinced that the God of the Bible was real."

"What did Mark Twain say?"

A page from his *Notebook* (1896) pops up in front of me:

"If I were going to construct a God, I would furnish Him with some ways and qualities and characteristics which the Present (Bible) One lacks ... He would spend some of His eternities in trying to forgive Himself for making man unhappy when He could have made him happy."

"Cute. But Henri never talked about his family. You'd think he would have mentioned Camille."

"She was still a Christian, Josh. She never suspected that Father Magloire was anything other than a faithful priest continuing to foster a vengeful male God."

"Ah, Henri's age and beliefs worked against him."

The Mark Twain notebook vanishes. Camille's diary is directly in front of me again. Dieter lies back on the hay wagon, his hands underneath his head. Before closing his eyes, he says, "I'm gonna excuse myself now, Josh. You have enough background on Camille. I'm gonna do an AfterL thing with my community and Henri's. I'll be back after you finish reading the diary. Just one last thing, the first bit of the diary wasn't part of the discussion between Henri and Jean, but you'll find it a good lead-in."

Dieter closes his eyes. His body takes on a more translucent glow, as if some of his energy is being diverted elsewhere. I sigh and then focus on Camille's diary and begin reading.

Today we talked again about God's vengeful nature, His Old Testament approval of genocide and slavery, and His New Testament consent to male domination. Dear Louis knows I cannot accept a God who sires and sacrifices an only child or denies him a wife and children. He also knows I cannot accept, carte blanche, a church that would advocate such as gospel.

I can accept a loving Jesus, who gathers children at his feet and advises turning the other cheek. I remain a Christian, but I will challenge those I love to revere a more compassionate deity—one that need not be identified as male or female.

God may have had a reason for dividing his creatures into male and female, but the purpose that serves in heaven? I may not be accepted there because of my views, but I cannot live a life obedient to or subservient to the deity our church portrays. Nor will I allow my son Jean to accept such rigid dogma, and Louis agrees with me!

As we must all go through passages and the Good Book gives little direction for us, male or female, to understand or better navigate the way through, I am writing my own, and after it's finished Louis can discuss it with Jean. I'm just sorry I didn't think of it earlier. I could have shared it with his brothers. Maybe it isn't too late?

The diary slowly dissolves in front of me and a folded letter replaces it. The papers open out, and I see it is the same handwriting as the diary—Camille's beautiful penmanship, a treat for my eyes. I note the date, 1909, and look over at Jean and Louis. Louis is unfolding the original of the letter I have in front of me. No doubt it is in French. I silently thank Henri for providing me with an English copy. The first page moves towards me. I grab it and begin reading.

Dear Jean,

It wasn't that long ago when I read bedtime stories to you: Jack and the Beanstalk, Hansel and Gretel, Little Red Riding Hood. *How wide your eyes would open when the giant told Jack he wanted to crush his bones; when the witch said she wanted to eat Hansel, and when you heard why the wolf told Little Red Riding Hood he had such big teeth. I told you not to worry. They were just fairy tales.*

Even then you were a smart lad and asked why I read such frightening fables. My answer: the children outwitted their foes without any help from grownups and lived happily ever after. Even young boys and girls overcome great odds. When you were young, these answers satisfied you.

When you were nine, you began asking more questions. Why were they called fairy tales? Why did ogres and giants and witches want to eat children? And after church, you queried me on the Bible: Why did David kill Goliath and cut off his head? Why did King Darius put Daniel in the lion's den?

I said there is good and evil in the world and fairy tales and Bible verses mirror life. I vividly remember how quickly you grasped this. You nodded and said, "Mama, that's why there's heaven and hell and God and the Devil."

I reach the end of the page. It doesn't vanish or make way for the next one. I look over at Jean and Louis. Louis sets Camille's letter on the bench and begins a conversation with Jean.

Louis: "Do you remember that day?"

Jean: *"Oui, Papa.* At school the next day, I told my friend, Thérèse. It was during recess last spring. Two boys had sticks and were fighting. One of the boys got poked in the eye and started crying. Thérèse said that was terrible, and she didn't know why boys had to fight. I told her what *Maman* said, about good and evil."

Louis: "What did she say?"

Jean: "Not much. She said her Aunt Marie didn't talk about such things. Her aunt thought God would look after them. They had a farm and plenty to eat. She should be thankful and not worry."

Louis: "Well, your *Maman* has more to say about many things other people don't discuss."

Jean: "I like it when she talks to me, Papa. She doesn't mind me stuttering. She listens to me."

Louis: "You two are very similar—curious about things—which is why we're having this chat."

Jean: "Normally we come to the woodshed to work, Papa. This is the first time we've come here just to talk, just the two of us."

Louis: "That is your Maman's doing. If she'd thought of it sooner, your older brothers would've had similar tête-à-têtes with me."

Jean: "Why're we reading this? Couldn't she just talk with me?"

Louis: Oh she will, but she made me promise to read this with you first, before you get too much older."

Jean: "Is it gonna be about sinning, Papa?"

Louis: "No, no. We get enough of that at church. Your *Maman* is a headstrong woman. On some things, you should be like me and agree with her. She has reasons to do what she does. She decided long ago to keep a diary, and now she wants parts of it read and discussed."

Jean: "Do you have a diary too, Papa?"

Louis: "One is enough between the two of us. She has always let me read it. I just don't get to change it. Now let's read on."

The page in front of me flips to the bottom. In the background, I hear Louis reading it in French. I focus on the English version.

When you said God and Satan, and Heaven and Hell helped you understand good and evil, I bit my tongue. I decided to pray for guidance before saying more. Fortunately, a gift and a dream gave me direction.

The gift came from Father Claes. Our bishop in Namur gave him tickets, donated by a wealthy parishioner, for the play, L'Oiseau Bleu. We watched it together while Papa and your older brothers were at the farmers' market in Bastogne. Tyltyl and Mytyl, the brother and sister, search everywhere for happiness, then find it in their own backyard, where a little blue bird is singing. You said it was easy for them. No one called Tyltyl "stutter boy."

That tore at my heart. I gave you a hug, told you I loved you, and said some people can be so cruel. I also said there was a reason the Good Lord sent us to see that play, and I needed some time to think about it.

It wasn't long after that I had the dream. As soon as I woke up, I knew it answered my prayers. I jumped out of bed and quickly wrote down everything I could remember, the sights, the sounds, the conversation.

When I was finished, I shared it with Papa. We talked about it for hours, set it aside for a few days, discussed it some more, and now Papa is going to do the exact same thing with you; read it, talk about it. He'll tell you why we agreed on this approach. We'll carry on our discussion of good and evil and cruel people later.

I reach the end of the page and all the text vanishes except for the words "a gift and a dream."

Before I have time to think about what I just read, or wonder what is coming next, I'm whisked off the hay wagon and plunked down inside the wall behind Louis and Jean. The wall is perfectly clear. Dieter or (Henri?) must want me to have a front-row seat, since a comfortable reclining chair pushes up behind me, forcing me to relax and sit down.

This is the first time I really get to see Henri's father and grandfather up close. They are both wearing coveralls and long-sleeved shirts. A large straw hat hangs from a nail on a pillar near Louis. I deduce it is his and that he doesn't wear it indoors. Jean is wearing a newsboy's cap. Louis sports a handlebar moustache, mutton-chop sideburns, and thick eyebrows and eyelashes. Father and son both have swarthy complexions and round, slightly bulging brown eyes. Like Henri, their ears are large with drooping auricles. The family resemblances are striking. Neither ugly nor attractive; there is still something about their faces that pleases me. It's the eyes—like Henri's they draw you in and make you want to stare without appearing rude.

Louis reaches underneath his coveralls and pulls several sheets of paper from his shirt pocket. From my vantage point, I can clearly see Camille's distinctive handwriting. I wonder why I didn't find any of her materials among Henri's keepsakes. Inside my head, I hear, *"You'll find out. Now pay attention."*

Not only is the handwriting worthy of a calligraphy prize, Camille's artistic talent is equally captivating. Louis holds out two illustrations: The Virgin Mary, and Tyltyl and Mytyl from *The Blue Bird/L'Oiseau Bleu* the play Jean and Camille attended in Bastogne. Louis looks at the Madonna drawing intently, and I notice the baby Jesus is also in the picture. It's such a riveting sketch that I want to reach out, grab it, and take it home with me to Bond's Hill. The conversation between Louis and Jean pulls me back from my reverie.

Louis: "You know how much Maman adores Mother Mary and loves Jesus."

Jean: "Yes, Papa."

Louis: "I'm sure if I took this picture to Father Claes, he would want to show it to the bishop."

Jean: "Then I think you should, Papa."

Louis: "Ah, no I won't. Your mother would never permit it, and I'm going to tell you why, but first a few questions that Maman and I have asked and discussed many times, most recently after her dream."

Jean: "Yes, Papa."

Louis: "Have you seen a picture of God in our home?"

Jean: "No, Papa."

Louis: "Does *Maman* ever talk about God?"

Jean: "Not much, Papa. Doesn't she like Him?"

Louis: "That's one of the reasons we're here, Jean, to talk about God, man to man."

Jean: I'm not a man, Papa."

Louis: "Ah, but soon you will be, and Maman and I ... well, we want you to be a good Christian. Look at this picture. What do you see?"

Jean: "It's Mary and Jesus."

Louis: "Yes, a special picture of them, Jean. It's drawn by your Maman, and as far as I know, no other such picture exists. It's the first one drawn by a woman."

Jean: "It's a beautiful picture, Papa. Why aren't there more pictures like this?"

Louis: "That's what your Maman learned in her dream—the reason why."

Jean: "Maman has done lots of drawings before. This is the first with anyone from the Bible."

Louis: "Yes and she drew it after her dream. She said Mary told her to get her drawing pencils and sketch pad and Divine Spirit would do the rest. Look at the picture again, at Baby Jesus' and Mother Mary's faces."

Jean: "They look healthy and happy ... and there's something about their eyes."

Louis: "Good, you see it. You've heard the expression 'the eyes are the windows into the soul.' Well, those eyes pretty much tell everything there is to say about their souls. Now look at the faces again. What do you see?"

Jean: "They both have the same colour of hair, but Mary's is longer. Their cheeks and noses look pretty much the same."

Louis: "I said the same thing to *Maman*. There's a strong family resemblance. She clapped her hands, danced around the room, and said, 'She told me so. She said you wouldn't see it. Mary said that's what was wrong with the world. And after she pointed out what I missed, and what you missed, I had to agree with her."

Jean: "What did I miss, Papa?"

Louis: "There is nothing in that picture that proves you are looking at Mother Mary and Baby Jesus."

Jean: "So it could be Joseph with a little girl?"

Louis: "Or Mother Mary with a little girl. The point of the dream and the picture was to confirm what *Maman* believes: God is *not* a man."

Jean's eyes open wide just before the scene disappears, and I'm all alone somewhere out in the universe amongst the stars. "Ode to Joy" bursts forth again, and the "Welcome to AfterL" banner encircles me; the word "Neutral" forms to its right and left, and then the banner vibrates and transforms from a circular band to a horizontal figure eight. It takes me a few seconds, but then I realize it's the scientific symbol for infinity.

Dieter pops up in front of me, a Cheshire Cat grin on his face. He claps his hands and silence surrounds us. Dieter raises his eyebrows and asks.

"Well?"

"I ... I don't know what to say. God is not a man?"

∞

The infinity symbol starts spinning around, sounding like a helicopter blade just before takeoff. Dieter watches it for a few seconds and then slows it down and makes all the lettering peel away and dissolve. The whirling symbol slows to a stop and shrinks to the length of a cheer-leader's baton. It floats towards him. He grasps the outermost ends and comes close to me. The Cheshire Cat grin returns and remains on his face. "Two questions for you, Josh. First, are you right side up?"

"I'm floating around out here in space with you. There's no gravity, and no frame of reference. Every which way is up. And it's disconcert-ing to hear you talk with that silly grin on your face."

The grin becomes even wider. I shake my head, and Dieter asks his second question, again without changing his expression. "This thing in my hands. Besides being the symbol for infinity, what's it called?"

"I don't know, and what does this have to do with God not being a man?"

The grin disappears from Dieter's face, and he transforms into a medieval clergyman wearing an orange-and-black gown, complete with cowl. In his hand is a Bible. At first, what I see is all in Latin. Dieter taps the page and the relevant section, Revelations 22:13, becomes English.

"I am the Alpha and the Omega, the First and the Last, the Beginning and the End."

I remember that Omega is the last letter in the Greek alphabet. The Bible closes, and a voice I don't recognize begins speaking. "Hi Josh. I'm John Wallis. I included some of my colleague Isaac Newton's work in my book on algebra. I'm the guy who came up with the infinity symbol and think it's ironic that some people believe it's based on the Greek letter omega—Ω.

He disappears, and Dieter is back before me, holding the large infinity symbol.

I'm still puzzled.

Dieter continues. "I could have stuck around as John Wallis and let his Oxford appearance add authority to this next bit of theology/geometry, but the demonstration will speak for itself. This infinity symbol is also known as a Möbius strip. Wallis almost certainly knew about it. It's been around since Roman times, but he chose not to disclose that, because besides being a mathematician, he was a high-ranking member of the Presbyterian Church back in the mid-1600s."

"Whoa, Dieter, aren't we getting far afield from Camille and her dream?"

"Not at all. I'm telling you the Church has been highly successful in controlling people who questioned dogma, whether it was Galileo, Wallis, or Camille Deault. Camille had her dreams. Galileo and Wallis and countless others had much more concrete foundations for their beliefs. That's what my group, aka The Magnificent Mind, has spent a lot of time on: learning why people believe in a God that doesn't exist. And now Henri is in AfterL, with Atlas Released, he's hooked up with Camille's community."

I raise my hand. Dieter cocks his head slightly, allowing me to ask, "What's with the Atlas Released and The Magnificent Mind?"

"It's the unique identity the twelve mortals who unite after death choose once they've shed their earthly woes and bonded as a community. I'd love to tell you more but Henri told me to drop it. Now let's get closer to your home to your own galaxy."

We return to the Milky Way, and then stars and asteroids and comets quickly zip past us as we return to the Solar System. We hang suspended in front of the sun, behind the moon, at an angle that has the Earth half in light and half in darkness. Dieter suspends the Möbius strip in front of me and tells me to look at it closely and describe what I see.

"What I see, Dieter, has a seam in the middle, like a welding join that fastens the top to the bottom loop. It appears to be made from steel. On either side of the seam are identical halves that look like eyes of knitting needles, except they're twisted. If it were made of fabric I'd say it was a bow."

"Yes, Josh. You'd get the same form if you took a ribbon or piece of paper, twisted it, and then taped the ends together. Now let's show you its mind-blowing property."

The seams in the middle disappear, then the right half of the bow twists 180 degrees and the two halves take the shape of a loop. Dieter grabs it, transforms himself into Hercules, and bends the loop into a straight bar. Grinning broadly he hands me a soapstone marker. "Draw a straight line from one end to the other, and then I'm going to bend it back into a loop with a half twist, so it is back in the same form we started with."

I do as he asks. When I'm finished, he grunts and groans, making a big deal of his performance. The image of a World Wrestling Federation performance comes to mind, and I shake my head. Dieter suddenly drips sweat all along his brow and shakes it all over me. I jump back, and he laughs before reverting to his regular body and the clothing of a forest ranger.

After he orients the bar into a figure eight, he asks me what I see. The soapstone line is visible only on the lower right side of the bottom loop and across the top of the upper loop.

I furrow my brow for a few seconds and then grasp what it is that Dieter wants me to understand: it's impossible for me to see the entire soapstone line or have its ends meet. Sporting a Cheshire Cat grin again, Dieter nods, and then spins the loop end over end into space. Just at the point where it disappears, a giant fireworks display dominates the sky. Once the fireworks end, an enormous white screen unfolds in front of us and what looks to me like a pineapple appears on the screen, in black and white.

Dieter shakes his head and corrects my impression. "That's not fruit, it's crustacean. I'm showing you what astronomers believe is the result of a supernova—like the fireworks display you just witnessed. It's called the Crab Nebula, in the Milky Way. Has been around for about a thousand years. The Chinese witnessed its birth in 1054 AD. Now I'm gonna put that crab on a Möbius loop. I want you to watch what happens to that big claw on its right side."

I do as he asks. The crab goes one time around the loop. When it gets back to its starting point, the big right claw is now on its left side. Not believing what I just saw, I ask Dieter to do it again. The crab does another lap, and now the claw is on its right. Dieter has the crab do several laps. After every lap, its claw is reversed.

"Isn't that cool, Josh? Looks like a magic trick, eh? Well, it isn't. It's just another plane that proves the universe is way different than Earth's teeny tiny part of it. We don't even have to go outside our own galaxy to see exceptions to accepted notions of reality. The Crab Nebula is in the Milky Way. Much like Arthur C. Clarke's obelisk in *2001: A Space Odyssey*, the Crab Nebula and the Möbius Loop both challenge conventional wisdom."

The crab does several more laps around the loop with "Ode to Joy" in the background, and then it waves its big claw at us before disappearing along with the screen.

Dieter now draws my attention back to Earth. "From out here, our planet looks flat, Josh. It took centuries before people accepted it was round. Same with many other beliefs that proved false: the sun revolves around the Earth; planetary orbits are circular; the universe is static; we are created in God's image—"

"Whoa, Dieter, I knew about the cosmic corrections but our resemblance to God?"

"A human attempt to simplify and relate. With what you now know about AfterL, there are many accepted facts and foundations on which faith is grounded that are poppycock. It's the human bondage to a single body and brain that accounts for most earthling beliefs. Better to listen to sounds, especially music, and gaze at the night sky to appreciate the basic fundamentals. At best, the human notion of love is the closest humans will ever get to an AfterL experience of rapture and community. As for knowledge, because you are limited to what your senses and instruments can register, you will forever be restricted. What you can't prove remains suspect."

Dieter claps his hands and two beer mugs with frothy heads materialize. He hands one to me and proposes a toast. "To the mysteries unveiled in AfterL!"

I clink my mug with his and join him in a hearty swallow. After wiping the suds from his upper lip, he hurls his mug off into space and a conductor's wand appears. A tiny asteroid floats into range. Dieter taps his baton on the rock, clears his throat, raises the wand high overhead, and then swiftly swipes it from right to left. Below, the half of the Earth covered in darkness begins to dazzle. Flashes of lightning illuminate the clouds and set off rolling thunder. Their intensity, brevity, and randomness captivate my attention.

As suddenly as they appeared, they vanish, and Dieter carries on. "After love, lightning is a close second to an AfterL experience. You can feel its electricity before you see it. For the milliseconds it manifests, you are drawn in, amazed, and awed at its unbridled power and beauty. You have nothing to fear from death, Josh, but when you get back home, don't entice people to commit suicide to get here."

"What? The thought never entered my mind. Why do you even say that?"

"I'm not aware of any AfterL communities whose founding members killed themselves."

Dieter looks deeply into my eyes. I feel him boring into my soul, exposing me, making me feel naked, vulnerable. Just as suddenly as this defenceless mood emerges, it fades, replaced by a powerful aura of security, bordering on invincibility.

"You have to believe, Josh. Otherwise ... "

"I get it, Dieter, I do. It's enough to want to go on."

"Well, that's oversimplifying, but it'll do for now."

Below us, Asia slowly fades into darkness, no longer gripped in sunlight. Clocks showing the time zones float in front of us. A long, straight bar forms vertically, going north and south from England, and Dieter tells me it's the meridian line. I see it's 8 p.m. over Central Europe.

Anticipating my question, Dieter answers. "Yep, back to the woodshed. It's time for me to move on, Josh. It's been fun. I think Henri's on to something that will forever alter the bond between AfterL and Earth."

Dieter embraces me, and before I can ask why the sudden departure, in a blinding display of light and music, he vanishes.

∞

"Over here, Josh."

I turn around. It's Henri. He's dressed in the white plasterer's shirt, pants, and cap he wore when he visited my boyhood home in 1964. He's beside the woodshed, smoking. He takes a big puff of his unfiltered, roll-your-own cigarette, and then in three exhalations, expels three circular clouds of smoke that tilt ninety degrees to reveal words now familiar to me: "rapture, community, knowledge." Henri doffs his cap, grins, and then disappears! Why am I being left alone so often? Surely they know I had too much of that when I was a boy and young man? Solitude, no solace, no serenity. Don't they care for chrissakes?

The door opens and Henri's father and grandfather are exactly where they were when Dieter whisked me away. As before, my anguish is abruptly ended and I'm once more an interested explorer of Henri's past.

Louis: "Your mother now believes what she thought for many years: God is not a man."

Jean: "What do you believe, Papa?"

Louis: "Maman's a God-fearing woman. She says this picture is from the hand of God, and Mother Mary guided her pencil. I believe her."

Jean: "Has Maman shown this picture to Father Claes?"

Louis: "No, and she won't. It's all part of her dream."

Louis carefully sets the drawing on the bench in front of the crock where it had rested previously. He makes the sign of the Cross, then backs away from the picture, as if he were in church and moving on to another religious icon. He picks up a wooden toolbox from the floor and sets it beside the jar. He props the other drawing I'd seen earlier in front of it.

Louis: "After Mother Mary told Maman God is not a man, Mytyl and Tyltyl appeared at her side. Maman says she immediately knew why."

Jean: "Why?"

Louis: "They repeated Our Lady's message: We aren't created in God's image. He never was flesh and blood, let alone male or female. The use of the word 'He' is wrong."

Jean partially closes his eyes, looks skyward for a few seconds, and then gazes quizzically at his father.

Jean: "Papa, every night we say our prayers and every Sunday we go to church and say *Our Fathers* and our *Hail Marys*."

Louis: "I know, son, and that's going to continue. Mother Mary didn't come to Maman to ask her to fight with the church. She asked Maman to accept a more personal quest: to preach to a small flock— her family. When Maman woke up, she knew why she'd had a Holy Visitor: to receive a message ... that no God worthy of worship would ask a woman to bear a child to hang on a cross."

Jean: "Then who is Jesus' father?"

Louis: "Joseph, Mary's husband."

Jean: "So Jesus was not the son of God?"

Louis: "No, Jesus preached Holy Spirit and never claimed to literally be the son of God. That's what the Madonna came to tell your mother. A Christian is someone who accepts Holy Spirit."

Jean: "Papa, Father Claes told me at my Confirmation I'd receive the Holy Spirit and be a true Christian."

Louis: "Father Claes has it half-right, son. Our Lady told Maman that God *is* Holy Spirit, and that's what we'll become a part of when we die." He picks up the drawing related to Maeterlinck's Belgian play, *The Blue Bird* of *Happiness*. "Holy Spirit isn't only in the Church. It's in many things that bring us together and fill us with joy."

CHAPTER 12

Convergence

Louis and Jean fade from the scene, replaced by the young Henri I saw in Timmins. The look on my face causes him to pause. "I'm not feeling very joyous right now, Henri. In fact I'm pissed. All this fluttering about in time and space. If I didn't love you and miss you I'd tell you to leave me alone!"

Henri sways from side to side. Chewing his lips, he never takes his eyes off me. He slowly moves back, transforming into the Henri I knew before the hospice lockdown. The look on his face is enough to banish my vitriol. He firmly plants his feet and opens his arms.

Tears of joy overwhelm me. Sobbing, I move into his embrace and put my head on his shoulder.

"I miss you too, Josh. That's why I'm here. A drowned little boy and a young man consumed by fire handed us a key. Now dry those eyes." Henri slowly releases me and puts his arm around my shoulder.

I tousle the little hair he has left on the back of his head and give him a love pat. "Dieter told me I didn't have a choice. He's a little more intellectual than I expected but given he's part of The Magnificent Mind. I get it. He's also a likeable young man, so my time with him has been fun, although I prefer being in the driver's seat."

"Yes, Josh, control is a big part of you. It was also a big part of me. In its place a good thing but when you stretch it to cover most of your life—not good. Besides, this is a dream. You're going to wake up so enjoy the ride. It's not a nightmare." Henri ruffles my hair and steps back. Seeing I'm now a willing passenger he picks up where his ancestors left off in the woodshed.

He picks up the drawings Louis shared with Jean. "When my father showed these to me, I was a troubled lad, Josh, thanks to Father Magloire."

"And you never shared that with anyone until you and Dieter talked about puberty and his fallout with Elie and Dan. Why then?"

"Dieter reminded me of my Mémère Camille because of his artistic talent. I also knew that his father, André, was not going to explain puberty well." Henri looks affectionately at Camille's drawing of Madonna and Child. "*Chère* Camille wanted her men to be in touch with their feminine sides but wrapped it in a religious package I couldn't accept. Now you know why."

"I see that, Henri. I also see from the other picture she left with your father that she believed happiness came from within, and you don't have to be an adult to get that."

Henri holds up the bluebird of happiness drawing. "Notice their smiles, Josh? Kids smile at least a hundred times more per day than adults. The things we do to suppress their natural joyfulness." He sighs, puts the pictures on the work bench, and motions for me to join him outside.

We leave the woodshed, and I can hear women's voices: Henri's mother and sisters in the house. Their laughter brings a smile to my face. Henri raises his arms in a gesture I know well. I join him in shouting, "Let what I see encircle me."

Henri peers through the window at his mother. "Her religious devotion didn't make it any easier, Josh. I'm just thankful my father, Jean, and Mémère Camille gave me a foundation I carried forward. Now, I'm in AfterL. Wow! How much of what's here was foretold? Rapture in happiness, Holy Spirit in community, androgyny in AfterLings ..."

For a few seconds, Henri is silent, and I begin to wonder about Dieter's sudden departure.

Why did Dieter leave so quickly?

A large, stone-lined doorway appears in the laneway beside the Deault farmhouse. Henri motions for me to enter with him.

∞

On the other side of the opening is Henri's apartment building in Timmins. Coming out of the main entrance, I see young Dieter.

"Remember when you last saw him at that age, Josh?"

"Yes, he was with you in your apartment. You asked him if he wanted to join you for dinner."

"Uh huh, and what had we heard just before that?"

"The fire alarm."

Henri looks at me expectantly.

I pause, reflecting on his silence. I shake my head and then answer. "A fire. There was a fire that had something to do with his family."

Henri nods and sighs. "At his home. Annie and André managed to escape unscathed, but the house burned to the ground. Nothing was ever the same again."

"I can guess. André kept drinking and fighting. Annie finally gave up and left him."

"Yes. It was a long time in coming, but when Dieter turned thirteen, Annie asked me to become his legal guardian. She told me she wanted a man she admired in his life. I was flattered."

"So the fire that day wasn't anything he wanted to bring up?"

"I asked him to leave that with me." Henri walks to the parking lot and opens the tailgate of his truck. He turns and leans against it, motioning for me to do the same. "Remember when we used to do this at break and lunch time on our plastering jobs together?"

"Yes, you'd have a coffee and a smoke. I'd drink water or lemonade. If your partner Gus Scheer was with us, you'd each have a beer."

"His wife was a teetotaler and staunch Seventh Day Adventist, sending their kids to a sectarian school and never letting them go to a Saturday movie. No alcohol, no tobacco, no coffee, or caffeine. She could never understand why Gus worked with me."

"You loved to tease, but I did think you were an odd couple."

"Not really. We both loved our trade. Everyone in the business knew we were the best guys for great finishes, especially if you wanted a fancy moulding."

"Why bring this up?"

"When Dieter and I left my apartment and saw where the smoke was coming from, I jumped in this old truck and headed for Dieter's home. When we got there, I parked far enough away to avoid the heat, popped the tailgate, and enjoyed the show."

"Knowing you, you probably asked Dieter if he wanted to get hot dogs and have a roast."

"I thought about it, but his mom and dad ran to the truck and pulled him away, saying they were okay and all would be well."

"But all was not going to be well."

"No. Dieter blamed his dad for the fire. Nothing any of us could do to temper his anger or make him forgive André. I could relate to that."

"How so?"

"Trauma, Josh. Had nothing to do with logic. It was all about emotion, feeling there was no escape. For me, it was Father Magloire. Everyone in my family thought he was a good priest making me a good Christian. For Dieter, it was his parents. Annie said she loved Dieter, but she wouldn't leave André."

"At least Dieter had you."

"Not the same thing, and he told you about my counsel."

"He said you were there for him."

Henri jumps down from the tailgate. He lights a cigarette and exhales. The smoke forms into a phrase that floats in the air in front of us. "Make a man on you."

I remember the AfterLing conversation Dieter and I had in the Château Frontenac. It was where Dieter shared this phrase with me—a translation of a French expression Henri had adopted in Canada.

"I believed that until the day I died, Josh. To me, the trauma was always there. No one could make it go away. No amount of sympathy or compassion or understanding because it's always there in your brain, stored as memories, experiences, feelings, thoughts. To me, building a wall around it was the best I could do, and I told Dieter the same."

The words shimmer briefly, then revert to a tobacco cloud dispersed by a gentle breeze. Henri rests up against the tailgate and Beethoven's Ninth Symphony begins playing. It's the fourth movement. The choral symphony is more than music to my ears.

"AfterL is a fitting realm for this musical masterpiece, Josh. Right away, it had an emotional impact beyond anything I'd ever experienced. I think the separation of mind and soul from flesh and blood also had something to do with it."

Henri is silent for several minutes, swaying to the music. After the soprano solo, the music ends and Henri slides over to embrace me. "Listening to that voice sure puts me in touch with my feminine side, Josh. Too bad I was caught up in all this manly nonsense while I was alive." Henri hops into the back of the truck and raises his arms high in the air. "To all my earthly male friends, don't waste your time making a man on you."

He jumps from the truck and stands in front of me. "Now you know why I'm your guide, not Dieter?"

"I think so. He's told me his story—enough of it for me to understand how it ties to your early years and the reasons you raised him as you did."

"Yes, so there's two bits of unfinished business; one is mine to carry out and the other is for Ronnie."

"Ronnie? Ronnie is gonna show up?" I'm tightly gripping Henri's arm as I say this. He puts his hand on mine and the acute pain in my head, heart, and gut disappear, replaced by a warm glow. Foreboding becomes anticipation.

I easily accept Henri's response: "Of course."

He claps his hands and changes into a blue, short-sleeved shirt, striped, white vest, grey trousers, and black shoes. "This is what I was wearing when I left Belgium in 1947. Farewell gifts from my grandmother."

"I remember you meeting up with Dieter's Uncle Gilbert in Timmins. He asked you why you left Belgium. You told him you wanted to put an ocean between you and a woman there."

Henri's eyes tear up. He looks towards the heavens, clasps his hands in front, slowly nods then continues without answering my question. "There's much more. Let's go back to Bond's Hill."

∞

We're immediately back in the bedroom in Henri's apartment. The cardboard box that I found in his dresser is sitting on the night table beside his bed. Henri pulls a picture out of the box. "You didn't see this one the day you blacked out, Josh. You only saw the picture of Dieter and Dorie." He hands the photo to me. It's a black and white, with several people standing in front of a field of corn. Judging from the height of the stalks, it's early summer.

"Is this your family, Henri?"

"Yes, in 1937."

The photo starts vibrating in my hand. Startled, I let it go. It expands and attaches itself to the wall beside us. There are seven people in the photo: two young girls, two women, and three men. From left to right, names and dates appear under each of them; Lise—1923,

Chantal—1923, Thérèse—1900, Camille—1875, Louis—1873, Jean—1898, Henri—1921.

"Lise and Chantal were my twin sisters, and Thérèse, my mother. Camille and Louis were my paternal grandparents, and Jean was my dad. My mother's mother, Adèle, died three days after my mom was born. Her father, Stefan, was heartbroken and left for Canada. He left Mom with his older sister, Elise, and her husband, Jacques. After he got to Canada, he stayed in Montréal for a bit, then got hired on at a farm near Joliette. He never remarried, and died on the Western Front in 1917."

"So your mom never knew her parents?"

"No, and she had no cousins to grow up with. Her aunt Elise lost three children and could have no more. My mother also lost a child, Michel, three days after he was born. I came along a year later."

"So you also lost a brother."

Henri has a pensive look on his face. He points to the wall adjacent to the family photo, where the following headline and bulleted text appear:

Key Events and Facts

- August 4, 1914—Germany invades Belgium
- May 10, 1940—Germany invades Belgium
- More than 120,000 military and civilian deaths
- December 16, 1944—Battle of the Bulge

"My parents were teenagers in the First World War. My sisters and I were teenagers in the Second World War. Imagine what life was like during those years. I was working in a Krupp munitions factory in Germany during the Battle of the Bulge, but everyone else in my family was on the farm. The fear, the uncertainty, the atrocities." Henri waves his hand and a newspaper replaces the figures on the wall. It's the front page of a Belgian paper published in 1917.

"During the First World War, my father was sent to work in Germany until 1917. When he returned, he told *Pépère* Louis, who was a member of the Résistance, about the abuses he suffered there. It's documented in our underground newspaper."

The newspaper disappears, and Henri puts his index finger on Camille in the family photo still on the wall. "Through all of this, Mémère kept the faith and told us we were living through hell and a better life awaited us." Henri sighs as the picture on the wall reverts to a faded, sepia-coloured photo. He puts it on the top of the dresser. "Very few Canadians who returned from the wars talked about their experiences. All you have to do is read any of the stories published to know why the silence."

"You didn't tell Dieter's Uncle Gilbert it was to get away from all the reminders of the war that you left Belgium. You told him it had to do with a woman."

Henri waves an arm in dismissal. In a calm, reflective voice, he says, "I'm dead, she's dead, we have eternity to catch up."

"You can't do this to me, Henri—just leave me hanging. You told Dieter and me the past often explains why people do what they do going forward. Who was that woman, and why did you become a confirmed bachelor when you came to Canada?"

"Josh, remember why you're here. Mine was the last death I wanted you to deal with as a reminder of past sorrows and losses. Every death since Ronnie's has opened old, deep wounds in you. Now is the time to get rid of them. It was too late when I met you. There was never a time when it was right for me to help you deal with Ronnie's death. You were shut tighter than a nun's knees."

"For God's sake, Henri, what else could you expect? I was a ten-year-old boy when I lost the only person I loved! The only person who cared for me! You're damned right I closed up!" I'm staring at Henri, surprised at the intensity of my outburst, at the fear welling up inside. A fear that always turned to emptiness.

Henri puts his hand on my chest. As if he's a Reiki healer, warmth flows into my body, lowering my heart rate and eliminating the acidic churn in my stomach. In a soothing voice, he carries on. "We're here for you, Josh. Very soon, Ronnie will be with you, in a good way, the rest of your life. But there's more to the healing than memories. I didn't cure myself entirely while I was alive, but well enough to make a difference to many people—just not to you, at least not as much as was needed. I knew that, and *voila*, a door opened and Ronnie was on the other side. Once I accepted his presence, two things became clear. You blamed yourself for his death, and we could fix that."

Henri stands in front of me and puts an arm on my shoulder before continuing. "For you, thinking about the past almost always triggers a feeling of guilt and a return to the funeral parlour and Ronnie's grave. Well, Ronnie's body, bloated as you remembered it, was all that was in that coffin. But when his coffin was lowered into the ground, you buried all the memories, the wonderful memories of the time you shared with him. You couldn't even recall what he looked like. If it weren't for the photo I saw when I came to your house the first time, I probably wouldn't have known about Ronnie, either. It was your secret. You saw him get buried, but you just couldn't let the memory of his drowning go. I know why now. Ronnie helped me to understand. He knew."

"Henri, I'm not ready for that. I want to know about the woman."

Thunder shakes the walls and windows in Henri's bedroom. A deafening crackle and flash of lightning fill the room. Henri smiles. He couldn't have found a better way to emphasize his point. "Dieter told you. You're not in charge here, Josh. All will be revealed as promised."

Henri leaves his bedroom and motions for me to follow. In minutes, we're standing on the corner where the main street intersects the one where I grew up. Before I can say anything, Henri has me in my parents' backyard, behind the garage. "Time to unearth the truth of your brother's death, for you to see what really happened. Ronnie will join you. I'll be back later."

CHAPTER 13
Youth Revisited

I'm alone beside the pear trees, apprehensive and frustrated, feeling like a prisoner without any choice of events—hopeless and helpless. Why do they keep abandoning me? As if reading my thoughts and feeling my emptiness, "Ode to Joy" begins playing. At first barely audible, the volume keeps increasing and my eyes are tilted to a fork in one of the larger trees. A blue circle appears between the boughs, pulsating to the music. Besides pumping blood, my heart infuses me with serenity and anticipation. The blue circle floats down and expands. When it reaches my height, my long-dead brother, Ronnie, appears. Brown curly hair, a pixie face that would melt any tyrant's heart, and bright peacock-blue eyes that drink deep. There is no angelic scent or heavenly aura. Just a young boy, smiling at me with trust and faith and love.

Before I can say anything, he pulls a wand out of the back pocket of his shorts, waves it in a sweeping downward motion, and opens his arms. Suddenly, I'm four and a half feet tall and in his arms. He whispers in my ear, "Welcome back, brother. I'm so glad we made contact. I got a lot of memories to give back to you."

I bathe in the warmth of his embrace, wanting him to stay forever. He pinches my bottom and steps back. When I say, "Hey!" I notice my voice is that of a ten-year-old.

"I've turned back the clock, Josh. You and me, boys again, back before ..." He doesn't finish. He looks at me sheepishly. "I know, you still have some poop to deal with, but that's why we're here." He sticks three fingers in the air. "Your wife, Jackie, says three is her lucky number. I'm your third visitor from AfterL, Josh, so I think I'm your lucky number, too. I'm here with poop repellent."

He laughs and sprays me with an aromatic stringy, red yarn. A mirror pops up in front of my face. My hair is completely covered. I look like a Raggedy Andy doll. Ronnie sprays the yarn on himself, and then makes the can vanish. He jumps up and down, claps his hands, and then does several cartwheels. "Remember when we used to do cartwheels and handstands together, Josh?" Ronnie is suddenly upside down. He puts his arms close to his body and is standing on his head. "Couldn't do that back in 1961, eh?"

I can't speak. Somehow, Ronnie, like Dieter and Henri before him, can alter my sense of self, alter my emotions. Ronnie floats into an upright position and slowly walks close to my side. "I can see you've forgotten it all. That's why I'm here." He combs his fingers through the Raggedy Andy curls and walks towards the garage. "Come on, let's go inside and get started."

He walks through the wall, and I follow him, pulled along by a force I can't control It's dark inside this seldom-used workshop. The only windows face east, towards the cornfield Ronnie and I last walked together in 1961. I avoid looking through the spider-webbed and dusty panes. Instead my attention is directed to the hoist. Rusted, massive, it could easily have lifted the largest motor out of the biggest semi. Then my eyes are forced up towards the ceiling. The hoist is mounted on a long I-beam that spans the concrete blocks on either side of this over-sized family garage.

Why such a big hoist? I never saw it used.

Overhead a voice quietly says, "Dad had this garage built for the truck he was going to buy."

"Ronnie?" I can't see him anywhere. Where is he? What is he talking about? I don't remember anything about a truck.

"Dad was pretty happy when Barry and his men finished this garage. We were here—you and me." He floats down from the I-beam and puts his hands gently on my shoulders. "You never recalled any happy memories, Josh. You never had any pleasant dreams after I died. A complete shutdown once I was buried. We were happy, carefree kids. What was going on around us was adult stuff. We had each other. The rest didn't matter."

The hoist starts moving along its beam. I try to grab it. Nothing. My hand goes right through. A long silence. Then the hook at the bottom of the pulley begins swaying on its own, gently, almost noiselessly. I take a deep breath, raise my arms, and say, "It's been almost forty years, Ronnie. I lost my youth when I lost you."

"I know, Josh. But you became an adult child much earlier, being the oldest and taking care of the rest of us as much as you did."

A faint, almost translucent aura shimmers around him. I can't help but smile. His Raggedy Andy look is calming.

"You were nine and I was eight when Dad had this place built."

"I don't remember."

"I'll fix that."

I'm suddenly sitting on the concrete floor, cross-legged, in a Buddhist position. Ronnie stands behind me. His hands are warm on my shoulders.

"Close your eyes and relax. We're going to watch a movie, sort of ..."

I put my hands on my legs, palms up and ask, "What kind of movie?"

He squeezes my shoulders gently. A slight heat and vibration move up both sides of my neck, meeting at the top of my skull and then radiating back down. "Now that you're relaxed we can begin the show."

∞

There's a low humming sound, then the grey mist—becoming familiar to me—replaces the dark nothingness in front of my eyes. Seconds later, it too vanishes, giving way to a scene of my father, Gord, and my grandfather sitting at the kitchen table at Grandpa Don's house in Courtland.

The pendulum clock on the wall is just striking one o'clock. The calendar beside it displays the month and year: June 1959. Between Grandpa and Dad are a bottle of rye and two shot glasses. Ronnie and Eddie are sitting on the floor, petting Grandpa's dog, Tandy. As Eddie runs his hands behind Tandy's ears, he wags his tail, opens his mouth wide, and tries to lick Ronnie's arms.

I wonder where the rest of the family are. They have to be in the house. Dad's parents didn't have much of a back yard. The garage where Grandpa keeps his big semi takes up most of the space; the rest of it is a tiny garden, where Grandma Bev grows vegetables.

The scene shifts from the kitchen to the living room. It's odd to suddenly see a young me, sitting on the couch with my Grandmother, watching her knit a sweater. Annie is in her crib, sleeping. I can hear Willie, Luke, and Ben in the front porch pushing toy cars along the carpeted floor. The toilet flushes, the bathroom door opens, and out comes my Mother, very pregnant with my brother, Matt. Mom eases herself gently into Grandpa's rocker, then pulls a cigarette from the pack on the table. Grandma says nothing, just looks at her kindly and pulls out a cigarette from her silver case.

It's quiet. There is nothing to distract me from staring at the nine-year-old me. My ears stick out, my toothy grin shows a lower jaw filled with crooked teeth. I have a clear complexion, before the acne and ensuing scars. I seem happy, content to be there instead of in the kitchen with the men.

It doesn't feel right to see myself as a carefree child.

The scene shifts back to the kitchen. Dad is filling Grandpa's shot glass. When he finishes, he says, "With another child to feed, things are going to be different, Dad. I'm tired of working for somebody else. If you co-sign the loan, I can buy that truck I've had my eye on and be an independent again."

Taking a sip of his rye, Grandpa looks at Dad and then puts the glass on the table and starts turning it in his hand, slowly. "Maybe I can help, Gord, but things didn't turn out so good last time."

Dad sits a little more upright in the chair, takes a drink from his glass, and then sets it down. Not looking at Grandpa and staring at the table, he says, "Things will be different this time, Dad. I know they will. Mary has seven kids to look after. Soon there'll be eight. She's learned her lesson. So have I. We can have your bookkeeper manage the accounts. You know I'm reliable and can get plenty of work."

"I know, son, but like I said, things didn't work out so good before. Maybe you can do something to convince me."

"Like what? That was four years ago, and we're back on our feet now. We have our own house; we've never missed a payment. You can check with the bank."

"No, Gord, I see things are better, but trucks are expensive. I know. I've been in the business over twenty years—gas, oil, maintenance, repairs. You don't even have your own garage."

"There's plenty of room in our yard for a garage."

Grandpa raises his eyebrows, lifts his glass once more and says, "Well, build the garage, and we'll talk again."

Dad raises his glass too and says, "I will!"

The scene slowly evaporates, swallowed by the grey void.

I'm back in my dad's garage. Staring at the hoist, I realize for the first time what it symbolizes: Dad's proof of commitment to Grandpa. With this hoist, he could do his own engine maintenance and show Grandpa he was serious and deserved a family loan. Dad could once again be the owner/operator of a semi—like his father and two older brothers.

Ronnie squeezes my shoulders. "So now you know why Dad built this garage. How does that make you feel?"

I look out the dirt and cobweb-encrusted window, past the yard and field and forest beyond, to the weathered barn on the side of the hill, half a mile away. From my vantage point, I can dimly see the front and one side of the old, abandoned structure. Its grey tin roof is still intact, but many of the grey sideboards as well as the door to the loft are missing. It's been that way as far back as I can remember.

Ronnie tugs on my arm. "Never mind the barn, Josh. That's somebody else's story. Tell me how you feel about this place."

"I don't feel a darned thing, Ronnie. I never thought about it before, and now I don't see any reason I should. It's just an old garage, for God's sake." My heart rate speeds up, and my reflection in the window shows my eyes are narrowed.

"No, it's more than that. Don't play dumb with me, Josh. I know what you're thinking and feeling. Say it." Ronnie moves out from behind and faces me, waiting. His eyes look deep into mine. I try to look away but can't. Some force is making me look at him.

I feel him, some part of him, probing inside my head. It feels weird, uncomfortable. I want him out. I sigh, straighten my shoulders, say aloud what he probably already knows. "I don't feel anything, but obviously this old garage is Dad's second and final broken dream. That still doesn't forgive him his trespasses against me, against us, and you can't make me feel any sympathy for him. He shit in his own nest—our nest."

I look at Ronnie. His eyes are closed, his head bowed. The sensation of his presence inside me intensifies. It's as if he's attached himself to the back of my head, deep in my brain. From there he creates gentle waves that spread slowly throughout my skull, vibrations that resonate and relax me—that extend down farther to my chest and abdomen.

Spontaneously, almost against my will, I say, "Poor Dad. He probably regretted what happened the rest of his life."

It's enough to stop the feeling that Ronnie is inside me. He slowly rotates his shoulders and moves his head from side to side, then back and forth. Was this part of some re-entry routine?

He doesn't give me the chance to ask. He opens his eyes and fills in another blank in my memory when he says, "Dad never said anything, never complained. The Friday after the garage was built, he went over to Grandpa's after work, to tell him the good news—"

I interrupt, shaking my head, protesting, "I don't want to hear any more." I push Ronnie away and try to escape. An invisible force pins me in place.

As if I'd said nothing, Ronnie continues, "As usual, they talked and they drank. It was late when they finished. Grandma asked him to spend the night, but Dad insisted he was fit to drive—"

"I remember the rest. Dad wrapped his car around a telephone pole on the way home and ended up in the hospital for two days. When they let him out, he was wearing a cast and his arm was in a sling. He lost his licence and his job. He and Mom sat around drinking for days afterwards." I laugh and raise my arms, palms up.

Ronnie hops up onto the workbench and says nothing.

I carry on. "When Dad finally sobered up, he started working as a bartender at the hotel. How ironic!"

Ronnie quietly says, "It paid the bills."

I turn away. "Maybe it paid some of them, Ronnie, but not all. I remember the Christmas after his accident."

I turn around to face him. He's nowhere in sight and a misty void slowly unfolds. I look up to see if Ronnie is on the beam supporting this hoist. Not there. The hoist starts swaying from side to side while everything around fades to a hazy grey.

Now what? What is Ronnie doing? It's hard for me to believe we lived through this together. How come he sees things so differently?

Hell, we were only a year apart in age. Didn't he feel the same bitterness, shame, and anger?

I understand why he made me witness the conversation between Dad and Grandpa. I also understand what happened earlier when Dad owned his first semi. Mom hadn't made the monthly payments, and the truck got repossessed. Dad filed for bankruptcy. We had to stay with relatives until Dad got full-time work and we could afford the house in Bond's Hill.

Is Ronnie doing this on purpose?

The grey mist once more envelopes me. When it dissipates, I'm back with Ronnie outside our childhood home in Bond's Hill, in the back yard, looking away towards the fields. It's springtime. The radiant sun has melted the last snows of winter and the pear and apple trees are sprouting with new growth. I can see and hear the robins. Childhood memories of our searches for polliwogs in the nearby ponds suddenly return.

A red-tailed hawk soars overhead, riding on the thermals from the newly plowed furrows. I wonder if Ronnie has anything to do with the bird's appearance. His words confirm my suspicions. "Free as a bird, Josh. When you were ten and I was with you, the booze didn't matter. We're gonna relive some of the events that happened before I drowned. Besides, what better way to relive them than in the same body?"

Ronnie makes a large mirror appear, like one you might see in a dressing room in a department store. In it, I see us, kids again but no Raggedy Andy hair. I stifle a sob. Ronnie smiles, grabs my hand, and off we go into the field. He stops just when I'm beginning to sink into the soft spring soil.

"Let's get you in the right clothes, Josh, and turn the clock ahead a few weeks."

Now there's grass along the fence, corn shooting up from the fields, and Ronnie and I are in sneakers. He motions for me to come closer—within whispering distance.

"Josh, it will feel a little weird, this part. You're inside your body, and you'll see and hear everything you and I experienced all those years ago. Literally, we'll relive the past, but I'm in charge and everything we do will be recorded."

"What? What's with the recording?"

"It's the best word I could think of. Let's try this. Consider what happens in a dream. You're asleep in your bed, the room is dark, and you're unaware of anything going on around you. Inside your head, it's different. You could be slaying dragons, wooing fair maidens, lots happening. Sometimes you wake up and remember the dream." He checked to see if I was following him.

I nod; he continues. "When this is all over, when you open your eyes in the hospital, everything we're about to relive will be back in your memory. You won't think of it as dreams. You'll remember it very clearly. It will seem a bit strange, because you're in the dream, but Henri and Dieter have things fixed so you're witnessing the dream at the same time. Ready?"

"So, I'm cameraman and actor at the same time? Is that what you're saying, Ronnie?"

"Sort of, but you can't change what's recorded 'cause it's a record that's already been made. You just don't remember it. Let's just put it on play, and you'll get what I mean."

Ronnie snaps his fingers, and two chairs appear beside him. He motions for me to join him. A pulsating bubble appears—at least thirty feet in diameter. I feel a part of me drawn inside it. Ronnie laughingly says, "Lights, camera, action!" He's also drawn in.

Whoosh!

We're in the field on the other side of the bubble. It's closing. Behind it, I see two young boys in folding chairs.

Scene I

I feel like a marionette, being drawn to the fence, pushed gently into a crouching position. I hear myself say, "Ronnie, look at this one." I'm looking at a circular spider's web, its owner sitting motionless. Ronnie comes over and crouches beside me.

"It's a yellow garden spider, Josh. Mrs. Black told us about them in science class. See those spots in its middle. Don't they look like eyes? That's a pretty big spider, prob'ly a female. The male's web will be close by. Let's go find it."

Ronnie remembers a grade-three science lesson and is inviting me to explore it with him. I just assumed being the older brother I was in charge and knew everything.

Scene II

Ronnie pulls two stalks of grass from their root tips and hands one to me. Each of us then strips off a large blade and cups it between our thumbs. Both of us count to three, then blow hard, changing the angle until loud, raucous sounds, country sounds, fill the air.

"Mine was louder than yours, Ronnie. I get first dibs on the swing at the crick. Come on, grab the towel and let's go swimming."

I grab the towel (we always share one) and run through the burgeoning corn stalks in the field behind our home. I am taller with longer legs. Halfway to the creek, I slow and turn to see how far Ronnie is behind me. He runs into me, and we both fall to the ground. I feel the warm, soft soil cushion my head. Ronnie is on top of me, pins my arms, and starts counting to ten.

"Oh no, you don't," I say. "Whipper Billy Watson is the champ, always will be."

I plant my feet in the dirt, anchor my elbows and push. Ronnie loses his grip and rolls over beside me. I scamper on top of him, pin his arms, and we both start laughing.

"Keep trying, Ronnie. Now let's get to the creek."

But that's where Ronnie drowned.

Ronnie quickly holds up three fingers, says, "Scene III," and whisks us back to 1955, when he was just four years old, before we moved to town.

Scene III

We're in front of our rural, three-bedroom bungalow outside Bond's Hill. A plain white clapboard building, it sits alone along a country road in a farmer's field. Our dog, Sandy, is licking Ronnie's face. Ronnie is laughing, his eyes smiling.

I say, "Lick him, Sandy; he needs a good wash."

Ronnie grabs Sandy's front paws and down they go. Sandy shakes himself free and runs towards me. "Oh no, you don't," I say. I'm taller, and Sandy has to jump up and stick his tongue out farther to reach my face. I turn from side to side, then stick my hands under his legs and pick him up. He barks and then, as I turn my head, he licks my ear. "Yecch," I say and let him go. He begins circling us, then runs toward the faded red barn down the road.

Ronnie yells, "Come on, Josh, let's follow him," and off he goes on his stubby legs. I follow. By the time we reach the side door, two minutes later, Sandy is sitting on his haunches, his head cocked like the Victrola dog, his mouth open. Ronnie grasps the latch but isn't strong enough to pull the door ajar. I sweep him aside, flip the handle, and then tug it open. Turning, I raise my arms, flex my biceps and shout, "Superman!"

Ronnie rolls his eyes, skirts in front of me, and races up the ladder to the loft. I hold the door for Sandy, who immediately lowers his head and starts sniffing the ground. I leave him to search out mice and rabbits and head up to join Ronnie. By the time I reach him, he's on tiptoes, peering out the window at the hay field below. A barn swallow dives towards him, an insect in its mouth. Ronnie ducks, and shrieks, "Hey!" and covers his head with his arms. The swallow alters course.

"Don't worry, Ronnie," I say. "They won't hurt you. There's a nest in here somewhere. Let's see if we can find it." I raise a finger to my lips and whisper, "Quiet."

Pushing aside leather straps, baling twine, and rope, I shuffle across the floorboards in the loft, searching beams and crevices and listening for the sounds of hungry nestlings. Ronnie taps me on the shoulder and points to a corner beam. We approach. I hear a "chirp, chirp, churee" and the "whoosh" of a swallow close to my head. I say, "Ronnie, let's go," and head to the ladder. I let him go first. The swallow doesn't chase us. Sandy is waiting below with that Victrola dog look again.

We leave the barn and sit under a nearby tree. A gentle breeze rustles the leaves above us. Ronnie has Sandy between his legs, patting his head. We watch the swallows swoop and dive, catching insects on the fly.

Ronnie says, "Don't you wish you could fly, Josh?"

Before I answer, the scene fades away. Ronnie and I are back in our yard, two young boys in another dimension.

Ronnie puts his hands under his legs and leans towards me. "This's better than flying, Josh. But you still aren't ready for the creek ..."

Is there anything going on in my head that he doesn't know?

"We're starting our next journey in darkness, Josh, before dawn, December 25, 1957, after we moved to Bond's Hill. Merry Christmas!"

Scene IV

Ronnie nudges me in the tiny bed we share. Slowly opening my eyes, I see Dad silhouetted in the doorway. More asleep than awake, I don't hear what he's saying. I try to pull my pillow over my head, but Ronnie stops me, saying, "Come on, Josh, let's go open presents."

Dad turns on the bedroom light; a pale yellow bulb magically accents his and Ronnie's glowing faces and broad smiles. "Santa's been here. Josh, Ronnie, everybody—time to get up and see what Santa brought!" Dad then breaks into *Jingle Bells*. He has a child's rattle in his hands that he uses to keep time with the music.

Ronnie jumps out of bed and pulls on my pyjama sleeve until I get up and follow him. Barefoot, clad in stained, worn long johns, Dad leads the way down the stairs, where Mom's waiting. She's in a flannel nightgown that barely shows under her fluffy pink housecoat. With her hair pulled back by a kerchief tied in a bow, she looks like Lucille Ball. Her slippers are open-toed, also pink. She hands her cigarette to Dad as he passes, throws out her arms, and says, "Merry Christmas, Josh! Merry Christmas, Ronnie!" We try to dodge around her, but she blocks the way. "Oh no, you don't." She puts one arm around Ronnie and the other around me. She kisses us on the foreheads but doesn't let go until we both say Merry Christmas.

Ronnie is first to squirm out of Mom's embrace and run to the Christmas tree. Mom and Dad quickly follow, and I trail behind. Dad grabs a Santa hat and then gets down on his knees to reach under the tree. Our cat, Ginger, is lying on the back of the couch. He opens his eyes just far enough to see what the commotion is about, yawns widely, and then closes his eyes. By this time, Ronnie has our dog, Sandy, in his grip, left arm around his front legs while the other holds on to his collar. They are snug up against Dad's butt, intent on seeing the present Dad grabs.

Mom puts her hand on my shoulder. I feel the gentle pressure she applies to steer me to the couch. We sit down. Ben is in his playpen beside us. Eddie, Willie, and Luke are sitting in the three chairs between the kitchen and living room.

"There's hot chocolate on the table next to you, Josh." Mom says. She tousles my hair and continues. "You're such a sleepy head, but this should fix you up."

I smile at her, say thanks, and reach for the cup. Ronnie is looking at me, a twinkle in his eye.

He then winks, and his open eye transforms into a camera shutter. The shutter expands and slowly closes around us, encasing us in darkness. Ronnie says, "Scene V, same day after lunch."

Scene V

The shutter opens, and we're together in our bedroom. Ronnie is facing me, dressed as Tonto. He's playing with the leather strips on the front of his deerskin jacket. I'm trying to fit the leather strap across his forehead. The strap hangs off his ears.

"It's too big, Ronnie," I say. "Let's try this." I tuck his ears under the band and nod. "Now it's okay. You look real good. What about me. How do I look?" We both face the mirror. My Lone Ranger hat is slightly cocked to the right, its stampede string tightly knotted under my chin. As we grin at each other, I fast draw my cap gun out of its holster, fire it twice at the mirror, then hold it under my chin and blow on the barrel. "That'll teach 'em to mess with us, Tonto."

"Yes, Kemosabe. Let's mount our horses and ride off into the mountains."

We grab our horse poles and head for the stairs. Our younger brothers wait at the bottom of the stairs to ascend for their afternoon rest. When we get down to the kitchen, Dad is opening the front door. He gives Grandma Bencet a big hug, and they both step aside to let Grandpa in. He fills the doorway. Mom rushes up, embraces him, and says, "Merry Christmas." He spots Ronnie and me at the foot of the stairs and boisterously says, "Ahh, my *bees*, look at you. Come say Merry Christmas."

Ronnie and I run to greet them. Ronnie gets there first. "Merry Christmas, Grandpa! Merry Christmas, Grandma!" Grandpa scoops him up in his giant left arm and motions me to join him on the right. I jump up, and Grandpa tilts us towards Grandma, so she can put her hands around our faces, kiss us on each cheek, and look deep into our eyes as she says, "Merry Christmas!"

Grandpa puts us down and hands his cap and winter coat to Dad. Grandma has already given her black fur coat and blue bowler hat to Mom. Grandpa wears a suit and tie. Grandma is in a bright red dress and shiny black shoes.

"Grandpa, how do we look?" Ronnie asks.

Grandpa answers, "Like two guys I wouldn't mess with." Then he reopens the front door and brings in two giant shopping bags from the front porch. He hands them to Dad, who puts them under the Christmas tree in the living room. Grandpa reaches into his jacket pockets, crouches in the archway leading from the kitchen, and motions Ronnie and me to join him. He hands each of us a present wrapped in wrinkled and worn, plain brown paper and then steps back.

Looking at us mischievously, Grandpa winks at Mom and Dad, puts his arm around Grandma, and steps back to watch us open our gifts. Ronnie and I tear away the wrapping, look at the boxes in our hands, and then stare at each other wide-eyed.

"Cigarettes, Grandpa?" I say. I hold up a cigarette pack: "Players Cigarettes Medium," is printed on the front, with a picture of a bearded sailor inside the circular life saver.

"Open it," said Grandpa. "You're never too young to smoke!"

Again, Ronnie and I look at each other. Grandpa doesn't smoke, never did, never will. He always has a sad look on his face when Grandma, Dad, and Mom light up.

I push on the bottom of my pack and a roll of black tape pops out. I look over at Ronnie. He has a roll of white tape. We gaze at each other, then turn towards Grandpa. He laughs and says, "Go look under the tree, in the bags. There's one for each of you. Yours is the green one, Josh."

Ronnie and I each grab our bags. "Hey, Grandpa," I say, "This is heavy." I drag my bag over to the couch and start pulling the wrapping paper out. Ronnie sits down beside me and does the same. In seconds, there is a pile of paper on the floor. Ginger comes out from behind the Christmas tree and starts batting the paper around and then pouncing on it. Sandy and Annie join him. Sandy bites at the paper and Annie crawls on top of it, crinkling it in her fingers. Ronnie and I are totally distracted.

"Look, look, Josh!" Ronnie says. He holds up a pair of shiny black skates and a helmet. "And there's more." He reaches into the bag again and pulls out hockey gloves and a Montréal Canadiens sweater and matching socks.

"I've got this stuff too, Ronnie!" I whip off my Lone Ranger mask, hat, and gun belt and hold up my Montréal Canadiens sweater. "Mine says I'm Jean Béliveau. Let me see yours." Ronnie holds his up. "Richard" is stitched on the sweater.

"Wowee, Josh! I can be Henri or Maurice," Ronnie says.

"Oh no you can't," I say. "It has number sixteen on it. That's the Rocket's number, but that's good, Ronnie. You and me are both centres. We can face off against each other."

We don our sweaters, then go say thank you to Grandpa and Grandma.

"Ronnie, Josh, look what else Santa brought." Dad holds out two brand new hockey sticks. Ronnie and I start jumping up and down.

"You like your smokes, eh, boys?" Grandpa asks.

∞

Ronnie takes my hand, says, "Hi Ho, Silver!" and we're sitting in the chairs in our back yard. Ronnie gets up from his chair, stands in front of me, cradles my head against his chest with one hand, and puts the other one on top of my head. "Our whole past is now in there, Josh. All the good times we shared and you have blocked—until now."

Our whole past will be there? For nearly forty years, every time I thought of Ronnie, my heartbeat quickened, my stomach filled with bitter acids, and I felt alone, a guilt-ridden little boy. Like a mill wheel forever forced to turn in circles by the endless incoming water, my feelings, memories, and thoughts repeated themselves in an unending circle. I wasn't there when he needed me.

... but now it ends ...

My heartbeat is slow and regular. Wonderful memories of Ronnie and me flood through my mind's eye. Each butts up to the other and comforts me.

"I love you, Ronnie."

He pulls me off the chair, and we hug each other. Our heads rest on each other's shoulders until he gently backs away a few inches. There are tears in his eyes.

"I know that, Josh—always did. Now you remember the same things and will recall them when you think of our time together. It wasn't a long time, but it was a good time." He wipes away the tears and winks at me.

"Hey, you sound like Henri. He always said that!" Tears well up from deep inside. They're tears of joy. I'm taking deep breaths, letting the feelings overwhelm me.

"When Henri was in the hospice, I told him you only remember what happened on July 10, 1961. Now you have the same memories as me."

"I don't feel anxious."

"I'm happy about that. Josh. Henri says for this to work, *you need to be freed.* He first called it a *catharsis,* but then he remembered I'm a young squirt."

"So like Henri, even in his last days, to come up with more slogans."

"The eulogy you wrote mentioned that. Henri, Dieter, and I were there when Paul read it at the funeral home. As Paul said, you're good with words. Think back to 1961. Everything you remember. Don't worry, your emotional baggage has been removed."

As if I'm recounting a story relayed to me by someone else, with no emotional involvement on my part, I set down what I remember about Ronnie's last days.

CHAPTER 14

Our Last Summer

Ronnie and I swim where all the poor kids swam in the summer of 1961, in Morgan's Creek, south of town off Main Street. We call it "the creek"; teenagers refer to it as "Morgan's hole." It is an idyllic but raucous gathering place. By foot or bicycle, from midmorning to mid-afternoon, kids from eight to sixteen would come and go. There are no adults, just a dozen or so kids and teenagers.

Ronnie and I walk from home, preferring a shortcut through the field to the longer route along the streets. We always go together, just the two of us, enjoying the solitude, the smell of the corn pushing skyward, and the sound and sight of grasshoppers, beetles, and mice scurrying out of our way. We look skyward, watching the hawks, hoping to see one dive for a meal.

Eventually we climb a fence, return to the street, and walk through a tunnel under a railroad overpass. Exiting the tunnel is like entering a different world. It isn't a mountaintop view, but our town is named Bond's Hill for a reason. It is elevated, and the tunnel is at its highest point. When you come out of the tunnel, which is about fifty feet long, you get a panoramic plain that ends at the lake. We can look straight down the valley to the trailer park where the older kids go nightly to dance in the hall next to the swimming pool. They put money in the jukebox and make friends with the kids in the trailer park.

"I'm glad we don't have to swim in the trailer park pool, Ronnie. Chlorine and kids' pee, yuck."

We are content with the creek. When we arrive, the creek is in direct sunlight, warm and inviting. We are never first; older kids are already there, at least one of them swinging across the deepest part of the water hole on a thick rope that hangs down from the maple. Others are on the bank, yelling, laughing, waiting impatiently for their turn.

When the freight trains roar by over the bridge, the younger kids wave and yell, hoping the conductor will blow the whistle. He never does, but they always hope. Ronnie is among the boys who hoot and holler. I consider myself too old for that kid stuff.

Our routine is simple. Invariable. We walk down the path, Ronnie in front of me, both of us holding on to the single towel we share for balance. He reaches back over his right shoulder. I put one end of the towel in his hand, then pull it tight so we support each other. At the bottom of the steep hill, we take off our sneakers and socks, roll up our pants, and walk across the stream via the concrete mouth of the tunnel. Safely across, we then rush into the bushes to change, racing to see who is first into the water.

Too small to compete for use of the rope, Ronnie and I go back up the tunnel at the edge of the stream, and then see who jumps farthest into the pool. It's a game we never tire playing. Sometimes we get in each other's way, slowing each other, pushing, and tickling, anything to get an advantage. We also have to watch out for bullies, kids that want to push us into the deeper water or wet our towel, anything to spoil our fun.

That's how it is until July, with nothing to break the endless pattern of eat, play and sleep. Ronnie and I, less than a year apart in age, are always together. Happy to be away from a home too often filled with the sounds of our siblings crying, or our parents partying or fighting, we have no thought of the future. Every day is ours to idle away and savour. It's enough.

But then it all ends. July 10th is our last day together—and our last words are less than an hour before his death. Ronnie dies and a part of me dies with him. Three incidents are burned into my memory the day he drowned. Each of them replays as part of the interminable nightmare evoked whenever I think about him and that day, his lost life, and my lost youth.

The first scene:

It's a Monday morning, all sunshine and heat. Too warm to stay in bed or inside, we dress and eat before going out. I make the toast and spread it with jam and peanut butter. Ronnie pours us glasses of milk. After we eat and grab a towel, we leave the kitchen by the side door. On the adjoining porch, I see the familiar high stack of empty beer cases and smell the stale alcohol residue. I become upset and irritable. I yell at Ronnie when he doesn't hold the door for me. I push him, and he falls on the cement patio. He scrapes his arm and starts crying. I call him a baby.

The second scene:

It's late afternoon, and we're at the creek. The sun has moved behind the big maple and the water starts to cool. I tell Ronnie it's time to go and head into the bushes to change. I wait for him to give him the towel, but he doesn't show. I get impatient and return from the bushes. He's standing on the sand where the sun is still shining, smiling, enjoying the light and the warmth. I throw the towel at him and leave, never once looking back.

I mutter to myself, "You can drown for all I care."

The last scene:

I don't want to go home without Ronnie. I don't want to find a babysitter with my sister or discover my mother at home, probably half drunk. The school Ronnie and I go to is on the way from the creek to Main Street. I go to the playground and sit on one of the swings. It doesn't feel right to be there by myself. I get off the swing and walk through the cornfield adjacent to the school. Every now and then I climb one of the fence posts and look back towards the creek.

Tired of being alone, I head for the community park and sit in the stands to watch older boys play baseball. When they finish, I go to the corner store where Ronnie and I usually go when things are unpleasant at home. One of the older boys, Big Roy, one of the town toughs, is standing by the door. He looks at me, sneers, and says, "Your brother's dead, and you're hanging out here? Un-fucking believable!"

It doesn't click. He's a ruffian, mean, vicious, and insensitive. I back away from him and then turn towards home, just a block away. I walk quickly, shaking my head, cursing him, eager to prove he's wrong. Then I see the police car in front of our house. I tell myself not to panic. The police have been to our house many times before.

Then Ronnie's teacher, Mrs. Black, opens our front door to let the policeman out of our kitchen. Mrs. Black holds out her arms to me. I just stare at her. She says, "I'm sorry, Josh. I'm very, very sorry." Then she starts to cry. I've never heard a teacher cry before. Then I hear my mother sobbing in the living room. Our next-door neighbour, Mrs. Gobhan, is sitting next to her, an arm around her shoulder. Our dog is on his haunches beside my mother, his head cocked to one side. He turns, looks at me, then heads toward the door. I let him out. It's the last time I ever see him.

I remember nothing more of what happened that day. Did I run into the back yard as I usually did when things got unbearable? Did I get any solace from my mom or dad? I don't know. I can't tell you where I went or what I did—only that I was grief-stricken to the point of amnesia for about forty-eight hours.

The nightmare fast-forwards two days. It's mid-afternoon, and Mrs. Black is coming out of the funeral parlour with her husband. I hold the door for them. After they express their sympathies, I hear Mrs. Black say, "It's a real shame. Doesn't look like him at all."

I don't grasp her meaning right away, until my mother pulls me inside and firmly steers me to the front of the light-brown casket and tells me to say goodbye. I see a bloated face and bloated hands on a bloated body inside a blue suit, surrounded by white satin. I run out of the building, chest heaving, tears streaming down my face. I go to our car and get in the back seat, crying, thinking, *"That's not him! That's not Ronnie!"*

One other memory in the chain of scenes embedded in my nightmare is at the cemetery. It's July 12th, a sunny day. I am graveside with Grandma and Grandpa Bencet. It's not the tiny Bond Hill cemetery— that's been closed for years. We're in the large city cemetery some five miles from Bond's Hill. It, too, is an old cemetery with bushes and huge pine and maple trees throughout. An ornate iron fence surrounds it. There are marble monuments everywhere. Some are purple, some are brown, others are grey. Many of them are taller than me.

Ronnie's casket is already set on the green carpet covering the burial plot. There are flowers on top, along with a wooden statue of Jesus on the Cross. Ronnie's grave site is in the shade of one of the maples close to the intersection of two gravel paths. It's a windy day and when Grandma Bencet, all dressed in black, sees me shivering, she moves me into the sunshine and shelters me from the wind. A black veil covers her face, but I can see tears in her eyes. She has a rosary and in her left hand, a white handkerchief embroidered with her initials. She wipes the tears from her eyes, softly reciting *The Lord's Prayer*. Then she puts her right arm around me and asks me to join her in the Hail Mary.

I start crying. I can't accept there is a God and a Holy Mother that would take Ronnie away from me. I am the one who was bad the day he drowned. I am the one in the wrong.

I am the one who should have died.

The nightmare ends on that thought. It is tightly bound to the last words I muttered when I left him at the creek: "You can drown for all I care."

CHAPTER 15

The Healing Process

Ronnie stands in front of me. He has a wistful look on his face. I sense he sees the same look on mine. "For all these years, Josh, thinking about me made you replay those scenes and feel guilty and sad. You didn't see me for who I was or what we were to each other. You never told anyone about our last day and you didn't remember anything else. You forgot I was your best friend. How close we were and how much fun we had."

"I think you've changed that for me, you and Dieter and Henri. Now I have the memories and the good vibrations Dieter talked about ... and the guilt and sorrow ...."

"Yeah, well that's why Henri got interested when Dieter and I visited him. On your last evening with Henri at the hospice, do you remember what he said?"

"Uh huh, he heard strange, ghostly voices; he had strange thoughts about numbers and music, and he wondered if he had made enough of a difference."

"We were there, Dieter and I. Henri said those things, but he said something else too. He said he left something for you to resolve. He gave you a picture of Dieter, and he told you to look after his things— that all would become clear."

I snorted and said, "After Henri died, I went to his apartment and what was inside that cardboard box led to my blackout. The only thing clear is that Henri suffered a loss the same day I did in 1961, and revisiting that memory put me in a hospital bed. How long have I been out?"

"That's not important, Josh. You'll be home with Jackie and the kids before anyone there gets too worried."

"Well, Ronnie, I'm still confused. Why did Henri think the contents in that cardboard box would make things clear to me? There was a picture of Dieter with a young blonde, a medal, and a letter saying Dieter died on July 10, 1961.

"Yep, Dieter died the same day as me, and it was only during Henri's last days that he learned—from me—what made you sad and quiet most of the time. You thought you should have died. I told Henri what happened. Dieter was there. He heard it too."

"So, once Henri understood my secret, he thought he could change me somehow?"

I'm out of my chair, standing close to Ronnie. I'm about to lash out, but I feel him inside my head, calming me. My heart rate slows, and I take a deep breath. Ronnie gets a satisfied look on his face and backs away until we're five feet apart. He snaps his fingers, and the tall mirror that had been with us before reappears. Ronnie says, "We were boys when I died. You got hung up by my death, Josh. You never got over it. Come stand by me, look in the mirror."

I see the two of us; young boys in 1961. We're wearing shorts, ankle-length socks, sneakers, and T-shirts. Ronnie's shirt has blue and white stripes. His shorts are black with an elastic waistband holding them up. My T-shirt is white, and there are faded letters and pictures of young boys and girls tugging at the letters. My shorts are light-green in color. Instead of a belt, a cloth cord tied at the front keeps them from falling.

Ronnie asks, "What do you see, Josh?"

"I see two boys wearing second-hand clothes that tell everybody they're poor."

"Is that all?" Ronnie points at his face.

In response to his wide grin, I break out in a smile too. I get his point. "We were happy, despite being poor and the sons of alcoholics."

"While we were together, Josh, that was all that mattered. After I died, you changed. I wasn't there so the two of us could grow together. Watch this." Ronnie points at the mirror, and the two of us start to sprout. At the top of the mirror numbers—years—begin to fade in and out in sequence: starting in 1961, to the year 1974. As each year slowly flashes by, Ronnie and I morph from boys to young men. I easily recognize myself, but a grown-up Ronnie stands beside me. He puts his arm around me and asks, "What do you think?"

"You're a handsome dude. Grandpa wouldn't approve of your long hair and moustache, but you'd fit right in with the guys I was hanging with."

Ronnie smiles and the mirror gradually disappears. In its place, another young man takes shape. It's Dieter wearing the forest-ranger hat, vest, and short-sleeved shirt he was wearing when he first visited. Ronnie goes over to him and gives him a hug.

Dieter smiles, looks at Ronnie, and replies, "Henri wanted this 'dream world' we're in to be as real as a dream can be, Josh. He told us before we came here, if it wasn't, we wouldn't succeed in our mission." Dieter puts his arm around Ronnie's shoulder, and the two of them have expectant looks on their faces, eyebrows slightly raised.

I say, "It's working so far, but there's still some healing to do. Ronnie has restored some wonderful memories of our time together, but the sorrow and guilt I have related to his death are still here." I put my right hand, clenched into a fist, on my chest.

Ronnie and Dieter look at each other. I can sense they're having a telepathic conversation that excludes me. I lower my right arm and take in the scenery around us. As I look across the fields, memories of the convivial times I spent with Ronnie flood my thoughts. The feelings of sorrow and guilt fade.

Is this how it's going to be? Any negative emotions about my childhood that surface will trigger visions of Ronnie and me enjoying each other's company?

I smile and recall what Henri told me the first summer I worked with him and Gus, his partner, as a plasterer's helper. It's my first week on the job. We're having a morning break. Coffee and doughnuts in hand, I just returned from the diner in Henri's truck. I'm angry. I tell Henri and Gus another driver cut me off when I was exiting the parking lot and I had to swerve and brake hard to avoid a collision. The coffee spilled and soaked the doughnuts. Concerned the paper bag might rip apart, I hold it up with my left-hand underneath. Henri takes the bag from me. He removes the coffee cups and set them on a nearby bench. He then pulls out a doughnut and bites off a coffee-soaked portion. After swallowing it, he passes the bag to Gus, who does the same thing. Neither of them say anything about my anger.

I exclaim, "I could have been hurt or your truck could have been damaged! Aren't you going to say anything?"

Henri and Gus look at each other, shrug, and then start smiling. Gus says, "You weren't hurt, and our truck can be replaced. I've been telling Henri for years it's time to scrap that old rig. You would have been doing me a favour. Aren't you going to have a doughnut?"

Henri brings the paper bag and a coffee cup to me. He sits next to me, and after he finishes his doughnut, he says, "You can't deal logically with emotion, Josh. Have a doughnut, then get back outside and load the mixer. Gus and I have to get the mud coat on this room today."

I think about what Henri said. I had not heard anything so profound in my intro-psychology course the previous term at university. I think to myself that working with Henri is going to be rewarding in more ways than one.

As I'm coming out of this reverie, Dieter nods and says, "I see you're starting to fit things together, Josh. I think you know this already, but we AfterLings can read your thoughts. We were there with you when you reminisced about that first week on the job with Gus and Henri. You heard what Henri said about logic and emotion, but hearing it and applying it ..."

Sensing what I am about to say, Ronnie picks up the thread. "When it comes to other people, Josh, you often quote what Henri said. And you apply it to others—just not to yourself."

Dieter adds, "Opening up the past—about Ronnie—is a bit of a Pandora's box for you, Josh. You think you are releasing evils into your world with no way out. You can't see what's in the jar when Pandora closed it."

"I don't remember that anything is left in the jar."

Dieter and Ronnie raise their hands and a large jug appears. They each take a handle, and with his free hand, Ronnie grabs the lid. Dieter motions for me to look inside. Seeing the hesitant look on my face, Ronnie slowly lifts the lid. As he does, I hear soothing music in the background and four letters slowly waft out of the jar:

H ... O ... P ... E

The letters pulsate as they grow from inches to feet in height. Ronnie and Dieter put down the jar and begin dancing under the letters. The soothing music—something you would probably hear at a yoga retreat—fades away and the "Ode to Joy" choral from Beethoven's Ninth Symphony replaces it.

Ronnie and Dieter each grab one of my hands, and we form a circle. They join in the tune with la, la, la, la, la, las and hop and skip to the beat of the song. I am caught up in their ecstasy. We are all in sync with the music and the moment. Tears well up in my eyes.

I can think of few past experiences that elicit so much emotion and feelings of well-being.

We continue singing and dancing, and I see delight and rapture in their faces. When the chorus ends, the music fades to silence, and Ronnie and Dieter let go of my hands and stand facing me. Their expressions are unchanged. Dieter asks, "What do you think, Josh?"

"Right now, I'm not thinking about anything. I'm looking at you two and letting what I see encircle me."

They laugh. Dieter picks up on it and poses as Henri did whenever he saw a beautiful woman walk by: right hand on his heart, left hand high in the air, palm extended toward the sky, his eyes locked on the woman's behind. Ronnie follows his example and so do I.

In unison we say, "Let what I see encircle me."

I quickly add, "None of the ladies took offence. The way he said it and the pose he struck ... well, I'm sure they were flattered."

"Henri didn't say those words and adopt that stance only when a shapely lady passed by. When we were working on a country home, putting on an exterior finish, for example, high atop the scaffold, facing the morning sun, his trowel in his right hand, hawk full of stucco in the other, he would say the same thing."

Dieter takes off his ranger hat. As if it's a sign, Ronnie reverts to a young boy, wearing a Superboy outfit. He grins up at Dieter, shouts, "Up, up, and away!" and streaks off into the sky. Dieter waves at him, puts on his hat, and motions for me to walk with him. He is silent the entire time. I sense he is with other AfterLings.

We go back to Henri's apartment and sit in his kitchen. This is where Henri spent most of his time with me. The furniture is like what Henri had in Timmins. He never was one for décor.

"Ronnie showed you what he would have looked like had he lived, Josh. He's still a child, happier being Superboy in his AfterLing community than revisiting Earth. Henri just told me what we have left to do isn't something Ronnie can do. Ronnie knows that. His is a child's perspective that won't change."

186

Dieter opens the fridge and pulls out a soft drink. Henri always had plenty of pop and juice on hand. He offers me one and floats it over when I accept.

"I'm not up to what remains either, Josh. I made it through puberty, was engaged and only had one alcoholic parent that Henri helped me deal with. What you now know about AfterL and Henri should get you where Henri wants you to be."

"Where's that?"

"On the other side of your guilt and emptiness. It's still there. You feel responsible for Ronnie's death, and no amount of restored memory is going to change that, or your feelings toward your parents. As Henri's already discovered in the brief time he's been an AfterLing, there's more to it, and he's going to be your guide."

Dieter stands beside the sink and folds his arms. He nods. A letter pops out of the toaster into his hand. He brings it over to me. I take it and begin reading. I recognize it as Henri's distinct hand.

Dear Josh,

Early on, I discovered I could only drink so much, which is why you never saw me drunk. It was easy for me to enjoy beer and wine. I knew when to stop. So did my parents and their friends. The fact that we were poor farmers who lived off the land further limited our intake. Until my late teens, I had never seen anyone intoxicated.

That all changed in May 1940 when the Germans invaded Belgium and King Leopold surrendered less than three weeks later. I was two months shy of my nineteenth birthday. Along with thousands of others in Europe, I was shipped off to Germany to work in a munition's factory. That was where I saw drunkards for the first time.

I understand now, having spent years with Dieter, your family, and others, and the myriad experiences and memories merged into my AfterLing identity:

Your parents never meant you any harm.

I read on:

Your parents were like many others, Josh. They spent their early years on farms and were lured from rural to urban areas by the promise of good jobs and a regular paycheque. What they didn't fully appreciate, until it was too late, was the sacrifice required. They gave up their family ties, several generations living close together: cousins, aunts and uncles, brothers and sisters, nieces and nephews, parents, and grandparents. They didn't realize it, but they gave up those bonds for bondage. They became captives to time clocks, schedules, and rules and processes they had no hand in creating or changing. Value was measured in dollars, by the hour.

They left behind their network of friends and relatives on the farms and in nearby villages. That network came with many benefits: a sense of belonging, being cared for, feeling loved, being part of a community that valued each other's ideas, opinions, and abilities. There was a healthy balance between independence and interdependence.

Your parents were products of their time and place.

I feel Dieter's hand on my arm and look at him. He sees I'm puzzled and says, "Henri understood, Josh."

"Is he saying Mom and Dad were victims of circumstance? I find that hard to accept."

"Henri was very clear in what he told me to say. He said he understood." Dieter cocks his head, nods, then adds, "He didn't say he agreed."

I reflect on this. "I guess that's what made him Henri. He wasn't one to criticize people. From what you've shown me so far, he was a man of action, doing what needed to be done. He didn't bear grudges; he did what he thought was right."

"Remember what he said to you at your mom's funeral when you were at the cemetery? He said he wanted to be buried upside down—"

I grin and interrupt him. "Yes, yes, I do." He joins me in finishing Henri's sentence,

"So the world can kiss my ass!"

"You know why Henri asked me to share that memory?"

"I'm sure he told you, but let me guess. It was typical of how Henri behaved in emotional situations. He would make light of them. There we were in a cemetery, surrounded by headstones and grieving people, and he's cracking jokes. If I didn't know him as well as I did, I might have been offended. Come to think of it, if he didn't know me as well as he did, he wouldn't have said it."

I look over at Dieter, and after nodding, he adds, "That's part of it. There's more, which you included in the eulogy you wrote for Henri's memorial service. Paul had to read it because you were in hospital. I'd like you to read it to me. Paul did an okay job at the service, but he didn't say it as well as I know you can."

Dieter hands me three sheets of paper.

I begin reading.

Thank you, Reverend Lockhart. And thank you all, friends and family, for being here today where we've gathered to say farewell to a very good, very dear, memorable, unique man and friend: Henri Deault.

Who would dispute—who would dare dispute—that he was a good and dear and memorable friend and more ... much more? Many, if not most of us in this room, would and rightfully should take issue with the description of Henri as simply a friend. Because the truth, the honest, deep-down-in-the-heart truth of the matter is that, and will always be that, despite his passing, Henri touched us more deeply, more closely than any mere friend could. Because Henri didn't treat us as friends. He welcomed us all and made us members of his personal family. And many of us are better people today for the unselfish, giving attitude that made Henri the special man he was.

So we are not here to mourn the passing of a good friend. We are here saddened by the fact that we have truly lost a member of our family—a loss as close, and as personal as the loss of a brother, father, or grandfather. Henri had a special relationship with us, and no doubt with many who moved away from our community. Seeing how many people are here today, it's obvious how many lives he touched. How can that be? Wasn't he just an old man, quietly living out his time in a little apartment in a little house in a little village, looking after a laundromat in his final years to make ends meet? No one here today thinks that. Everyone here today is here because of who and what Henri was and not what he appeared to be or how he looked.

Henri did not live in a big house at the top of a hill on a treelined drive. He didn't have a big car or smoke fine Cuban cigars, or take winter vacations. He didn't run for office or join committees or do things to merit getting his picture in a newspaper or his life story on television. But he did a lot of things for a lot of people, over a long time, that many of us will never, ever forget.

Anyone who knew Henri when he was younger would agree he was an unforgettable, larger-than-life character. He had a big heart, a unique laugh, an accent that some people simply could not understand, and a complete and utter disregard for what others thought of him. He was a man's man, who worked hard, lived hard, and for many years, exhaled more smoke than the stacks in steel mills.

Henri told me that, by his own standards, he lived well. Can anyone here ever remember him saying he was worried about anything? Can anyone remember him being ill or down in the dumps? I don't. He was one of the most positive thinking people I have ever met, if not the most, and as I said earlier, he didn't care two hoots what others thought of him or his lifestyle or his appearance. He was what he was, and if it was good enough for him, then it just had to be good enough for everyone else.

Could you imagine trying to change Henri in any way? Okay, maybe you could imagine trying, but could you ever imagine succeeding? Henri was Henri, and anyone who avoided him because of how he looked or how he talked or how he lived ... well, that person probably wasn't worthy of his time anyway. And the loss was not his. It was theirs. Because underneath that plaster dust, inside that squat frame, and behind that distinct and unusual face was a good mind, a golden heart, and an unsinkable spirit.

Would that there were more people like Henri in this world? ... Because the world is poorer by one very good man since he left us.

We know little of his life before he made his home among us. He seldom talked about it, and if he did, it was a few words at best. He had closed the door to his past when he moved here, and no amount of probing would make him re-open it. But if his past was mysterious, there was nothing cloaked about his life here in Bond's Hill ... for his door was always open and anyone could enter and see Henri for what he was. Not what he had been or why he was who he was.

Henri never professed to be a romantic or sentimental man. In fact, I remember what he used to say about relationships. He'd describe some particularly nasty separation involving kids and neglect or physical abuse. Then he'd roll his eyes and say, "And that's love?!?!" But he didn't fool any of us who knew him well. Somewhere along the path, Henri decided he was going to dedicate his life, his passion, his earnings to making this world just a wee bit of a better place. Especially for children who were hungry, needy, or in want of a safe shelter, whether it was for days, weeks, months, or years.

Henri's generosity, his willingness to help, wasn't limited to children. If Henri knew someone needed a ride to work or wherever, he'd drive him or her. If he knew someone was down on their luck, he'd take them in. Not only would he take them in but he'd feed them, offer them a job, or help them find one, give them money, and give up his own bed if he had to.

Henri would tell you he wasn't a religious man—and he would tell you exactly how he felt about religion, just as he would tell you how he felt about politics, government, the legal system, marriage, medical care, or anything else he'd read about or seen on television. He was very opinion-ated, and it didn't take much to get him going, but it was all talk. As Paul said when he called to tell me that Henri had passed, Henri had a heart the size of this town, and he gave of himself willingly, without strings.

Henri may not have been a religious man, and he was certainly an irreverent man, who marched to his own drum. To get his respect, you had to earn it. He tolerated no man or woman who tried to save him, change him, or influence him to be anything other than what he was. He never looked down on anyone, but he held his head high, proud of who he was, even if he never, ever boasted about his good deeds.

Henri never turned his back on any one in need. The only thing we think he turned his back on was his past, because he never talked about it—wouldn't talk about it, even to a nosy person like me. All Henri ever said was that he came from Belgium, still had some family there, and as far as the war went, it wasn't the German soldiers who were cruel; it was the Gestapo that committed all the atrocities.

So Henri, your past, about forty years of it, remains a mystery, and we'll bury you with those secrets. But we will not gloss over your life here; it was too important to let it go with you, too important to those of us who learned from you, by your example. You left us with some lessons and some great memories, and it is those I will share today.

I think Lesson One from the Henri Deault Book of Life was: be bold! Some examples I can think of:

- *One summer, I worked for Henri. It didn't matter where we were working, Henri liked to have a beer or two, and if he could get the customer to supply it, so much the better. When we started a new job, he would very casually say to the homeowner, "Got any beer?" If they said, "Yes," then he'd say something like, "Good, I'll have one at break time and at lunch!" If they said, "No!" or sounded offended, he'd say, "Fine, I'll bring my own." Then he'd say to me, "That one is a poor sport, no sense of humour."*

- *My sister Annie used to drive Henri to the local barn dance every Saturday night, and she didn't even have her learner's permit when this started. Fortunately, she had one when a policeman pulled them over one night after the dance. What had Annie's heart racing was that Henri had a bottle of beer in his hand! Annie told me, "I was a nervous seventeen-year-old. I was almost in a panic. But Henri, well, he just folded his arms so the beer was hidden and sat there cool as a cucumber."*

Lesson Two, and equally important, was "have fun." And Henri excelled at this:

- *He was a practical joker and especially liked to play tricks on those who were just a little too full of themselves. For instance, he worked on a job with one carpenter who never stopped talking about all the big fish he caught on the weekends. So, one Friday, Henri decided he'd had enough of this guy's boasting. Henri bought some condoms and slipped them into the guy's lunch pail before quitting time. I can only tell you that, after the guy's wife opened his lunch pail that night, there was no fishing that weekend and probably little of anything else!*

- *Another time, Henri hired a labourer, but quickly discovered the young man worked at a snail's pace and took long and frequent breaks. Any of you who know anything about Henri or plastering, know he was a hard worker in a demanding profession. So he nailed this guy's lunch pail to a bench one day before quitting time. The guy never came back to work after that.*

Lesson Three, and the last and most important lesson I will cite from Henri's Book of Life—the lesson that fills most of its pages—is this: others before self.

- *Henri was a father figure for most of the children in Bond's Hill. Not only did he treat our family like relatives, but every child who was underprivileged was welcome at his home. If you needed a ride anywhere, he would always be there regardless of the weather or the time. He was a babysitter, a big brother, and often the man who set some of the children on the straight and narrow. This man, who seemed to be without a lot of life's material assets, was rich in gifts he gave, such as patience and understanding. Henri didn't ask for anything in return, only that you grow up with respect for your fellow man and respect for their property. The fond memories we have of Henri will stay with us till the end. He taught us that it's okay to laugh and forget about life's little ups and downs.*

Henri's golden rule of others before self was rock solid, non-negotiable, cast in stone. He was an unselfish guardian and friend. Only three things made him angry: injustice, laziness, and pity. Henri never ever wanted or accepted anything from anybody, and he would never let anyone down. As Paul said to me, "It would kill Henri to think he had failed someone in need."

Henri's golden rule of others before self meant his house was seldom empty. He'd be first up in the morning to feed you and pack you a lunch for school or work. All the while, he'd make small talk, ending always with a laugh, on a note of optimism and hope. On Saturday nights in the summer, he'd gather all those who wanted to go and take them to a drive-in movie. On Sunday nights, it would be to a restaurant. If all was quiet, no one to look after, then—and only then—would Henri go out on the town.

Well, Henri was here for a long time ... and I thank God for making his life full and ours richer from knowing him. I think Henri also had a lot of good times and many of us are the better for sharing them with him. I'm glad—so very glad—that he had eighty years to enjoy life and share that unshakeable love of life with us.

So how do we close the book on such a man? Well ... we don't. We may have come here to pay our last respects, but at the same time, we're here to light a torch to a life that lives on through us. Through our feelings, our sorrow, and our love, he remains with us forever.

As we leave today, I encourage all of you to recall a treasured moment with this earthy, outspoken, selfless, carefree man, who many of us knew fondly as "Old Henri." Think about his gentleness, his thoughtfulness, *and his contribution to your life. In this way, we preserve his memory and ensure he lives on both in this world and the next.*

May his infectious enthusiasm for life live on in us all!

Dieter smiles and gives me a hug. "Henri is glad you wrote that, Josh. You couldn't read it at his memorial service. You didn't see Paul give a copy of it to the funeral director, Mr. Dewer. It was put in Henri's coffin, along with the pictures that were in Henri's apartment."

"So, Paul must have known how important they were to Henri."

"Not really. When Paul came to Henri's apartment, you had one picture in your hand. I was there, too. I planted the thought in Paul's mind."

"Thank you, Dieter. I'll bet Henri asked you to do that. What about the picture that Henri had with him in the hospice? Where did it go?"

"It's at your house. Paul gave it to Jackie. When this is all over, you'll know why." A bell rings and Dieter nods his head. "Time for me to go. Josh. We'll have eternity to get to know each other better. I'm going to leave you with Henri. It's been a pleasure. Henri had a way of finding people who benefited from knowing him, and I'm glad he managed to find a way to bring us together." He gives me a big hug, transforms into a Canada goose, and disappears.

Bars from "Ode to Joy" startle me with their loudness. Henri pops out of nowhere. For just a few seconds, he's an older man. His belly sticks out over his belt buckle and the words "Molson Canadian" appear in a tattoo around his navel. His stomach pulsates to the beat of the music. When it ends, Henri reverts to the younger body he had shortly after his arrival in Timmins. A Champagne glass pops into his hand, half full. Another hovers in front of me. I grab it. Before I can say anything, Henri proposes a toast: "To AfterL and its amenities!" I join him in the toast, but before I can say anything more, the glasses disappear and Henri has me in a bear hug, hopping around the room, laughing, and lifting me off the ground, saying joyfully. "This sure beats our time in the hospice."

When he lets go, I have to wipe tears from my cheeks and catch my breath. It's as if a heavy iron door in my chest is creaking open. I can hear hinges break free of rust, and see two hands slowly emerge.

"I see them too, Josh. They're your hands. Before we're through the door will be gone and you'll be released, totally free." Henri opens his arms and embraces me. "How's it feel?"

"Great and unusual, Henri. It's like I'm getting a tune-up and transfusion at the same time. I'm tingling and my sense of self is changing. Ronnie and Dieter made me feel this way, too. There's a bond unlike anything I've felt before. I'm not alone. I feel like you're all a part of me. I'm glad you came back." I tighten our embrace.

"Me, too. I didn't know it could be done but thanks to Ronnie and Dieter, here I am." He slowly releases me and guides me to the window, his arm around my shoulder. It's late afternoon and I can see long shadows being cast in the parking lot beside The Sacred Heart of Jesus Church. "When I lived here after Dieter moved in with me, we used to go to that church with his mother, Annie. Despite Father Magloire, thanks to Mémère Camille I still had some affinity with religion. Like my grandmother, I share my beliefs with few others and don't accept a vengeful God." Henri moves away from the window and closes the blinds. He motions for me to sit down. He turns a chair backwards and sits on it, his arms resting on the back rest.

I interject. "It seems Camille knew some things about AfterL."

"Dieter told you AfterLings have been trying to communicate with humans for centuries. Mémère is one of many who learned some of its attributes but filtered them through their own beliefs. I won't be surprised if you do the same when this is over. You've travelled the universe, and met my family. Even better, you know what to look forward to. All thanks to three spirits."

"Well, it isn't what I signed up for. You coulda told me what I wanted to know years ago when we were both alive. Why didn't you?"

Henri sighs. A slogan I'd seen before appears outside the window: "There is no future in the past but it often explains the present."

"I carried a heavy load for years, Josh. Not anymore. Shortly after my death, while my community was forming, all the crap causing my earthly silence vanished. Dieter told you the same thing happened to him. In my case, well ... I thought I'd send this to you via Dieter. Something I think you knew but never said. It was new to Dieter, too."

"Yes, we didn't talk about it much, and I haven't had any time to really think about it. Dieter was so busy telling me about AfterL, and you kept making brief appearances, interrupting him, and distracting me."

"Distractions and interruptions? No, they were a key part of my transformation."

"So, why didn't you or Dieter just say that?"

"AfterLings can't see around corners or into the future, Josh. We can pile up an incredible number of memories and experiences, but we don't exist in any kind of perfect paradise. Our communities— Dieter's, Ronnie's, mine—are on a unique journey. What we're doing's never been tried before, and it's kinda exciting."

"So you say you learn as you go?"

"Yep, we're explorers, and so far our only missing talent is foresight. Like earthlings, we can guess about results from our actions but that's all we can do, speculate. What we do know is that we can do no harm. That in itself is a real heady notion, quite intoxicating."

"Sounds like you're enjoying AfterL."

"What's not to enjoy?"

"Dieter didn't really go into a lot of detail. He said he became part of a group of twelve and twelve is a heavy duty number."

"You don't really need to know more now. All will be revealed. For the moment just accept that many of the things humans think are important are human distractions, male or female, sexy or celibate, old or young, popular or recluse. Irrelevant here. Dieter told you that those are earthly things, necessary there but part of the problem. Of course, I have memories of my earthly experiences and relationships; physical, emotional, spiritual, social—positive ones only. All the other stuff that stopped me from sharing my past? Poof, it disappeared when Atlas Released formed."

"Dieter said you were shaking things up in AfterL."

"AfterLings have been communicating with humans since Neanderthals disappeared 50,000 years ago."

"Is that when AfterL formed?"

"Good question, Josh, but remember what Dieter told you about language; it limits what earthlings can understand. The short answer is that AfterL's earliest community has been around forever."

"Okay, you're making my head spin. Physics isn't my thing. When I get back home, I'll just tell Jackie there are mysteries beyond human ken."

"Einstein and Steven Hawking couldn't reconcile the contradictions. Philosophers and theologians haven't done any better. They can't. We just wanted you to know that's okay. The world you know sucks."

Henri laughs and points to the ceiling. A brilliant rainbow appears. Atop the apex, I see the characters from *The Wizard of Oz* and hear Dorothy singing *Over the Rainbow*. When she gets to the part of the song where the words, "*why can't I?*" are sung, they appear in an arc; three flashing question marks end the phrase, the song, and the light show. In their place, beer mugs with the Molson logo appear.

One floats into my hand, the other to Henri's. He grabs its handle, takes a mouthful, swallows, and continues. "There are some things about being a human that are worth keeping. Dieter said life is not linear, Josh. Neither is AfterL. AfterLing communities don't ascend some kind of spiral staircase with evenly spaced steps to a static plane of enlightenment. We grow in leaps and bounds and can be on several different levels at once. It's hard for you, or any earthling, to grasp."

"I think I get most of it, Henri. A lot of it has to do with the soul; that's what survives."

"Perish the thought! Soul, spirit, essence, psyche ... they're all tied up in the notion of 'me,' a sense of self. One of the first things an AfterLing community realizes is how limiting the concept of 'me' is."

Henri transforms himself into Atlas with a giant replica of Earth on his back. He spins around three times, and on his last twirl, the Earth swirls off into space, travelling at the speed of light. Grinning, Henri reverts to the body I'm used to and exclaims, "Atlas Released!" and then holds up the placard I've seen before, with one change:

No us and them—only WE

On an endless journey

The banner rises to the ceiling then disappears.

Before I can acknowledge, Henri has us back on his family farm in Belgium, outside the shed. A freshly lit cigarette pops into the air. Henri takes a long drag. While he's exhaling, he walks away from the shed, sits on a large rock beside one of the fence rails near the pig pen, and motions for me to join him. Seeing there is no place for me to sit, Henri conjures up another rock for me and an upended packing crate for us to rest our beer mugs.

When I get close to him, the smell of pig muck makes me hesitate. Henri rolls his eyes, mutters, "City boy," waves his cigarette, and the pig-shit pit turns into a bed of clover, its sweet, pleasant smell quickly dispelling the poop odour. Once I'm sitting, Henri puts down his beer mug and holds up a picture of Atlas with the heavens on his shoulders. He points to Atlas and says, "In some ways that's you and me for most of our lives. We weren't holding up the sky, but we were carrying lot of shit we couldn't release. That was the first thing to go when I got to AfterL. If all goes well your burden will disappear sooner."

∞

A dawning sun appears, and the picture vanishes. Henri stands and motions for me to follow him into the farmhouse, walking through the walls. He goes into the pantry and takes an apron and chef's hat from hooks on the wall. After putting them on, he points to a wooden chair in the kitchen and I sit down, facing him next to the wood stove.

I remember coming to Henri's house in Bond's Hill on the weekends when I was in my late teens, after my mother died and several of my brothers had moved in with him. Often, there would be other children and sometimes a man or woman sitting at the table, waiting for Henri to serve up sausages, bacon, eggs, toast, pancakes, milk, and coffee. Invariably there would be a cigarette in his hand, a plasterer's cap on his head, and a white T-shirt underneath his apron.

Reading my thoughts, Henri magically covers the table with mugs, plates, and cutlery. A coffee urn, butter, and maple syrup in a glass serving jar appear on the table. "I enjoy cooking too much to have everything ready, Josh. Help yourself to the coffee, while I make some breakfast."

As the bacon and sausages cook in the frying pan, Henri stands next to the porcelain sink beside the stove and expands on his earlier comment. "A priest, a young woman, the war, and Dieter's death made me the man you knew and described so well in my eulogy. Of course you couldn't expand on my past because I buried it. Ronnie and Dieter exposed you to many experiences and memories you suppressed. That's what we had in common and wouldn't discuss. For both of us it began at an age when there was no one to help us understand or overcome so we never let go. It was always there. What we learned was that men don't talk about such things."

"I remember Dieter saying I was shut tighter than a nun's knees. None of the psychology courses, counselling or group-therapy sessions made a difference. If anything, they made things worse because talking about them just reopened the wounds and in some cases brought back memories I'd completely buried."

"Like your puberty experiences."

"Yes, thank God I was never physically harmed but the emotional scars and lack of trust ..."

"Don't tell me; I see the scene with the psychologist when he was giving you his assessment. You were about twenty-five at the time. He said, based on the tests, you were a 'cautious lover.'"

I laugh and reply, "Yes but like you I never gave up on love. It's just that we looked for it in different places."

Henri winks and goes back to the stove to turn the bacon and sausages. He puts another pan on the stove, and four eggs appear on a plate beside him. I take a mouthful of coffee, and before I can ask, a pitcher of orange juice and two glasses appear on the table. Henri fills the glasses, sits his on the counter and resumes. "If only we'd known. Life and love are so different in AfterL."

I sip my orange juice and watch Henri. A hunk of butter goes into the frypan and he swirls it to cover the surface. With his other hand, he cracks an egg and plops in yolk and white, losing nothing.

"Sunny side up and over easy for you, Josh, right?"

I nod. Seeing Henri in one of his elements comforts me. Caregiver, plasterer, chef, I feel privileged to have known this man, and now I have the chance to peer behind the veil to his past and new life.

"Tell me more about AfterL, Henri. Dieter said there were some things you had to do before you could join me."

"Breakfast is ready. Let me sit down, and I'll tell you why entering AfterL is rather exciting."

Carrying our plates to the table, Henri sets them down, removes his apron and cap, and sits opposite me. I note there is no bread. Henri points to a spot beside me and out of nowhere a plate full of toast appears, already buttered. Henri smiles, and then between bites of bacon, eggs, and sausage, and sips of his juice and coffee, he tells me about his first experiences in AfterL.

"Dieter already told you, as part of the welcoming ceremony, everyone becomes part of a community, based on sex, age, and cause of death. Our first task is to toss aside our collective traumas and decide on a name."

"Well, he told me some of that, but not those specifics."

"Mm, easy to understand. I'm a new arrival. He's been here forty years. Still, a lot of the things he and Ronnie did with you tie to AfterL welcoming activities: rides, flights, taking on other identities, living their dreams. Some of the things out in the yard just now, they tie to trauma-tossing too."

Henri snaps his fingers, and a projection screen lowers from the ceiling at the end of our table. Curtains lower in the windows and reduce the light in the room. Henri takes a sip of his coffee and lights a cigarette. On the display, the number twelve appears. "There're many different 'ologies' in your world, Josh: theology, biology, anthropology. One I didn't know anything about until I got here was numerology. Look up the number twelve sometime. It helps explain why a dozen souls meld into a unique community shortly after they arrive in AfterL. Boom!"

On the screen I see: "Now it's We, in our first twelve D."

Henri explains. "AfterL is about memories and experiences of twelve people combining. Suddenly, sights I've never seen, places I've never been, sounds I've never heard, encounters I've never had are part of 'me.' Who and what I was transformed—from caterpillar to butterfly. But even the butterfly comparison doesn't work because it's one for one."

"Okay, on the screen, I assume the D is for dodecagon. What I don't get is why I'm only seeing you. Where are the other eleven members of your community?"

Henri finishes his sausage before answering. On the screen, a large forest appears. The trees have white trunks. They look like birch. Henri interjects. "What do you know about aspen trees?"

"Not much."

"What you see when you look at an aspen isn't a single tree with its own roots; underground is where the main life force is. In Utah, there's an aspen forest that's been around for over 80,000 years, all part of one entity! Dieter told me—part of his ranger training. My community is like this aspen forest. What you see is a small part."

The forest fades from the screen. In its place, I see Henri's rendition of his community, a dodecagon with several squares and triangles inside it.

He asks me what I see.

"From back here, it looks more like a circle than a polygon. Besides the twelve triangles on its perimeter, I see three squares. And I just noticed, not one of the triangles is inside any of the boxes. You mentioned numerology a minute ago. Is there some symbology in the shapes on the screen?"

"The only two relevant to our talk are the triangle and the circle. I've explained the triangle. Each one represents one of the humans who bonded with the other eleven. To say anything more would get very esoteric, and only a few AfterL communities get it. The circle, now that's something very related to our discussion."

A coffee percolator and mug appear out of thin air. The percolator fills the mug and floats over to my side of the table. Henri grabs the mug, takes a sip, and gazes at me mischievously. Knowing him as well as I do, it isn't long before I get what he's up to.

I take my mug and hold it up next to the percolator. I get a refill and the percolator disappears along with his Afterling drawing. Carnival sights and sounds tie into the images that begin to fill the screen: rotating roulette wheels, wooden rings thudding onto metal pegs, arrows swooshing then piercing archery targets, dice rolling across craps tables, flippers clanging back and forth in pinball machines.

The display continues until Henri finishes his coffee. Then he gets up from the table and stands beside the screen. The number twelve reappears at the top. Henri asks, "How much trauma trash you carrying around, Josh?"

"Huh, trauma trash? I've never heard that expression before, certainly not from you."

"No, because shit happens. Men get over it. Women get away from it. Simple as that."

"Well, if it were that simple, Henri, I don't think we'd be having this conversation."

"No, probably not. Humour me. How much trauma trash do you carry around?"

Henri looks at the screen and a question mark appears beside the number twelve. Thinking this is meant as a cue, I answer, "Nope, not twelve. Not that many. Ronnie's death, seeing his bloated body in a casket, acute teenage acne, and puberty, watching my grandfather die, dealing with alcoholic parents, being downsized. How many's that?"

"Six. You still feel guilty about Ronnie?"

"Yes, but I've got pleasant memories back from Ronnie. It's just that ..."

Henri nods and a familiar phrase appears on the screen: "You can't deal logically with emotion."

"Your Grandma Camille gave you that, in a letter. She told you not to open it until you left Belgium."

"Oui, and you know how much I learned from that?"

"I think you learned a lot, Henri. I wasn't at your funeral, but Ronnie told me the chapel was packed."

"But I never married or shared my past ... until now."

"I'm beginning to understand. You asked how much trauma I'm carrying. Not much. Even less now. Still, it acts as a wall, always there. I find it hard to relate to people. They even have a term for people like me: Adult Children of Alcoholics*—ACOA."

For a few moments, Henri lets me recall my ACOA meetings and private counselling sessions. He then bangs on the table, points to the screen, and in a calm, compassionate voice says, "ACOA, AA. Those are just two of more than thirty twelve-step programs. By the look on your face, I can tell it didn't work for you, and it's not what happens in AfterL. Pure coincidence that twelve souls meld in each new community. Besides the numerology stuff, the only thing we AfterLings have related to the number twelve back in your world is the number of eggs in a carton and the number at the top of your clocks."

"So, there are some mysteries in AfterL?"

"Of course. Anything we don't know or can't explain is a mystery. But consider this: because we trash our trauma when we enter AfterL, it's moot to think about it once we name our community. It's an earthly thing, totally irrelevant, like tits on a bull. And we have fun doing it."

"Okay, you're gonna tell me that, but what about that phrase up on the screen? How does it fit?"

"You've heard the expression: 'With the possible exception of this one all generalizations are false?'"

"No, I haven't."

"Well, you have now. We'll make sure you take it back with you. Now let me modify the message."

The words on the screen change: "Oil Floats on Water."

Henri snaps his fingers, and three transparent glass beakers appear in front of him. A miniature oil rig materializes above the left beaker. Overtop the right beaker, the Manneken Pis from Belgium briefly appears, gurgling as he relieves himself.

"It's not willy water, Josh. Good old potable water from Brussels."

Henri pours some of the water into the larger beaker in the middle. Next he adds oil. Smoke, steam, sparks, and hissing and sputtering sounds emanate from the jar. I stand up and back away from the table. Henri laughs, and the disturbing sights and sounds end. Once the smoke and steam clear, all I see in the jar is oil the colour of gold, floating and shimmering above the water. I guess what just happened.

"You did that as a joke. Oil and water don't flare up."

"We're not bound by all the rules you are, Josh."

"Well, you scared me."

"A human emotion. Doesn't apply here. Relax. What do you see?"

"There's black oil from the derrick in the beaker on the left. It was black when you poured it in the middle beaker, but after all the commotion and chaos, I see it ended up a golden colour."

"Very observant, Josh. It's like dying and going to AfterL. Your black trauma goes poof, you hook up with eleven other souls, and *voila*, an AfterL community—pure gold! The AfterL universe exists right next to yours, but there is no emulsifier that allows you to mix them and make a nice dressing, like for a Caesar salad."

"So you're floating around the universe?"

"Dieter told you it's hard to describe AfterL to humans. We're in a parallel universe, but the portal only opens to dying people. Which souls combine is one of the mysteries, but it doesn't matter too much."

"Why's that?"

"Because we have eternity to hook up with other communities to exchange knowledge, memories, and experiences. Also as many as 13,000 communities form each day. Plenty of new ones for Atlas Released to hook up to, plus all the ones already here."

The plates, cups, cutlery, and all the beakers, except the middle one, disappear from the table. The middle beaker rises and with a sucking sound it transforms into a two-dimensional object slurped onto the screen. It ends up below the "Oil Floats on Water" banner. Henri takes off his lab coat. Two diving suits with scuba gear, fins, and oxygen tanks appear. Before I have time to ask what he's up to, I find myself fully dressed and swept up in a current that forces me into the beaker on the screen. Around me, water; above me, the golden liquid.

Henri is beside me, also in a diving suit. We don't have an intercom. He talks inside my head. He asks me if I remember the 1966 movie *Fantastic Voyage*. I remember it involved a shrunken submarine being injected into some guy's bloodstream with some people whose mission was to save him. Before I can ask how that is relevant, Henri and I begin shrinking. *"What the hell, Henri, what're you doing? Where are we going?"*

"You're in a beaker of water, and I want you to see AfterL the way Atlas Released can see it. Right now, all you see is that golden liquid above you. When I'm done showing you what Ronnie, Dieter, and I did to contact you, I'll explain trauma-trashing."

We're tiny divers surrounded by whirling and sloshing objects I don't recognize. I freak out and begin flailing and thrashing about.

Henri swims close. His diving mask butts up flush to mine. The glow in his eyes fades. He blinks, and then everything around us disappears. Suddenly Henri has me back in Bond's Hill. I see my comatose body lying in the hospital bed. The ghostly me is out of the diving suit. I'm in a hospital gown, an IV tube taped to my arm. Henri is in a lab coat. He reaches out and puts his hands on my shoulders. I have the same feeling I had in the Belgian farmhouse when he touched me earlier: warmth, and positive, loving energy.

"Ronnie wants me to help him change your life, Josh. That's why I'm here. We don't have to learn about my past or how we made the connection, or about trauma-trashing. Are you ready to go back?"

"I'm sorry, Henri. I felt trapped. Under water, in a diving suit, in a subatomic world. Totally out of my depth, I panicked. No, I don't want to go back, not yet. Please, forgive me. Somehow, being in that beaker reminded me of rolling myself up in a carpet when I was a young boy and then thinking I couldn't get out. For a few seconds, I was terrified, thinking I was going to suffocate and die. It also reminded me of how Ronnie died."

Henri lets me go and waits. His head is tilted as if he's listening to someone whispering in his ear. Jackie and my two sons, Josh Jr. and Jessie, enter the room. Henri switches from lab coat to diving gear. His flippers slapping noisily on the linoleum floor, he quickly shuffles past my family and out through the wall.

I wait, expecting diving gear to replace the gown so I can follow. Nothing happens. Jackie goes to one side of the bed and my sons go to the other. I feel myself being drawn back towards the bed, into my inert body. I feel like an abandoned puppy, alone between worlds with no one to talk to. I sigh, tears well up in my eyes, and I begin swaying back and forth.

Inside my head, I hear Ronnie. "Sorry, Josh, some technical difficulties on our side. Henri and Dieter are taking care of it. Seems you need a break. We slipped some good stuff into your IV tube to relax you. Don't worry. Listen in on the family chat, have a restful night back in your bod. Henri'll be back tomorrow, after you and your brain get some time together. The gauges you're about to see will both be all-green by then. You're in good hands. Love you, bro."

The tone of his voice, the fact that he's still around, reassure me. I feel the bedsheet and pillow against my skin; one more wash and they should both be dumped. I smell soap and ammonia. I can't move, but that doesn't bother me. I see two gauges. The one on the right, all-green, has the word CALM above it. The one on the left, with about a quarter of it in red, is labelled CONNECTED.

An immaterial but spiritual part of me is still off on an ethereal journey with my ghostly guides. Take too much of it away for too long and you risk a disconnect. Henri sent me back for a recharge. Confident and reassured, I accept the hiatus and comatose state my family observe. Although I cannot see anything—the two gauges disappear—I can listen in on my family's conversation.

Josh Jr.: "They didn't shave him today, Mom. He looks kinda scruffy."

Jess: "Maybe they shouldn't shave him. I've always wondered how Dad would look with a beard."

Jackie: "He'd look ratty. I know. He tried growing one when we were dating. I made him shave it off."

Jess: "Well, we know who wears the pants in this family."

Jackie: "Mind your tongue. Josh, help me put your father on his side. Jessie, grab those cushions on the table. Prop one between your father's legs and put the other two behind his back."

Josh Jr.: "Did you hear that, Mom? Dad grunted when you grabbed his arm."

Jackie: "Better than no sounds at all. When he starts talking, I'll feel a lot better."

Jess: "Hey, did you see that twitch? In his elbow?"

Jackie: "No, but I'll tell the nurse about it on our way out. I have a meeting with the doctor tomorrow, and we'll see what he says. So far, your Dad hasn't opened his eyes. When he does, then you two better clean your rooms."

Josh Jr.: "Ah, Mom. Why is Dad such a neat freak?"

Jackie: "Too many years in a messy home. I know he doesn't talk about it, and you two think it's sissy that your Dad does dishes and laundry, but it's part of the reason I love him."

Jess: "Oh Mom, you're not going all mushy on us again?"

Jackie: "I miss him. It's been ten days now. If we're going to help him recover, we have to talk to him. I brought your Dad's notes from when each of you was eight years old. I want each of you to read them to him."

Jess and Josh Jr.: "Okay, Mom."

As soon as Josh Jr. begins reading from my journal, the "Connected" meter reappears. I see a noticeable increase in the amount of green liquid in the tube. Family makes a difference.

The meter slowly dissolves and a full moon appears in its place. A message scrolls underneath it.

"Nightie night, Josh. See you in the morning." Henri's face appears inside the moon. He winks at me and smiles.

I listen to Josh Jr. reading from my journal. Throughout the years when our boys were growing up, I took lots of pictures, videotaped our vacations and celebrations, and kept all their drawings in a cedar chest.

Before their birthday I would review all the memorabilia from the past year and write in my diary, a father's reflections on good times we had, missing from my own childhood. When they were sixteen I gave them each a copy. A lump caught in my throat. Tears welled up in my eyes. I wished I could emerge from my coma and tell them how much I loved them. Jackie and Jess are smiling, enjoying the moment, reliving the good times. I fall asleep.

∞

"Wake up, Josh. Time to go."

It's Henri. Is it time to go to work, another day of mixing mud and carrying a hod? I open my eyes. I'm in a hospital bed. What the ...?

Henri appears at the foot of my bed in a diving suit, his mask on top of his head. It takes a few seconds before I remember that he's in the same garb as the last time I saw him. He explains. "Had to do some Caesar salad work in that beaker you and I were in. Seems getting you that close to AfterL in a teeny, tiny state was a wee bit dangerous. Good thing you asked to skip the demo."

"So, it's a good thing I asked you to get me out of that beaker?"

"Yes, there're still some glitches. When Ronnie and Dieter got to me in the hospice, and we mixed up a mental coma cocktail to knock you out ... we thought we'd broken a barrier. Turns out we were a little further along than Newton and Einstein, but they never believed Harry Houdini pulled off a post-mortem contact with his wife, Bess. They're still skeptical."

"You're in touch with those guys?"

"Not those guys. Their communities. Big difference. Those guys are in communities that normally don't come anywhere near the likes of Atlas Released. I was just a survivor from the war who had an open mind. When they found out we contacted you and were able to mess around with your brain and soul, they got interested."

"All right, I'm intrigued, but do you still need that diving suit?"

"If you want to go back to the beaker, yes. There're some interesting things going on, and you've got nothing to worry about now."

"I think I'll pass. Maybe you should leave well enough alone yourself."

"I'm in AfterL, Josh. No community can do any harm here."

"Well, Henri, I'm still an earthling. Seeing Jackie and the kids just now reminded me why I want to go back, more so since Ronnie came and—"

"Josh, we're on the edge of a great breakthrough."

"Are you sure it's a breakthrough, Henri? You said yourself that the likes of Einstein and Newton have their doubts."

"They have questions and concerns no one in AfterL or on Earth has been able to answer or resolve. Remember what Pope John Paul II said at the Vatican Conference on Cosmology in July 1985?"

"No."

Henri's diving suit disappears. He's back in a plaid shirt, dungarees, and plasterer's cap, its peak raised. A folded sheet of paper materializes in front of him. He holds it out for me. I take it. A lit cigarette shows up in the corner of his mouth. I open the article. One sentence has been highlighted.

The more we know about physical reality, about the history and structure of the universe, about the fundamental makeup of matter and the processes and patterns which [are] at the roots of the material world, the more we can appreciate the immensity of the mystery of God, the more we are in a position to grasp the mystery of ourselves—our origin and our destiny.

"So the Catholic Church changed its position; instead of refusing to embrace science, it was trying to use science to support theology?"

Henri takes a puff of his cigarette. The smoke he exhales forms into the word "Bingo!" The look on his face tells me he's excited and deeply committed to telling me more. He goes on. "I can imagine what's going to happen when Pope John Paul II gets here and his community meets up with physicist and theologian communities for a chinwag. I gotta feeling they'll want to know what we've been doing."

"Henri, you're into things I never heard you talk about when you were alive. What's going on?"

"A nine-year-old boy is what's going on, Josh. Ronnie's innocence led to my interest. When I was alive, I thought religion was hooey; Father Magloire, Mémère Camille, the war ... other stuff. Being here, a lot has changed. It does for everyone. The 'mystery of God ... the mystery of ourselves' takes on a whole new dimension. Ronnie put Dieter and me onto something theologians and physicists missed."

"What's that?"

"Life, as earthlings know it, is like a womb, a place with all they need to survive while they're there. Once they're born, all that changes. It's the same in AfterL."

"I think I understand. It's a whole different milieu. In the womb, without the umbilical cord, a fetus would not survive. In AfterL, the gestation period sounds like it's shorter. It's the time required for a community to name itself and trash the trauma that marks its birth."

"Yes, then AfterL provides forever the conditions necessary for growth emotionally, spiritually, socially, and intellectually. Life is just a way station, a place to acquire sight, hearing, feeling, taste, smell—the things the brain needs to store memories and experiences sufficient for a community to form here."

"Okay, Henri, what you're telling me is that humans are inside a body. One body, one mind, one lifetime. In AfterL, no bodies, no death, a fusion of twelve minds into a community with endless possibilities to hook up with other communities. Body and brain, corporal stuff, are abandoned and sense of self takes on a whole different meaning."

"And sense of God too."

Henri finishes his cigarette. He flicks its short stub into the air, where it vanishes.

It prompts me to ask. "You're smoking, and Dieter enjoyed a few beers with me at the Château Frontenac. You must miss earthly pleasures."

"Miss them? I can smoke anytime, sip on a beer. What's there to miss? And nothing is bad for my health. Remember, you're seeing the Henri you knew, doing things you remember. I can only give you an inkling of Atlas Released. Until you become part of a community, there's no way I can give you an appreciation of its identity—its connectivity and potential."

A nurse comes into the room. She checks my IV, replaces my urine bag, pinches my thumb—no reaction. Despite the time I've been out of my body, I'm still having difficulty accepting the separation.

Henri moves to the window. The blinds open. He looks outside, raises his arms, and shouts out one of his favourite expressions. "Let what I see encircle me." He goes to the nurse's side, acquiring medical scrubs, a stethoscope, and an ophthalmoscope along the way. He sits on the edge of the bed, then flings the medical instruments into the air. They disappear. "No need for health checks in AfterL, Josh. Physicians, theologians, physicists, they all missed the mark. For them, it's all about saving a life, having a God, finding the indivisible building block of the universe. Fine on their side of the lifeline, not applicable where I am."

"I remember one of my books from university days. The author was a guy named Thomas Kuhn. The book was *The Structure of Scientific Revolutions*. He talked about paradigm shifts. That's what you're talking about. Ronnie and Dieter put you on to something that no one else saw. They were blinded by their own concepts of reality."

"Understandable given their experience and context. Still, what scientists know from the world of the very small is a clue. It's the octet rule."

"How do you know this?"

"'Because when I was still alive, in the hospice, I asked a question of Dieter's community, The Magnificent Mind: How could they make contact with you?"

I'm still in a hospital gown. Seeing Henri sitting beside my tubed body in a doctor's cloak feels strange. Sensing my discomfort, he whisks me away to the second beach in Bond's Hill, where I spent many a day watching the waves, listening to the gentle rhythmic wash of the sand and pebbles along the shore. I'm barefoot, wearing sandals, blue jeans, and a hooded pullover.

Henri's wearing a sailor's cap and striped shirt. He has tattoos on his arms: an anchor on one forearm; a dodecagon on the other. He holds them out, making sure I notice. "Like Dieter told you, in AfterL we can take on pretty much any physical shape we want to. Are you comfortable?"

There is a log about twenty feet from the shoreline. I sit before answering. "Yes, but you're losing me. I don't see the connections: anchors, dodecagons, sailors ..."

"What did I say when I opened the shades?"

"Let what I see encircle me."

"Uh huh, fitting eh?" Henri points to the tattoo. It's the one he showed me in Belgium, with the twelve triangles.

"Ahh, not only are you encircled, but you're also part of the circle. Now how do the anchor and sailor's suit fit in?"

"Until sailors circumnavigated the world, there were still people who thought the Earth was flat, even though a Greek scholar, Eratosthenes, proved it was circular 2,000 years ago. As for the anchor, besides the nautical relevance, it symbolizes hope and the soul."

"Circles and symbols, science and religion. You make it sound like they have some common threads tying them together."

"They do, Josh and here in AfterL we get that."

"Up to a point. You had to reconnect me with my body yesterday."

Henri ambles to the shore, arms folded in front of him. He has his back to me. I stand and go to his side. Hearing me approach, he turns and the dodecagon tattoo on his arm lifts off, expands to the size of a beach ball and hovers in front of us. As it moves forward, Henri follows it and motions for me to do the same.

"I got caught up in our success, Josh. Ronnie, Dieter, and I thought we'd made a great breakthrough. Maybe I can't take you back to that beaker. Perhaps the mind–brain connection has a link that can only be severed at time of death and prevents lengthy visits to the sub-atomic world."

"You got me back and I say we leave well enough alone, Henri."

"I won't make any promises, Josh. Now that we've made the connection, we might be able to visit you in your dreams and get back to the octet rule and everything else I'm learning about AfterL."

"Dieter already said no one is going to believe me."

"Some people will, Josh. As Dieter also said, it's up to you to decide what to do with what we've given you. If people want more, we'll know. Don't be surprised if we show up in your dreams."

"So, when I come out of my coma and tell Jackie about my time with you, what do I say?"

"Dieter already covered that; AfterL is inexplicable to a human trapped in a body in a universe dependent on the Big Bang theory."

"Alright, Henri. Dieter told me I'd be in a coma for two weeks. We've got another three or four days before you send me back. What's next?"

The dodecagon ascends skyward, pulsating to the beat of Beethoven's Ninth Symphony. It soars towards the sun and for a second or two, it looks like it is being absorbed into the sun. Transfixed, I keep watching as it starts expanding, behind the sun. Ten seconds later, it dominates the sky, hurtling lightning bolts back towards the Earth and off into the cosmos. Every conceivable lightning pattern is part of the display: bead, ball, blue jet, forked, dry, heat, red sprite ....

Suddenly, without any transition, we're back in the Deault family kitchen in Belgium. A banner with the words "Trauma-Trashing Tools" is behind Henri, now a young man in his mid-twenties. He

215

holds up a mirror. I'm also in my mid-twenties, standing by the table. Henri smiles. "Trauma can get you at any age, but you and me, we both had the damage done by the time we were twenty-five. Here, have an Affligem."

A frosted mug full of Belgian beer is on the table. I pick it up. Henri already has a mug in his hand. "*A votre santé*—to your health!" After swallowing a mouthful and releasing a hearty belch, Henri sits opposite me. Three roll-your-own cigarettes appear on the table in front of him. He picks each of them up, then sets them back down, making sure I'm watching. "I asked you earlier how much trauma trash you were carrying. You gave me six examples: Ronnie's death, seeing his bloated body in a casket, puberty and teenage acne, watching your grandfather die, dealing with alcoholic parents, being downsized. That's three related to death; three related to living."

"Is that why you have three cigarettes on the table?"

Henri nods, then takes another swallow of beer before he picks up one of the cigarettes. He lights it, takes a puff. The smoke he exhales turns into a cameo of Ronnie, smiling. "Any trauma left related to Ronnie?"

"No, he, you, and Dieter ... you took care of that."

"How?"

"You replaced it with good memories, made me recall the good times by revisiting them with Ronnie."

"What about the trauma related to your grandfather's death?"

"Now that I know he's in AfterL, not a problem."

"No more death-related trauma?"

"No, it's gone."

Henri snaps his fingers, and two cigarettes on the table move away from the third one.

"No more guilty feelings about Ronnie, right?"

When Henri says his name, images of playing cowboys and indians, celebrating Christmas, and playing hockey swirl around in my head.

Tears of joy, and the sounds of our shared laughs make me smile. I'm almost giddy. I give Henri a big hug.

He picks up one of the cigarettes. It grows a wick on one end and a cone-shaped top at the other. Henri lights the wick. To a whooshing sound, it streaks off toward the ceiling where it explodes, releasing multi-coloured streamers like the ones you see at a Grey Cup parade. After the streamers fall to the floor, they attach to each other, forming a three-foot-long banner that displays the words: "I wasn't on Earth for a long time, Josh, but I had a good time."

Inside my head, I can hear Ronnie saying those words as I read them. A lump forms in my throat. The banner slowly dissolves, and Henri holds up the second roll-your-own. He taps it with his index finger. With each tap, it expands until it's the size of a fence post. Henri stands it near the stove, close to the Trauma-Trashing Tool banner. He sits beside me on the bench and takes another sip of beer. After he sets his glass down, he gets up, straddles the bench, and puts his hands on my shoulders. "The traumatic examples you gave me, Josh ... A lot of them were based on incidents or events that took place over weeks, months, or sometimes years."

"Yes."

Before I can say any more, the banner folds itself around the post Henri formed—to the sound of a chain on a steel winch. When the pulley sound ends, Henri looks into my eyes and moves his right arm to the back of my head. "That post against the wall, that represents your biggest remaining trauma, Josh."

"Mom and Dad."

Henri nods.

Out of nowhere comes the memory of a late-night conversation with my parents after they return from the hotel late. I'm thirteen, left alone again with three siblings, two of them below the age of two. It's a weeknight. I have to get up early to catch the bus to the Catholic school I'm enrolled in. I'm in bed but can't sleep. I hear my parents stumble through the side door, close to the stairwell. I come down-stairs. They're now in the living room on the couch, laughing, hugging, and kissing. They pay no attention to me. I run into the living room sobbing, shouting, crying, "Why did you have children?"

They don't answer. The glaze in their eyes tells me they're drunk.

Henri gently applies pressure to my shoulder. After giving me a minute to recover, he picks up the post formed from the banner pole and sets it on the table. "That recollection, it's just one of hundreds you're carrying around. Maybe you'll still be carrying them when you wake up, but I'm going to show you how we deal with trauma in AfterL."

Henri stands up. Along the outside wall, a giant wood-turning lathe appears. Henri picks up the post and removes the Trauma-Trashing Tool banner. He places the banner above the lathe and then sets the post inside the lathe's head and tail stocks.

After tightening the hand wheels, Henri smiles and returns to my side. "Okay, Josh, now we get to have some fun. One of the things you enjoyed as a young man was eight-ball pool, right?"

"Yes, but I was never good at it."

Henri shrugs, and the kitchen table turns into an empty pool table. The post in the lathe begins turning and transforms into a pool cue. When it's finished, Henri grabs it. He twirls it in his hands and then holds it towards me. After I grasp it, Henri transforms into a ringmas-ter; his top hat is at least a foot high, his bow tie and jacket are royal purple. His shirt and gloves are white and his pants black. A cue ball appears in his hand. He wipes it with a cleaning cloth, then hands it to me. The words "Josh's Trauma-Trasher" are imprinted on it. I give Henri a puzzled look. He puts the ball back on the table and hands me a solid-yellow billiard ball. I expect to see the number one in black ink, inside a small white circle. Instead there's a question mark.

"What's your biggest remaining trauma, Josh?"

"I told you: my alcoholic parents."

"This went on for many years, and what you have are a lot of horrific memories that made you an ACOA. Shame, an overdeveloped sense of responsibility, living life as a victim ... all the classic signs. You were the oldest and took care of your sister and brothers. You cleaned up before they got out of bed, so they didn't see what you did. Look inside that ball, where the question mark is. Tell me about the movie clip in there."

It's a familiar sight.

"The family kitchen table is full of beer bottles and unwashed glasses, some with cigarette butts in them. Dirty plates, full ash trays. I come around the corner at the bottom of the stairwell. I'm about six years old. I scrunch my nose, shake my head, gag. It gets worse when I go to the bathroom. The chemical toilet pail is full of urine, floating turds, and tissues. I turn around, go back, put on my winter coat, my mitts, and boots, and go to the outhouse to pee. I'm sobbing."

"Your first traumatic memory as a child?"

I nod. I get why this recollection is inside the ball, and remember why I never invited anyone to our house.

Henri snaps his fingers, drawing me back. "All right, Josh, put the ball on the pool table."

I do as he asks. All the other solid and striped balls that make up a standard rack appear on the table, scattered randomly. I give Henri a questioning look. He smiles, takes off his white gloves, puts his thumb and index finger in his mouth, and lets out a shrill whistle. The door from the pantry opens, and a smiling, balding man in his mid-thirties enters, cue stick in hand.

"Josh, meet Harold Worst, inducted into the Billiard Congress of America Hall of Fame in 1970."

Harold shakes my hand and looks at the handle on my cue stick.

Seeing my raised eyebrows, Henri explains, "You can tell a master by his tools, Josh. That's one of Harold's sticks. The lathe was just for show."

Harold takes the billiards cue from me and balances it on the index and middle fingers of his right hand. Next he places it on the table and rolls it back and forth several times. "If you can't balance it or have it roll smoothly across the felt, Josh, you're beat even before you go near the table. Shooting pool is like most sports, as much mechanical as mental."

Henri chimes in. "Not only sports, crafts and trades too. I may have had an old, beat-up truck and mixer, but my plastering tools were always clean and well-maintained."

Harold nods and then puts the cue on the table and snaps his fingers. Vertical, horizontal, and diagonal chalk lines appear on the felt tabletop. "When I was learning to play pool, I drew these lines on the table and spent hours just hitting the cue ball and making it stop on a chosen spot on one of these lines. That's how I got a feel for stroke and distance. When I could pretty much make the ball stop anywhere on the table from a straight shot, I got myself a special cue ball."

Harold snaps his fingers again and a white cue ball with black dots spaced every quarter-inch appears in his hand. He passes it to me and explains, "When you put spin on that ball you're holding, you have to hit it off centre. Where the ball will spin off the rail depends how far off centre you stroke it with the cue. I spent hours getting a sense of spin and distance, first just off one rail, then off two or three."

I begin to see what all of this means. "Mastering the game takes a lot of practice with special tools."

"Yes, and you keep upping the complexity until you have all balls on the table in many different places. Once your comfort level goes up, you take away the special tools, play against yourself, and then think about competition." Then he puts his hands on my head and starts massaging my temples.

"My God, omigod … you're doing a transfer. I'm receiving your experience, knowledge and emotional memories."

Harold nods. Henri beams. For the next five minutes, Harold walks around the table with me, explaining how he would run it and where the cue ball would end up after he pocketed the yellow one I placed on the table.

"You get it, Josh?"

"Yes, I do, Henri. In AfterL, trauma-trashing is a game. You recall your worst experiences, line 'em up, and dispose of them once and for all."

"I knew you had a love of pool, which is why I chose it for you. Whether that will be one of the ways you get initiated into AfterL remains to be seen. Harold, run the table for Josh, and show him why you were nicknamed 'The Best.'"

Henri sips his beer and leans against the window overlooking the fields behind him. I join him, and together we watch as Harold chalks his cue, scrutinizes, and then makes his shots. The thwacking sound from each carom, followed by the plopping sound of each ball falling into a pocket, are hypnotic.

As he plays, Harold talks. "I was thirty-seven when I died—brain cancer. If I'd only known what AfterL held in store. Most of us say that. Anyway, I'm glad Henri got in touch. I love to share my passion and grow my community." He nods.

I sense there is something more to his comment. When there is one ball left, I suddenly find myself seeing the room from his perspective. I can feel his cue in my right hand, the soft green felt on the table under my left fingers. I'm making the shot.

I gently strike the cue ball, watch as it softly kisses the eight ball, sending it slowly, truly, into the corner pocket.

Henri sets his mug on the ledge of the window and claps his hands. "Bravo, Josh. How do you feel?"

"Like this moment will be forever burned into my memory."

"Exactly. The trauma vanishes, replaced by moments of glory."

I'm back beside Henri. Harold sets his cue stick on the table and gives Henri a hug before disappearing, accompanied by the sound of a cue ball breaking a rack. His cue rises and floats over to stand beside me. The pocketed balls resurface, rolling to the point where they were last struck. The solid yellow ball with my first traumatic experience rises off the table, and a radar screen encircles it and begins emitting a beeping sound. After a few seconds, the screen disappears, the ball softly descends to the table, and the traumatic memory appears as a photograph. It's our chemical toilet in Bond's Hill. I smell its disgusting stench, and see the revolting waste products and discarded cigarette butts.

Almost as soon as the memory invades my thoughts, I hear a bell begin to peal.

"Go ahead, Josh, take the shot."

To the bell's joyful celebratory sound, I take a slow, calming breath, feel all the muscles in my arms, legs, and eyes align to my pool cue, and become one finely tuned instrument. I exhale and hit the cue ball. It takes the path already burned into my brain to hit the solid yellow, forcing it to slowly roll into the side pocket. Just as it starts falling, the traumatic image transforms. A banquet table replaces it. It's one filled with all the food and beverages Grandpa and Grandma Bencet served at our annual Christmas dinner—the ones Ronnie and I used to attend.

"A great trade-off eh, Josh? Trauma for treasure. Shit for sumptuous meal."

The bells toll for another minute as family gathers around the table and Grandma Bencet fetches hot chocolate for Ronnie and me.

Henri steps to the pool table. The scene at the holiday gathering freeze-frames, and Henri lifts it high into the air, waving it as if it were a victory flag you see at a racetrack. "See how it works?"

"I do. In AfterL, I get absolutely everything I need to trash the trauma and replace it with something memorable."

There is a passion and awe in my voice that has Henri looking pleased.

Like the solid yellow ball moments ago, the blue ball rises off the table, a radar screen encircles it, and it begins to emit a beeping sound.

"What trauma does that ball have inside, Josh?"

The ball floats over so I can look inside. It's me in front of the mirror, looking at my teenage acne blemishes, oily skin, and black-heads. Dozens of memories accompany the image: disgust on others' faces, whispered conversations between passersby; children's gasps and taunts; my own repulsion from touching my blotched face. The image mists over and the ball returns to the felt. As with the yellow ball, a radar screen appears and a beeping sound begins.

"Remember what Dieter told you about the brain, Josh? It turns energy into information. The disturbing things you see, smell, hear, feel ... they became traumatic experiences clogging up your mind and soul. Once you die, the cleansing process begins, replacing those negative events with positive ones."

"So all the sensations behind the trauma turn into things like radar screens and pealing bells that enable the process?"

"Like I said before, language doesn't do AfterL's trauma-trashing justice. I conjured up Harold and all this other stuff because I knew you liked the game of pool. If your thing was archery, then it would have been different."

"You're now an AfterLing, Henri. What were your trauma-trashing tools?"

∞

Henri laughs hysterically and briefly transforms into a young boy wearing vestments, but carrying a wand. "I was seven when I became a server to Father Magloire. When I got to AfterL, a baton instead of a cross or Bible became my tool of choice. I had a wonderful time."

"Are you saying some of the trauma gets neutralized with experiences you make up?"

"I'll show you how we neutralized some of my pain. Part of the formation of an AfterLing involves the merging of twelve ghosts. I drew on some of their experiences, and collectively, we neutralized some horrible memories." Henri snaps his fingers and a printed copy of an email pops into his hand. He gives it to me.

On the subject line, I read the title: "If the World were 100 PEOPLE." Henri has highlighted these lines from the thirty or so on the sheet: There would be:

- 70 non-white
- 61 Asians
- 50 suffering from malnutrition
- 33 Christians
- 17 people with no clean, safe water to drink
- 1 with a college education

Before I can look at the other facts, Henri takes the email away. "Your brother, Paul, gave me that in 1992. When Dieter and Ronnie entered AfterL in 1961, the statistics probably weren't much different. Dieter didn't make a point of the fact that we are minorities in our initial AfterLing communities. You can imagine how much we absorbed about other cultures, other lives."

"Wow, Henri, most of your fellow Atlas Released members have nothing in common with you."

"*Had* nothing in common, Josh. That was very quickly remedied in the magic of the AfterLing orientation process. Like Dieter said, it's hard to explain, because it's so foreign and beyond a Western human brain to absorb. What we have shown you is tailored so that you can understand and relate to it. The same with what I want to share now. Come outside and watch this."

We exit the farmhouse. Henri looks like he's fiddling with a dimmer switch, and we're now looking at a night sky. Three giant screens pop up, all blank. In the centre, a large church rises from the ground in Bastogne and fills the screen.

"That's Église Saint-Pierre, built in 1756. It was enlarged in my grandparents' time, 1895, before my parents were born. It suffered from dry rot and was damaged in an earthquake in 1983, but that's not a problem in AfterL." Henri snaps his fingers, and the church is restored to its 1895 grandeur. Lightning flashes down to the Romanesque tower and its circular counterpart at the other end for a few seconds, taking my breath away.

"A church, Henri? After all you've been through?"

"I don't have anything against churches, synagogues, mosques, temples, shrines. They're among the most inspirational of earthly monuments. And the music! It's what people like Father Magloire did in the name of God and Holy Spirit that are unconscionable and clearly wrong."

The lightning ends, and the church lights up from within, exposing all its Romanesque features: semicircular arches, barrel vaults to support the roof of the nave, massive piers and walls, and side aisles with galleries above them.

Music, scarcely audible, starts playing in the background. "Now watch this." Henri raises his arms, like a maestro at a concert.

On the left screen, a four-storey building appears. "That's the Theater am Kärntnertor in Vienna, Josh. Let's peek inside."

The exterior shot is replaced by an interior one. We can see from the back that the theatre is packed with a large orchestra, four soloists holding up sheet music, and a choral group. A text box appears above the conductors: May 7, 1824—Fourth Movement.

"Okay Josh, are you ready?"

The right screen changes. Horizontal and vertical lines divide it into twelve identical panels. A variety of images pop up, mostly battlefields with Axis and Allied soldiers in trenches; some church vestries and sacristies with one priest and one altar boy in each. Besides the soldiers shooting across the frontlines, bombs are exploding and airplanes are strafing. In the vestries, the priests and altar boys are removing their vestments.

On the left screen, the theatre image changes to a movie, the last of the orchestral recitatives ends, and the baritone soloist sings, in German, words that appear at the bottom of the screen in English: "Oh friends, not these sounds! Let us instead strike up more pleasing and more joyful ones!" Henri tells me the soloist is Joseph Seipelt, who premiered Beethoven's Ninth Symphony in 1824.

All the soldiers and congregants stop what they're doing. Their uniforms change to choral gowns matching those in the Viennese theatre. The same thing happens to the priests and altar boys. Once the transformation is complete, they walk out of their panels to the centre screen. They fill the Église Saint-Pierre and join the chorus in singing "Freude! Freude!"

Henri cranks up the volume, and I'm completely transfixed, totally immersed. At the end of the concert, the screen with the battlefields shrinks and disappears. The other two panels expand to fill the space vacated. In the Viennese theatre, the jubilant applause and standing ovation are awesome. The soprano ("Caroline Unger," says Henri) goes to one of the two conductors and touches his shoulder, making him face the audience. It's Beethoven.

In the Église-St-Pierre scene, everyone clears a space around the sanctuary where a priest and an altar boy have centre stage. The priest descends the steps in front of the altar boy and stops. The altar boy opens the gate and the priest exits. Once he's on the parishioners' side of the communion rail, the priest kneels and bows his head. The altar boy raises his hands over the priest's head and claps three times. The priest evaporates, transformed into a cloud of grey smoke before disappearing. Everyone else present begins clapping, and their applause merges with the audience in Vienna.

Circles of bright, pulsating purple surround the altar boy in Bastogne and Beethoven's co-director, Michael Umlauf, the theatre's

Kapellmeister in Vienna. They both expand to fill their respective screens and then merge. I give Henri a quizzical look. He raises his eyebrows and shakes his head, expecting me to guess what happened.

"That's you, Henri. You're in both those scenes. You're the altar boy in the church and the conductor in the theatre."

Henri nods, encourages me to continue.

"To trash your trauma as an abused altar boy, and nuke the memories of the Second World War, your AfterLing group, Atlas Released, put that whole production together and got a lot of help from some very well-established AfterLing communities with roots in Vienna and other parts of Europe."

"Yes, all of us who became part of Atlas Released were inspired. Out of the gate, we had a trauma-trashing blockbuster. After Winston Churchill's community heard about it, they raised a giant V for victory, and a banner entitled 'Their Finest Hour' unfurled below it."

Henri beams.

"How did that work, Henri? Did all the members of your community agree to the scenes you just showed me?"

"It doesn't work that way. That church scene was me and Father Magloire, unique and only applicable to me. If you were one of my fellow Atlas Released AfterLings, it would have been quite different, because of limited knowledge or exposure to Caucasians, much less to Canadians."

Henri waves his baton. The screens shrink and disappear.

"You said you banished your tormentors. Where did they go?"

"Damned if I know, Josh. From what Dieter's community shared with me, there are many mysteries unique to AfterL. Maybe they'll never be explained. Maybe mysteries are part of what make it so wondrous and awesome."

"Without any God ...."

"No community in AfterL is mourning the loss."

The tone of his voice tells me Henri has no interest in pursuing this further. His baton morphs into a dimmer switch, and the night sky is replaced by early morning sun. He nods, casts aside the control, and hurriedly returns to the farmhouse, turning briefly to explain what's next. "Let's get back to trashing your trauma."

The pool cue is back in my hand. I stop. "Henri, I don't think that's necessary. Like you said, it would be a simulation and at best an iffy one."

Henri is silent a few seconds, and then he takes the cue stick from my hand. He goes inside, waving for me to follow. There are still several balls on the table. He pockets each of them as masterfully as Harold Worst did. When the final ball, the eight ball, drops, Henri whistles, claps his hands, rushes over, pulls me into his arms, and gives me a hug. "No sense bringing Harold here and foregoing the experience of being an ace pool player. I really enjoyed that."

Around us, I smell lavender, hear water gently swirling in a brook, and sense Henri's embrace transferring to me a serenity and tranquility I've seldom experienced. My eyes are closed, but inside, I see wondrous, pastoral images. After he slowly releases me, we are no longer in the Deault family kitchen. We are on a hillside, under a beech tree, over-looking a grassy meadow and meandering stream.

"This is where I spent my last morning in Bastogne, in 1946, before heading north to Antwerp and boarding a war brides' ship to Québec City."

"I like it Henri. It reminds me of the creek behind our home in Bond's Hill."

"Mémère Camille used to bring us here for picnics—me and my twin sisters, Lise and Chantal."

"Is that why we're here?"

A wooden stool and an easel appear. On the easel sits a canvas painting of the meadow and the river flowing through it. "That's the Wiltz River. After our picnic, my sisters and I would play in the meadows while Mémère painted it."

"She was an artist, Henri. I remember seeing some of her sketches when Dieter left me in the woodshed with Jean and Louis, your father and grandfather."

"So, now you know why I never told anyone about Father Magloire, and why I've had a love/hate relationship with the Church for so long."

"You were a young boy, Henri."

"And so were you when Ronnie died."

The canvas painting breaks into tiny pieces that sparkle and float away in a silvery shimmer. In its place, familiar words, unfurl on a scroll: There is no future in the past, but it often explains the present.

"Those are your words, Henri. I've seen them before, Dieter showed them to me."

"Yes, and when you shared them with Dieter, you both learned something."

"Not the reason for your silence. You had to share your story, and the way you're doing it ... Wow!"

"Thank you. Do you think you can go back now?"

"I can, but you haven't told me about the woman."

The words on the unfurled banner lift off the paper and drop like tears to the ground. In their place, a hand in a white glove beckons me. As I go closer, I feel myself being drawn in.

Behind me, Henri says, "As you wish."

I'm alone, in the Deault family farmhouse, in the living room. Above the rocking chair where Henri's Mémère Camille probably sat, a giant flashing arrow appears. It's pointing to a notebook on the seat. I pick it up and see it has my name on it. I sit down and begin reading.

Josh,

It's best if this part of my story comes to you from the journal kept by Mémère Camille. In her will, she asked that her journal be given to me, which my sister Lise did. I got it in Montréal.

I read the diary, then I burned it. I was still an angry young man who didn't want any reminders of his past. I had come to Canada to start over.

Do you remember when Dieter's ghost brought you to Timmins to sit in on a conversation in my apartment? We were talking about emotions, and I brought out the letter Mémère gave me before I left Belgium—the one she told me to open when I was settled.

Why did I keep that letter but not the diary? No good answer, Josh, just that in the letter, Mémère had said you can't deal logically with emotion. I liked that idea, and I shared it with Dieter. The letter was about the wars and the suffering and humiliation we had gone through. It said nothing about Mireille.

Mireille? I had never heard that name before, only a reference to a woman and a story Henri had left behind in Antwerp, on the docks. That was all Dieter's brother, Gilbert, could get out of Henri that night at the local bar in Timmins.

From the diary on my lap, a faded yellow newspaper clipping falls. The title reads, "Local Girl Found Drowned in the Wiltz River."

I get up from the rocking chair, tears in my eyes and a lump in my throat. I swallow deeply and walk to the window, asking myself, "What do I know about suffering?" Outside, night is approaching. Dark clouds are closing in on the setting sun. In the east, I see lightning forks, followed by rolling thunder.

Behind me, I hear the rocking chair creak. Henri's grandmother, Camille, is sitting there. Her husband Louis is on the couch opposite. They both appear to be in their late seventies, stooped at the shoulders, white-haired, with wrinkled faces and hands. I walk closer to listen in on their conversation. Louis is reading from a newspaper.

Louis: "Camille, *écoutes,*. Two boys found a body in the Wiltz River yesterday. They recognized her right away: Mireille Colline. That's the girl Henri was going to marry."

Camille: "No, Louis, that's the girl Henri hoped to marry."

Louis: "There were no signs of violence, so the police think she drowned, a probable suicide."

Camille: "A suicide? *Non, cher,* a girl like that. I suspect she got drunk, fell in the river, and drowned."

Louis: "You never liked her."

Camille: "She wasn't a good Catholic girl, Louis. She didn't get confirmed, she seldom came to church, and when she did, she would be giggling and chewing gum. Henri's mother, Thérèse, didn't like her either."

Louis: "Well, Henri wasn't such a good Catholic after the war. After he came back from Germany, he refused to go to church."

Camille: "He was angry. I think if he met the right girl, settled down, and had children, he would have regained his faith, just like our son, Jean."

Louis: "You may be right. Jean was abused in Germany during the First World War. When he returned, he was withdrawn and bitter for a while. Thanks be to God, Thérèse was still here. Between the three of us, we got him to see that it was an evil German, not God or the church, that was to blame for his mistreatment."

Camille: "And you shared my views on the church with Jean. He had no reason to think the God you and I worship is the same God the church promotes."

Louis: "None at all, but Henri? After he was what … thirteen, fourteen … and stopped being an altar boy? Jean couldn't get him to talk about God or anything spiritual."

Camille: "I thought it had something to do with his adolescence and Jean's stutter. I noticed Henri became impatient with our Jean once puberty set in."

Louis: "Thérèse noticed a difference too. Henri still went to church, but just before service was over, he'd leave; he wouldn't wait for Father Magloire to bid him farewell in the narthex."

Camille: "Thérèse and I talked to Father Magloire about that."

Louis: "We've been through this before, *chère*. Please, let's not go over it again. You'll only upset yourself. Let me make some tea. Here, read this article. I'll boil the water."

Camille: "Tea, that would be nice. Where are my glasses?"

Louis: "Probably with your knitting. Let me look ... *oui*, here they are."

Camille: "I won't speak ill of the dead, Louis, but the Colline family ... ach, how many times did we help them?"

Louis: "We're Christians. It's what Christians do."

Camille: "Yes, but how many times when we offered them work did they show up? Whether it was you or Jean, or me or Thérèse, very unreliable. It was the same with their parents."

Louis: "But the Colline men had poor health and their wives ... all those children."

Camille: "The ill health and many mouths didn't stop them from having a pint too many in town almost every night. God, forgive me. Here, let me help you with the tea."

Camille sets the newspaper on the rocking chair and joins Louis in the kitchen. The faded clipping in my hand disintegrates, and the newspaper with the original article floats to where I'm standing.

Vers l'Avenir Saturday, July 10, 1948

Bastogne   Jordan Lejeune—Reporter

Local Woman Found Drowned in the Wiltz River
Earlier today, while fishing in the Wiltz River, two local boys found 25-year-old Mireille Colline floating face up under a fallen beech tree.

"We recognized her right away," Stefan and Peter Charlier told this reporter. "She was our babysitter for many years."

Mireille did not show for work at a local pub the previous evening. Her manager thought the severe thunder and lightning storm that swept through the area accounted for her absence. Whether the tempest had anything to do with her death is unknown at this time. Investigations are underway.

Family members were unavailable for comment.

When I finish reading the article, the newspaper returns to the rocking chair.

Henri left Belgium in 1946, two years before Mireille's death. Why the gap?

Camille and Louis re-enter the room, and I return to my listening post.

Camille: "Poor Mireille. Part of me was wishing Henri would be able to settle her down."

Louis: "After he came back from Germany, Henri was a troubled man. Jean tried to tell him about his experiences in Munich in the First World War, but he wouldn't listen."

Camille: "I know. Thérèse and I failed, too. Father Magloire wasn't much help, but I didn't think he would be, which is why I'm so thankful that Henri at least spent as much time as he did with me after the war."

Louis: "If you were young, single, and unrelated, the two of you would have made a lovely couple."

Camille: "Oh you. It's because we're related Henri is so close to me. It's the blood and the beliefs that made him come to me with his troubles."

Louis: "But he never had any troubles, really, before the war. None that we knew about."

Camille: "None that we *knew* about. Something happened, and I couldn't get him to open up. Sure, I knew he loved me, trusted me, respected me, but ..."

Louis: "Put down your teacup and let's have a cuddle on the couch. Remember one thing, *chère*, what Henri told you when he left Belgium."

Camille: "He said, "I love you, Mémère, and I love your God. In that, you must take comfort.""

Camille rises from her chair and joins Louis. He puts his arm around her, and she puts her head on his shoulder. She grasps his hand in hers and closes her eyes. Louis gently squeezes her arm. I smile and reminisce about similar scenes from my own past. A sign rises behind them.

"Time for Reflection"

∞

Alone, I'm back above the meadow overlooking the Wiltz River.

The sign above the Deault couch is on Camille's easel. A folding chair and table are assembled beside the tripod. A glass of red wine sits on the table, along with a pen, clipboard, and paper. It's mid-afternoon. A warm breeze wafts over me. I can hear the wind in the beech tree that frames the river and meadow. Billowing cumulous clouds roll slowly before me, kissing the horizon, looking like giant, inviting pillows.

The pen and glass rise from the table and position themselves beside the chair. I sit down and reach for the wine. The glass is lead crystal. Three smiley faces etch themselves around the rim, morphing into cameos of my AfterLing guides: Ronnie, Dieter, and Henri. I raise the glass. In front of the clouds, the words "Reflect" and "Write" appear in large purple letters.

The pastoral landscape around me reminds me of what I like best of life: its variety, splendour, and constant ability to provide solace and comfort. I propose my toast: "You've left me here alone now, with pen, paper, and potion for a reason. I hope I can do you justice."

The cameo images detach from the goblet, and to the plopping sound that stones make in a still pond, each of them infuses itself in its own unique God grain, then wriggles into the tip of the pen. Still suspended in the air above the table, the pen begins to vibrate and pulsate as if the God grains are giving the ink an energy and ability far beyond its original potential. From the nib, red ink in a continuous stream injects itself into my wine glass. Immediately, I recognize his sense of humour.

"The source of my inspiration, Henri, eh? No doubt there's a deeper meaning to all this. Well, thank you!"

Once the red ink stops streaming and transforms into whatever metaphysical mix my dear friends have added, the glass tilts, inviting me to take a sip. After I'm done and set the glass on the table, the clipboard and paper unite and join the pen in midair, but outside my reach. In the distant clouds, the word "Write" dims and the word "Reflect" shines and dazzles me. I smile, put my hands behind my head, and close my eyes. A host of thoughts and images parade inside, but not like dreams, somehow lodged in my brain, manifesting as normal dreams do. There are dreamlike sights and sounds, but they're augmented by sensations I struggle to capture in words. Then it hits me: *These are insights into AfterL, and I can only scratch at its full wonder and majesty.* Serenity permeates my mind and soul. The paper and pen come within my grasp. The words in the clouds reverse in intensity; "Reflect" dims and "Write" dazzles. I seize the pen and watch and feel as words tumble onto the page, guided by a force not altogether my own.

As I've just discovered, there are some things even AfterLing communities cannot explore. In trashing their traumas, the memories and experiences wiped out return to the material world, fragments for poets, writers, musicians, and other artists to weave into their explorations of the full scope of human depravity.

Henri, as part of Atlas Released, left me in Belgium when I asked why he never married. Alone then, I witnessed a conversation between his paternal grandparents. They talked about Mireille; a young woman Henri had never mentioned in all the years I had known him.

What was returned to Earth in the pen and the wine was for me alone to dwell on:

Should I tell Mireille's story?

When she drowned, I wonder what happened to her soul? Is she in some AfterL community endlessly pursuing rapture and knowledge, augmenting her own attachment to that eternal cosmos I can only partially understand?

The pen in my hand has all it needs for me to extract the events Henri expunged when he died. Shall I?

The price of admission to AfterL, surely one all humans gladly pay, is the loss of pain and suffering. Or do their tormentors, who've made others their victims, go into that part of the universe called Dark Matter, a place from which nothing escapes?

Dieter told me that, in his forty years as an AfterLing, he never ran across any evil spirits, so he couldn't tell me where they were or if their momentary appearance on an earthly stage was all they would ever know of the wonders of the eternal cosmos.

From what I learned reading the news clip and listening to Henri's grandparents, Mireille was not an evil person. The insight I got into her past tells me she was a sufferer, too. Her alcoholic family environment, like mine, was not the place to acquire the simple coping skills picked up in more congenial family settings.

I look around me at the pastoral scene, noticing for the first time how many pages I've written. The pages slowly assemble themselves, and a manila folder appears out of nowhere to protect them. I wonder if I'll find it back in Henri's apartment when I return.

I look up into the clouds. The words "Reflect" and "Write" dissolve, replaced by "Return."

CHAPTER 16

Return

A round me the entire panorama spins slowly. The word "Return" begins flashing. My eyes close. I can't open them. I feel myself being removed from the river's side, floating in the air, changing from a vertical position to horizontal, and then descending.

I hear a voice. It's Jackie. "Josh, honey, you're moaning. Wake up, dear. Oh sweet Jesus."

My eyelids flutter, and I see Jackie standing beside my bed, her hand on my shoulder, gently squeezing. I'm out of the coma. I'm back in a hospital bed. Back on Earth. Judging from the angle of the sunlight, it's early morning.

I hear *Frère Jacques* inside my head. When the bells peal *ding dang dong,* I see mental images of Dieter, Ronnie, and Henri. They smile, give thumbs up, then disappear.

Others for whom I've written eulogies appear. Why? Will they be back? Will they have stories they want me to channel?

Cymbals clash, startling me. The word "Return" flashes in red letters that turn green, then stop flashing. I open my eyes. Jackie is staring at me. I feel her eyes dig into my soul and open me.

I sob uncontrollably.

Jackie is startled, her head snaps back like she's been struck. I raise my arms, motioning for her to come closer.

The way her eyes and brows move tell me she's puzzled. "Josh, it's been two weeks. We were so worried. Josh, can you hear me? Are you awake?"

I want to pull her down on the bed. There's an IV needle in my left arm. Before I can say, *What the f—?* a billiard ball briefly appears behind Jackie's head, completely shattering my urge to swear. I point to the IV, then motion for her to come closer. I can smell her perfume, hear her shortness of breath.

Slowly she returns to my side and puts her hands around my face. She slowly turns my head, peering deep into each of my eyes. Her hands are warm. I can feel her energy pervade me.

I seize her right arm and slowly raise my hand to her chin. I draw her gently down and kiss her. At first, her lips are closed. I apply more pressure. She parts her lips. We remain locked together for ten or fifteen seconds.

Jackie withdraws, looks at me incredulously, then puts her hand on my forehead. "I don't sense any fever, but I think you may be delirious, Josh."

I caress her hand and sigh before answering. "Delirious? No, Jackie, not delirious. Disoriented like I've never been before, but in a good way. It's so good to be back!"

"Where've you been?"

"Many places, across many years, through some eternal mysteries. Now, please ask a nurse to remove this IV. Then get on the phone to Air Canada."

"Air Canada? What, why, where?"

"We're flying to Québec, to the Château Frontenac."